WHITE SHORE

by

Cyan Brodie

Enjoy the read

C/Brodie

Text Copyright © Cyan Brodie 2016

Cyan Brodie has asserted his right to be identified as the author of this work in accordance with the Copyright, Designs and Patents Act, 1988.

All rights reserved. No part of this publication may be reproduced, stored in a retrieval system or transmitted in any form, or by any means, electronic, mechanical, photocopying or otherwise without the written permission of the author.

First published February 2016

2nd edition January 2019

ISBN - 13: 978-1530036677

ISBN - 10: 1530036674

Cover Image © Mary King - www.sketchingholidays.co.uk

NATO conducts its Joint Warrior war games twice a year off the coast of Scotland.

This can involve the periodic jamming of GPS signals to a confined area - though this was suspended recently following complaints from North-West Scotland fishermen.

Claims that a trawler was snagged by a submarine have also appeared in the press, but to date there are no reports of any fishing vessel sinking as a result of the Joint Warrior military exercises.

WHITE SHORE

MAY

1

TWENTY-ONE-YEAR-OLD Matt Neilson didn't realise he was undergoing a life-defining moment until they drove him away in the prison van. He pressed his face against the Perspex window and watched people in the street go through their safe, day-to-day schedules. Not one of them imagining this could happen to them if things turned sour. None remotely aware that some faceless, omnipotent authority could destroy their future with the nod of a head. People like Matt were routinely despatched into oblivion as if they had no more relevance than a fallen leaf has to the forest.

His solicitor had taken the six-month sentence as a personal insult - begging a brief interview downstairs before his bruised client was transported away from the court buildings.

"They're trying to make an example of you, Matthew."

Matt still felt too numb to respond coherently. "Really?"

"A fine would have sent out the same message. You were hardly making a living pushing the stuff."

"So what? They still knew I'd been dealing."

The solicitor pulled a sheaf of forms from his briefcase. "That's as may be. You confessed everything to the police right from the start. It's your first offence and, given the mitigating circumstances, I think we should appeal."

Matt shook his head, suddenly coming to his senses. "No way. The last thing I want is another day in court."

He'd already accepted his fate before the sentence was handed out. The grim look on everyone's faces had made the gravity of the situation all too clear. From the moment he stepped into the dock, his life was on hold. He'd no longer be allowed to take part in the real world. Maybe the break would do him good.

"Matthew Neilson?" the custody officer asked.
"That's me."
"I need to take down some details before we ship you out. Date of birth. National Insurance number, etcetera."

The process of dehumanisation had begun even before the transfer from the holding cells inside Edinburgh Sheriff Court. They'd confiscated his belt and tie as soon as he was led away from the dock - presumably in case he tried to hang himself en route to Peterhead. Then came the three hour, bone-shaking ride North as daylight faded into night with street lights leaving trails of sodium flare in his wake. He felt like a stricken beast being trucked to the abattoir. A further hour's delay intensified the sense of doom before he was escorted into the empty shower block and ordered to undress.

"You've to hand over your clothes to me." From the smirk on his lips, the officer in charge of intake seemed to relish Matt's discomfort. The final stripping away of anything he might consider normal was no doubt intentional. New life new rules.

He tugged off his shoes first. Matt's solicitor had advised him to wear slip-ons. A detail he'd failed to understand the significance of until the custody officer in

Edinburgh had checked his shoes for laces. Jacket next. Shirt unbuttoned and pulled free, trousers dropped to his ankles. Socks tossed onto the cold tiles with everything else.

The bark of the pit-bull broke the silence. "Listen to what I said to you, Neilson. You've to hand over everything to me."

Matt tugged off his boxers, bent down to pick up his clothes and passed them to the guard. Then he reached for his clean kit stacked on a plastic chair next to the shower cubicle.

"I'll say when." Another snarled order. "Into the shower, then you get dressed. But first you need to bend over for me."

"Uh?"

The latex gloves made it clear what would follow. The final shame.

At least the water was hot. But as Matt lathered himself and watched the suds gurgle into the drain, it felt like everything he'd ever held dear was heading in the same direction. It only took that first sleepless night in his new cell to confirm how easy it would be to give up hope.

There was no other choice. He had to get a grip. Accept the fact he'd be sharing every intimate hour with creatures he had nothing in common with. Breathing in the same stale air, the same foul smells. Listening out for the same sounds. Trying to make sense of the routine while watching the hours drag by like storm clouds crossing an overcast sky.

Matt's cellmate had his own issues, as did most of the other boarders. Dack wore the same clothes day in day out, rarely bothering to wash. He even slept in the same gear despite the stifling heat. By the end of the first week, Matt barely noticed the stench - body odour tainted with the underlying reek of sour milk and the long-life bread rolls Dack squirreled away inside their shared locker.

The sounds took longer to fade into the background. Not just the hard, guillotine slam of the door and the scrape of the key in the lock as the screws settled them in at the end of each day. He'd flinched the first few times. And the screams and yells that echoed along the corridors following lights-out still kept him awake into the early hours. But sharing a confined space with his subhuman cellmate during interminable hours of lockdown made each minor annoyance increasingly unbearable. The belching and farting, the nervous cough, Dack's snotty nose and his energetic bowel movements were hard enough to stomach. The nightly ritual was the final straw - the frame of the top bunk rattling as soon as the lights dimmed.

"For God's sake, can you give it a rest?" Matt finally close to breaking point.

But it wasn't what he'd thought. The next morning, Dack had been more than happy to show off his body art. When he pulled up his t-shirt Matt had recoiled in disgust. He could see the guy's stomach hollowed out above his waistline and the skin deathly pale beneath the grime. It reminded Matt of an image he'd seen in an Art book one time - a Renaissance painting of a martyred saint complete with weeping, bleeding craters pockmarking his flesh. The saint had been spared the tattoo of a coiling snake wrapped around his torso.

Dack had used anything that came to hand. A dining fork, a broken ball-point pen, even the sharpened handle of a toothbrush. He swore the snake was trying to burrow through his stomach wall at night; chewing away at his guts as it searched for a way out.

Matt had complained to anyone who would listen. "Can't the doctors give him something to calm him down?" he'd pleaded. "He's doing my head in."

But no one seemed to take any notice. The screws had enough to do without nursemaiding some short-circuited junkie. And the others on the landing gave Matt grief for being such a soft touch. "Smack him one. That'll shut the fucker up."

Then came the night Dack climbed down from the top bunk and dragged Matt from his own bed. Straddling him on the floor of the cell; something shining in one hand. Accusing him of all sorts before begging for a fix. By the time Matt recovered his wits enough to retaliate, his cellmate was flat on his back, legs twitching and eyes rolled up in their sockets. Matt yelled until he was hoarse and eventually someone peered in through the spy-hole in the door.

While the medical team tried to stabilise their patient before carrying him out to a waiting ambulance, Matt was ushered to a holding cell next to the officers' station. But first they took away his t-shirt, splattered in blood, and the improvised blade he'd still been holding when they opened the cell door.

2

THE envelope lay on the worktop when I surfaced. Sun as bright as any summer afternoon had peeked through the blinds broadcasting unsubtle hints at the waste of another day. I'd rolled over and buried my face in the duvet. But ignoring the rest of the world took dedication, and eventually I became fed up with my own company and went in search of caffeine.

"You haven't passed away in your sleep then?"

I shrugged off my mother's unsubtle attempt at irony and went through the complicated routine of making a drink.

Clean mug. Teaspoon. Check the kettle for water.

"There's a letter come for you."

Click the switch on.

"I can see."

A heaped spoon of coffee granules. Into the fridge for the semi-skimmed.

"I'm only saying."

The kettle clicked off. I poured the boiling water into the mug and gave it a stir before adding the milk.

"Biscuit?"

I shook my head.

"So are you going to open it?"

"For God's sake, give me a chance."

I placed the teaspoon on the drainer then picked up the plain white envelope.

My name and address, written in slanting block capitals, stared back at me like a silent accusation. I hesitated - expecting to find another anonymous message inside. Three cryptic emails in the last couple of months followed by this. Except it contained something else entirely.

```
                            HMP & YOI Grampian

                                 Sunday 4th May

Hi Ames,

How's tricks? The last few days in
here have been desperately hard. I'm
not sure I can carry on without you.
```

I planted my mug on the kitchen table and dabbed at my runny nose with a scrunched-up tissue. The first sniffles of summer always seemed to coincide with the start of the Lochinver tourist season. When I was little, Mum had blamed the visitors for bringing their alien germs with them on holiday. But this time she told everybody I was run down - all due to the upset of the past months.
"Who's it from?"
The temptation to say nothing and crush it into a paper ball then dump everything in the waste bin was overwhelming. But I realised Mum would retrieve it the moment I left the kitchen. Looking out for me every opportunity she got - stalking me inside my own home. I know she sneaked in to my room whenever I turned my back. Checking my bedding for fresh cigarette burns perhaps or searching my drawers for weed or condoms. Who knows?

"Can I finish reading it first?" It took a while to digest; my face flushing as I realised who'd sent it and why. Matt still had feelings for me and expected the same in return.

```
That's why I'm sending you a VO. I
know it's a long shot but it would be
great to see your smiling face. I
really need to believe there's
something good waiting for me out
there or I'll go crazy in here.

Love ya always

Matt xxx
```

"It's from Matthew Neilson."
Silence for an eternity. I scanned the form. Someone had already filled in all the relevant personal details.

Name	-	Amy Metcalf
Age	-	18
Relationship with prisoner	-	girlfriend

That was pushing it.
Matt had even suggested a date to fit in with his busy schedule. A week away. Tuesday the 13th.
Right at the bottom of the Visiting Order was the number to ring to make an appointment and guidelines on what identification I'd need to take with me. All I had to do was make the telephone call then turn up as instructed.
Simples.
Even if Mum offered to drive me, there was no way I could put up with her company all the way to Peterhead and back.

Two hundred miles each way? Jesus!

"So what's he got to say for himself?"

I shook my head. Most of the letter had been about how hard done by he felt. I'd expected no different.

"Just the usual crap."

"Well I hope you're not going to start encouraging him," Mum continued.

As if.

I waved the form in her face. "He's sent me this as well. He's asking me to go in and see him."

I could feel tears forming in the corner of each eye. A half-day trip across Scotland, coast to coast, just to spend an hour inside some high-security establishment with all the other pond life. Matt was feeling sorry for himself. Nothing new there. He'd be looking for a shoulder to cry on but I'd already done my share of commiserating long before he got his stupid self locked up.

"He's got a nerve."

"I know." I folded both letter and form in half and tucked them into the back pocket of my jeans. "I'm going to get some fresh air. Clear my head a bit and see if I can shake off this cold."

"What about your coffee?"

"I've changed my mind, alright? I wish you'd stop fussing."

Back to the bedroom first to give my hair a brush and retrieve my phone. While I was there I hid Matt's letter with the rest of my personal stuff - photographs, letters, greetings cards and postcards from various exotic locations. Mum no doubt knew about the shoe box I kept at the bottom of the wardrobe. I trusted her to have enough discretion to allow me a tiny degree of privacy and leave its contents undisturbed.

Last year's Valentine's Day card lay on top of the pile. It had taken me a while to figure out who could have sent it. Presumably Matt meant it as a joke because I'd not suspected him of having romantic feelings for me despite the clumsy ambush shortly after. My rejection of the kiss hardly dampened his passion.

So did he really have feelings for me now, or was he just wanting someone to massage his fragile ego again? Words on paper - not always easy to read the emotions behind them.

3

TO his credit, Matt was the first friend to call round during those dismal days following my altercation with Gordon Paver. Everyone assured me I was safe. The doctors. The police. But safe from what? Once the memories began flooding back it proved impossible to come to terms with the idea that life would ever return to normal. How could I find the same level of safety I'd taken for granted before I got dragged into the whole Caddy Neilson mess? Lochinver had changed - or at least in my head it had. Changed in the space of two months from a cosy little fishing village to a battle zone.

Mum kept telling me the worst was behind me. But I feared different. I refused to venture far from the house after they discharged me from hospital. Matt brought me a scented candle for my bedroom one time and some organic chocolate another. But I could see right through his unsubtle attempt to coax me out of my shell.

Always the same question as he did his best to convince me these feelings wouldn't last for ever. "Remember what I was like, Ames?"

His spectacular meltdown had come shortly after Caddy's murder. A close encounter with Slippy and his cronies - some misunderstanding over the etiquette surrounding the local drugs trade. In the weeks that followed, I'd helped Matt recover in my own way. Never one to indulge his self-pity for too long.

But now I couldn't find the right words to explain how I felt. I wanted to fall against him and sob my heart out while he held onto me. To curl up like a wood shaving and become part of him.

"This is different," I said.

"Not that much. We're like a couple of rubber balls you and me - always bouncing back."

"If you say so."

But it hadn't been easy. He walked me to the end of Kirk Road one evening and we shared a bottle of wine to help reduce the tension a notch or two. But all the way there and back I kept wondering. What if we came across someone who recognised me? What would they think of me? What would they say? The thought of looking people in the eye and seeing what they knew etched in a glance was too much to bear.

There had been numerous cards and phone calls. Goodwill messages and an avalanche of 'Likes' on Facebook. A friendly word or two in the local shops and the pub. A day didn't go by without Mum reminding me how much everyone cared. But if things had turned out differently I'd be in Aberdeen now, flat on my back in some grotty bedsit. Drugged to the eyeballs and selling my body or worse.

A couple of days after our twilight trek to Costcutters, Matt and I spent an afternoon at the swing park at the centre of the village. I'd wrapped up despite the spring sunshine. Keeping a low profile. No eye contact. Staring at my feet for an age before lifting my gaze to watch the world crawl past. That's when he confessed all. Like most guys caught with their pants down, he glossed over the finer details of how he and Kay Jepson had exchanged bodily fluids. Kay meant nothing to him. She never had. I glared at the small sash window above the Picture Gallery. I half expected to catch her watching us now from behind one of the curtains. Smirking.

Mum was busy drying the dishes when I grabbed an empty Highland Spring bottle off the counter and filled it at the cold tap.
"Got your running shorts on? Well, a little exercise might do you good."
I didn't bother responding. Outside and away from prying eyes I checked my smart phone one more time. It had become almost an hourly ritual these last few weeks. Forever expecting something. Almost disappointed if nothing new appeared in my inbox alongside the three emails I couldn't bring myself to delete.
The first had arrived a week or so after they locked up Matt Neilson. I'd assumed it was spam from some random dating site I'd never even signed up for, as far as I could remember.

To : Amy Metcalf
From : loner@letstalk.co.uk

FEELING LONELY? I'M ALWAYS HERE

But the two that followed, each a couple of weeks apart, had taken an increasingly sinister tone.

WATCHING YOU WATCHING OVER YOU

WYWOY
WE HAVE UNFINISHED BUSINESS

4

DOCTOR Ross had prescribed tablets to help me sleep and advised me to take things slowly. There was no need to go back to school just yet. He suggested I take a complete break - returning after the summer holidays. I'd have got over it by then. His words not mine.

Most of the time, I craved anonymity. Even when I left the house I'd plug in my earphones but keep the iPod switched off - a good enough excuse not to have to strike up conversation with anyone who crossed my path. If I couldn't hear their blethering it meant they weren't there. What could they say that changed how I felt anyway? What could I say in return? There was no one in the village I could relate to anymore. No friend I could spill my secrets to with Caddy gone. No confidante to share confessions with beneath the duvet.

There had been a time when the evening run was an important part of my summer keep-fit regime. I might as well have attached a zipwire to my waist and let it launch me out as far as the breakwater and back most nights. But there were days now when I couldn't even muster the energy to venture beyond the bridge for a browse inside the newsagent's. And I'd only been as far as the White Shore once since February. That had been a pilgrimage of sorts.

But today the breakwater beckoned - a four-mile run with mostly flat ground all the way there and back. It would give me time to get my thoughts straight regarding Matt Neilson. I straightened the left strap of my vest and slowed down as I reached the narrow section of bridge crossing the Inver. No pavement here. Someone waved from a dark blue Volvo estate coming towards me. I stepped aside and waved back but had no idea who it was. Not remotely interested.

Now a right turn onto the main street. This stretch of road curving through the village from the Inver bridge to the Inverkirkaig junction had always been Caddy territory when we were kids. Mine had been Kirk Road and Inver Park. There had been summer days when Caddy hardly ever ventured beyond the bridge without me at her side. Afternoons at the play park, cycle rides as far as the Pottery to share an ice cream and study the mosaics, or a picnic above the Ardroe path.

All-night parties with Matt and his crowd had come much later, as had house calls on the two Bobs, staying up for the New Year bells at Moolie's, or drunken sleepovers where we'd get to share my bed and the latest gossip. Except, when it mattered the most, Caddy had kept the juiciest bits to herself.

I continued to jog beyond the car park adjacent to the Stag's Head with barely a glance at the shops on the opposite side of the road. Upstairs windows reflected the white hot sunlight glinting off the flat of the water. The loch had become miraged in late afternoon haze: A' Chleit afloat in its own liquid dimension. The spicy scent of low water and the lazy heat almost took my breath away. So many memories of better days than these.

An early season campervan with foreign plates sat next to the recycling bins. Next to the school bus.

Faster Amy.

I picked up the pace. Almost racing past the kirk despite my creaking joints. This was where my best friend's body had ended up one cold night last December after her supposed boyfriend strangled her and left her on the back seat of the bus for me to find. One tiny detail that everyone seemed to have overlooked at the time. I'd suffered as much as Caddy's family from the loss. As much as Matt frigging Neilson.

Each breath grew more ragged, caustic enough to burn my throat. The Cruamer bungalows on the left and the rocky foreshore on the right hemmed me in as I followed the long, straight stretch down towards the harbour.

Two small fishing boats were tethered to the wooden pilings at the back of the creel store today, wallowing hip to hip on the rising tide like a pair of spent lovers. Not a soul about as I crossed the road and passed the track leading into Caley Woods, the new trendy restaurant and the Caley Hotel - Matt Neilson's favourite watering hole. Then the industrial no-man's land of the harbour stretched before me. A barren expanse of baking concrete complete with its own convoy of beached boats gave way to the tiny marina and the breakwater beyond. A physical and psychological dead-end in this dead-end village.

As soon as I reached the breakwater, I sat on one of the benches to take a swig from my water bottle. This was where I'd generally stop to tighten the laces on my running shoes before turning and heading for home. Any excuse to savour the view back across the bay. It could be spellbinding when the light took on a particular quality. But other days it seemed the jaws of land were closing tight around me and there was no escape.

I gazed inland, remembering autumn evenings when the sun lay low enough to cast velvet shadows behind each ripple yet bright enough to bathe the white cottages in honeyed tones. On certain days the silhouette of Quinag's ridge overlooking the village resembled a cut-out from a postcard of the Rockies Photo-shopped in place. Spellbinding.

Matt and I had stood on the same skyline weeks earlier. It had been one of those glorious winter days. Sunburn in February. But closer at hand another memory intruded. The white bulk of Gordon Paver's boat, the 'Meera Rose', nudged its prow tight against one of the pontoons. I caught a flash of reflected light from somewhere behind the cabin windows. Someone watching me through a pair of binoculars maybe. There was talk Peter Paver had left the Army and was living on board Daddy's cruiser. The thought of seeing Paver Junior again was almost as distasteful as having to visit Peterhead.

I took my time walking back and paused as I reached the shops again. The sweat had already grown cold on my lower back and between my shoulder blades. A car slowed down ahead of me to pull into the filling station. Someone came out of the Gallery carrying a large package. Two tourists dressed for the hill stared in the window at framed photographs of this magical place I'd always considered home. A safe haven that had grown threatening and unpredictable almost overnight.

I caught a blur of movement in an upstairs window. Then a face, pressed against the glass: glossy dark hair pulled back, a cigarette in the left hand painting swirls of smoke. Our eyes met and I found myself crossing the street, pushing open the double doors at the foot of the stairwell and heading up to the first floor.

Kay Jepson meant no more to me than anyone else in Lochinver. She was just a name. We had nothing in common. Everything in common.

5

THE welcome was much as I expected. An overpowering aroma of Slacker Central greeted me as soon as Kay inched open the door. Patchouli combined with an underlying trace of weed from the roll-up in her left hand. Her eyes darted left and right even before I got a chance to speak. Expecting more trouble maybe. More sorrow.

"It's Amy. Amy Metcalf." I wasn't sure if she'd remember me from High School. Kay had been three classes ahead of me. She'd hardly seemed the studious type as I recalled. Working behind the counter at the local Spar probably the most she could ever hope for. "I'm a friend of Matt Neilson and I was wondering. . ."

"Hang on."

The door closed and I could hear her slide the chain free.

A cardboard carton of empties lay just outside the door. A set of wind chimes hung above it. They seemed out of place since no breeze was likely to reach the top of the enclosed stairwell. Then I noticed the length of cord attached to the top edge of the door and the chimes clattered a warning as she opened it wider to let me in.

Paranoia - I know that feeling.

"You'd better come in," she said as I followed her down a short passage into the living area on the left. Two stuffed armchairs and a collapsed sofa corralled a low table complete with empty cereal bowl, a joss stick holder and an overflowing ashtray. A couple of paperbacks lay face-down on the floor next to a pair of scuffed roller blades. '*AQA Chemistry*' and '*Plant-derived Natural Products*'.

"You know Matt's in prison," I began as Kay sank into the chair nearest the ashtray and stubbed out her cigarette.

"I had heard."

"Peterhead. Six months. That means he'll only serve three, if he behaves, so he'll be out before the middle of June."

A bookcase stood within comfortable reach of the sofa. A hundred paperbacks or more filled the shelves. I scanned the spines. Thick textbooks on chemistry and medicine and Tarot along with some lighter reading. Grisham. Rankin. And a few names I'd never heard of. Ballard. Murakami. Palahniuk.

"You've kept in touch?"

"Just the one letter – from Matt. It came in today's post."

"That's nice for you."

"It's taken him two months to get round to writing it, so no big deal. But anyway. . ."

"Is that why you're here? Is Matt Neilson finally bothered enough to find out how I am?" Kay obviously wasn't in the mood for small talk.

"Not really. I mean, that's not why I've called round."

I was tempted to recite Matt's letter word for word.

```
Just over a month to go by the time
you receive this, but it's feeling
like a life sentence. You realise this
won't be finished once I'm back
outside, don't you? I might be behind
```

```
bars in here but it'll be no better
once I'm home again. The real world
won't be on the agenda anymore. Not
for me. Sorry to go on but I wish I
could be more positive.
  The business with the drugs - that's
all behind me. You know that already,
I hope. This place is enough to remind
me how things could have ended up.
There are more junkies inside than
outside. But that's perhaps for the
best. If they made drugs legal then
none of this would have happened.
  Anyway. The thing is, I'm going to
change, and I need someone to believe
in me, Ames. Dad and Steff are no
help. I can tell they still don't
trust me. If Dad had been on my side
just once. But it was all about Caddy.
Always Caddy. So you're the only thing
that's keeping me sane in here. The
only thing I've got to look forward to
when they let me out - Friday the
13th. Can you believe that?
```

Words on paper, but clear proof that he needed me. More than he needed Kay maybe.

"So what are you after?"

"It's been hard, you know? Trying to put everything behind me."

She nodded. Kay knew, having also suffered at the hands of Paver's Ukrainian heavies.

"You don't look so bad yourself," she said.

My gaze lingered on her face - the haunted look in her eyes suggested the damage ran deep. "No. Well, they didn't attack me. I mean, not the same way."

Kay closed her eyes and took in a breath before giving a shudder. "We're both still here though, aren't we?"

"Yeah. I realise that."

"It could have gone the other way. The doctors told me, another hour and I'd have bled out."

I flinched. "From your mouth?"

She shook her head and I didn't need to be told what she meant. There were rumours that one of the Ukrainians had raped her. Torn her insides to shreds, according to the village grapevine.

"I'm sorry. I didn't mean to..."

"Look. If you've come round here to trade sob stories, forget it. I'm not in the mood."

"I haven't." I ran my thumbnail along my bottom lip. Time to come clean. "It was something one of the Bobs said last time I saw him."

"One of the Bobs?"

"Bob 2. He said you could get me some weed if I was wanting any."

6

KAY rolled the first joint then lit it and took a drag before passing it across.

"How much?"

She shrugged. "We can talk business some other time."

The familiar sensation took over. Summer afternoons at the White Shore. Water lapping against the rocks and sand shifting under my feet. The clink of bottles floating in the shallows close by and the music growing louder as more people turned up. Moolie and Sara. Caddy. Jed McKendrick. Peter Paver riding the waves like someone out of frigging *Baywatch*. White noise and whitewashed days of endless sun and laughter.

I pushed strands of loose hair out of my eyes before settling back into the armchair. "The two Bobs used to sell me what bit I needed after school. But I've not seen either of them since the start of term. And it's not something you can order off Amazon."

"Just shush and let it in."

Kay had already got another spliff alight and lay stretched out in her own chair with her stockinged feet planted on the edge of the coffee table. She wore a pair of black jogging trousers and a grey velour hoodie - both looking in need of a laundering. The sleeves were rolled up to her elbows and I could see a line of bare flesh where her top had ridden up high above her waistline. Her belly knot lay hidden within a seam of flesh but there were no piercings on show today.

Caddy had always been a bit wild. But rumours about Kay Jepson's lifestyle had been legendary, even before she dropped out of school. She hung around with an older set. Drugs and group sex something she bragged about on every social medium going. Yet she'd somehow retained a degree of childlike innocence. It had to be the little-girl-lost look. Matt said she reminded him of a manga doll. Those big eyes: dark pearls circled in darker mascara. And her black hair bunched up either side of her head. She'd worn dreadlocks not so long ago but now it was tied back in a pony-tail and shaven at the sides. Self-inflicted by the look of it.

"It's good stuff, yeah?"

"Mhmm. It's stronger than I'm used to," I said. "Smells a lot sweeter too."

"I know. Better than that imported crap the two Bobs are dealing."

She shut her eyes and inhaled. A stick of pale grey ash fell from the smouldering joss stick onto the table. Its scented smoke tapered into nothingness.

Kay was tiny - less than four foot six in her bare feet. Yet there was something about her that suggested an uncontrollable force playing beneath the surface. Her toes flexed and her body arched to take in another breath. Then her lips twitched once as her hips gave an involuntary squirm. Her sense of ease put me in mind of a cat on a window ledge basking in the sun.

"God, can you feel it? Sometimes it makes me horny as fuck."

I recoiled at the image of them together. It would have been so simple for someone like Kay to seduce someone like Matt. The double studs in both ears were the only evidence of body art on display. But I'd seen the photo on her Facebook page. A close-up of her tattooed breasts

- a pierced nipple - Matt spaced out and drooling right next to her.

"So, are you seeing anyone?" I said.

She shook her head. "As if. What about you?"

Ask me an easy one.

I delayed my reply long enough for her to take stock of the silence. "Not really."

She must have noticed the look of discomfort cross my face. "So you and Matt aren't together." Then her eyes opened wider as if noticing me for the first time. "I never had you down as a dope head. Caddy used to talk about you all the time. Bit up-tight, she said."

What exactly had Caddy told her? We'd both shared the occasional spliff, so this was nothing new.

"That's not fair. The last few weeks have been tough and Mum goes mental whenever she sees how much wine I'm getting through."

"She'd rather you smoke?"

"She's never said anything either way. But she must know what I get up to, even though I crack the bedroom window open."

"You realise this weed's a hundred percent organic. Right? So it's got to be better than most of the shit we put in our bodies."

"I suppose, yeah. I'm still on medication but that's not helping much. That's why I prefer this stuff."

"What you on?"

"Temazepam. It's supposed to help me sleep, but I still get the bad dreams."

"Tammies? Is that with Doctor Ross?"

"Yeah. I have to go and see him every couple of weeks. He's trying to get me to cut down."

"God. He put me on fucking Diazepam. He refused point blank to give me Tammies."

"How come?"

She grimaced. "Temazepam doesn't mix with alcohol and other recreational drugs, so he reckons."

"Christ. So he knows you were using?"

"I'm on all sorts. They started me on Ritalin when I was a kid. Just on schooldays. Borderline ADHD, the doctors reckoned. And I'll take anything I can get my hands on, to be honest. So if there's any Temazepam going spare we can maybe do a deal. Your tabs for top quality hash."

"Could do." That was unlikely.

"Don't worry, I won't let on where I got it from. My old man grows his own. It's the only thing that keeps me sane, if you know what I mean."

I shook my head.

"He brings me free samples so there's plenty more where that came from."

"Your dad grows weed?"

"He used to work at the Hydroponicum so he knows what he's doing."

"And he's still living at Achiltibuie?"

"Out at Rieff. It was years ago when he was dealing, but even then it was never on the same scale as Matt and his buddies."

"Yeah."

"So how come Matt's written to you if you're not an item? I know you used to have the hots for him, but still." She sniggered. "Something he let on. He thought it was so sweet the way you tried to pretend you didn't really fancy him. He told me he could read you like a book."

"Bastard." The idea of Kay Jepson and Matt Neilson having a cheap laugh at my expense was sickening even now. "Is that what you were talking about the night he was shacked up here? 'Cause if I'd known about you two then, I wouldn't have let him anywhere near me."

"Don't worry, it was nothing serious." She smirked as she watched me squirm. "More of a business deal."

"That's not the point."

"He practically dumped his stash on me and I thought I was doing him a favour in return - stepping in and saving him from a fate worse than death. Not that he ever had the decency to thank me."

"Saving him from me you mean?"

"Chill." She shook her head slowly. "I didn't even know about you and him. We were at the Caley. Me and Tracey Macleod. Our afternoon off. Matt waltzed in splashing the cash and he ended up steaming. We all did."

I studied her face and for a moment tried to imagine the way she might have looked that afternoon - sloppy drunk. Her dark lipstick smeared across her smile, mascara a blur and eyelids heavy with desire. That tiny body squirming as she got comfortable.

"She was all over him."

"Tracey was?"

"Gagging for it. But, you know what she's like."

"Not really."

"You must have seen her around. Rooster used to say she had a ripcord holding her pants up instead of knicker elastic."

"So you're saying you saved Matt from Tracey Macleod by dragging him back here, getting him high and shagging him yourself."

She blew smoke in my direction then fixed me with a stare. "Like I say, it was a business transaction. He was up for it just as much as I was."

"If you say so."

"Do yourself a favour, Amy. Matt would say anything to save his own skin. He doesn't care about anyone except himself deep down." She shook her head. "Christ, if I'd known what I was letting myself in for I'd have had nothing to do with him. Matt Neilson's a big boy so he doesn't need looking after by some soppy, love-sick teenager. Trust me."

I thought back to his begging letter.

```
It's going to be hard once I'm back
home again. Getting my shit together.
I just hope you haven't given up on me
because I haven't given up on us.
```

That's when I told her about the VO and my decision to go visit Matt in prison, despite what my mother or anyone else might have to say about it. Somebody had to look out for him. He'd watched my back in his own clumsy way not so long ago. Maybe this would be my chance to return the favour.

7

MY tea had developed a crust around the edges while I showered.

"I'd given up waiting. If it's spoilt it's your own fault."

"That's OK, Mum." I was in no mood for another argument. Besides, I was starving hungry so I tucked in. "I went as far as the breakwater then on the way back I bumped into Kay Jepson."

Not many in the village had a good word to say for Kay despite all she'd been through recently. "Is she back at the Spar yet?"

All the signs suggested Kay wouldn't be back at work any time soon. "Still off sick but she was asking after Matt."

"Really?"

Mum didn't pursue the matter for once, and I persevered with the curled up lasagne as the silence between us deepened. I'd need to telephone my sister Leanne and get her on side before announcing my desperate plan to visit Peterhead. Maybe Kay was right and Matt could manage without me. But I needed to feel needed by someone.

Pathetic or what?

I rinsed my plate clean then grabbed a yoghurt and retreated to my room. Three spliffs wrapped inside a tissue had been burning a hole in the pocket of my running shorts. I retrieved them and slid them under the paperwork in my shoe box. Then I pulled out Matt's letter again and thumbed the telephone number into my mobile phone. I'd ring up to confirm the appointment once I'd spoken to my sister. Maybe she could drive me there and back if she was free next Tuesday.

Then my eyes focussed on the writing. The letter. The envelope Matt had addressed to me from prison and the Valentine's card that lay beneath it. Two completely different styles of handwriting. I pulled out the card and read the inscription again.

```
I'd rather watch U any day than 100
sunrises or 1000 sunsets

xxx
```

Someone else had written this, and not necessarily on Matt's behalf. Someone enjoyed watching me - watching over me. The same someone who wanted me to know he was still out there.

8

THE guard escorting me into the visitors' room must have registered the alarm in my face. "It's not as bad as it looks."

"Christ!" I whispered as Matt gave me a lingering kiss then took the chair on the opposite side of the low table.

Almost exactly two months had passed since I'd last set eyes on him and he'd changed beyond recognition. Green and purple skin discoloured his left eye socket and abrasions ran down the same side of his neck before disappearing inside his shirt collar. Yet the broad grin suggested he wore his wounds with a degree of pride.

"I didn't expect this," I said. "You could have warned me."

The damage had already healed by the look of it. It was the new haircut that shocked me the most - Matt's head shaven down to the bone.

"It's nothing to get worked up about," he said, his eyes fixed on me as if desperate to imprint every memory of my visit onto his brain. "Just some guy kicking off. Random as fuck. He was off his head."

"On drugs, you mean?"

His gaze wandered across to where the nearest guard was stationed. "Not quite. If they'd let him have his drugs then none of this would have happened."

"What do you mean?"

"It was some loser junkie desperate for a fix. He

already had mental issues and I ended up in the wrong place at the wrong time. That's all."

"Right." I couldn't take my eyes off Matt's face. The wounds might have been superficial but behind the bruises and the two-day stubble he looked unclean, almost unsavoury. "I must be stupid 'cause I didn't even realise they shaved people's heads when they put you in prison."

"Shit, Ames," he laughed and ran a hand over the smooth surface of his skull. "It's not fucking Alcatraz. I paid someone to do this for me. Cost me a Snickers bar but it had to be done."

9

"IT'S all part of the act. I've got a reputation to protect 'cause most of the nuggets in here think I went and stabbed the nut-job who attacked me."

"You stabbed him?"

"Don't look so worried." He shuffled lower into his chair and began to chew one of his fingernails. "There's going to be an internal inquiry and all that crap but nothing's going to come of it."

I didn't know what to believe. "How can you be so sure?"

"It was accidental as far as they're concerned."

"And was it?"

"He was a coke-head, Ames. He'd come down from a self-harming binge and he went for me. The blade was still in his hands when he jumped me. So I lashed out and when they pulled us apart I was the one holding the shiv. But the screws already knew most of his wounds were self-inflicted. I'd told them what he'd been up to weeks before."

"What d'you mean self-inflicted?"

Matt told me every detail and he seemed to enjoy watching me cringe.

"God, that's gross."

"They'll never admit they were to blame by letting him carry on. It'll all be hushed up."

"So you're going to be OK?"

"You know me. Bouncy ball."

"I suppose." I realised he was trying to play it cool but there was more to it than that. I stared into his eyes expecting to see a flicker of regret but there was nothing. Not a glimmer of humanity.

"Shit, you should have seen the look on their faces when they saw this." He pointed to his black eye.

"Who d'you mean?"

"Everyone on the block. Once word got round, it went mental. I know people told me to keep my head down in here. But that's easier said than done. It didn't take long for the shit to start. All the 'pretty boy' crap. But I wasn't going to let this place break me like everybody thought it would. Dad, the solicitor, every man and his dog.

"I gave as good as I got, and once they heard my cellmate had been carted off with his guts hanging out. Well, I was in. Nobody thought I had the balls to knife anybody. I told them it was self-inflicted; of course it was. Every single wound except the final one. It won't be the first time some idiot junkie in here killed himself."

"You mean he's dead?" Something wasn't right.

"Nah." He grinned. "They don't exactly keep us informed of what's going on outside these four fucking walls. But we'd have heard something long before now if he'd checked out for good."

"You sure?"

"Defo. He's probably been stitched up and sectioned. But who gives a shit?" He reached out a hand as I surveyed the room in search of a clock. "Let me have a proper look at you. I never thought you'd bother coming all this way."

I wish I hadn't. How long had I been sitting here?

"So did you come on the train?"

"No. Leanne brought me. I stayed at hers last night."

He twined his fingers in mine as if desperate to keep

me under his spell.

"It took a lot longer than we thought. Five hours."

"I still can't believe you've come through for me, Ames. I mean. I know I've not written before now but I've never stopped thinking about you. About us."

"Right."

Ten to three. How much longer?

My head dipped as he raised my hands to his face and inhaled. "God, it's been that long, I've forgotten the way you smell. Let me breathe in some more of that perfume."

Try to smile.

"It's just moisturiser."

"Doesn't matter. It's something to remember you by. The way your skin feels. God, it's so soft."

I scanned the room again as he squeezed my hands in his.

Was anybody watching?

"You don't need to look so guilty. There's cameras everywhere in this place and Neanderthal fucking bouncers on every door, in case you haven't noticed. But you get used to it. They're only watching for anyone trying to pass on little packets of drugs or mobile phones."

"Are people that stupid?" I tried to pull my hands away but he refused to let go.

"You'd be surprised. There's women come in here with all sorts of gear stuck you know where. Up their arses or in their fannies."

Why was he telling me stuff like this?

I gazed at the untidy groups scattered around the other tables. Older women. Mothers, presumably. And young girls with infants barely old enough to walk. Each face drawn by the strain of trying to appear cheerful. Their smiles barely hiding the shared despair of passive acceptance.

"They only have to look at you to see you're different class."

I felt anything but.

"If the screws suspected we were up to something, they'd be onto me like a pack of wolves."

"Right."

"Just relax. Let me touch you." His hand reached behind my neck and I felt his fingers sift through my hair. No one else seemed to be paying us the slightest attention apart from one of the prisoners at a neighbouring table. I noticed he kept eyeing me up. Grinning as if he knew me. Then he flicked his tongue out and gave a wink.

Jesus.

"Can you stop mauling me, Matt? It's freaking me out."

He pulled away and began chewing another fingernail. "Fine." He rested both arms across the table and I could see most of the scarring had healed, even though he'd bitten his nails down to the quick. I reached out a hand and touched his arm. I'd never seen him as jumpy as this even when he first got home from his spell in Raigmore.

Think of something to say.

"So how are you coping? I mean, it must be hard."

He shook his head. "They feed and water us three times a day seven days a week. What more do I need? A couple of us get to spend our free time in the IT block. It's better than playing pool on the wing or brooding with the rest of the bottom feeders all weekend."

"That sounds good. Are you thinking of carrying on with your degree? On-line studying or whatever?"

"No chance." His head dropped a fraction. "They've put me on some drugs awareness course, if that's what you mean."

"Not really. Have your mum and dad been to see you?"

"Not since this." He pointed to his eye. "Dad acts like he's ashamed of being seen in here. As if he's the one doing time."

"Right."

"Steff's OK. Mother hen as usual. And I phone her every weekend. It breaks the monotony having someone else to talk to 'cause I'd go mental otherwise."

"I suppose. And the food's OK?"

"We had tuna baguettes for lunch with the usual stash of rabbit food on the side. Then we had corn chips to take away the taste of the tuna. Then we had pink custard to take away the taste of the chips, but nobody eats that shit in here."

"The custard?"

"Not the pink custard. Pink custard's for queers."

"Christ, Matt!"

He reached for my hands again but I snatched them away almost as quickly.

"That's what they think in here, it's the God's honest truth," he said. "The lads who work in the kitchen spit in it on purpose. That's why nobody ever eats it."

"They spit in your food?"

"It's not that big a deal," he laughed. "They're not exactly looking for a five star review on Tripadvisor. You've no idea some of the stunts they get up to. Bleach in the milk. Ground glass. Napalming."

"Napalming?"

He told me what that meant and I shuddered at the image.

"Has anyone put ground glass in your food?"

"No, but you hear stories. That's why I stick to the religious menu most of the time. What they feed the Muslims and the other ethnics locked up in here. Curries and vegetarian stuff. Fuck me, they get treated like royalty. It's better than living on burgers and chips and mince and tatties because half the time they mash up the skin and all the black bits into the potatoes on purpose.

It's gross."

This wasn't what I'd been expecting. To be truthful I hadn't known what to expect but I felt out of my depth. Why exactly had he asked me to come and see him?

"There's only so many ways you can fuck up a plateful of rice." He finally got a grip on my right hand and raised it to his lips. Then his tongue began to trace the tips of my fingers and somewhere to our right I heard a chair scrape as another shaven head turned our way.

Another wink. *God.*

"There's a couple of lads from our neck of the woods in here. Barcode and Bubble. We have a laugh."

"Right," I said, trying to picture Matt's idea of having a laugh.

"Barcode's been moved into my cell now, and we're due out the same week so get ready to party."

"I bet you can't wait."

He kissed each knuckle. "Counting the days. And every night I pray that the two bastard coppers who put me in here get cancer and die."

I managed to tug my hand free and stuff it into the pocket of my jacket, staring him out as he looked on with defiance. "What the hell's come over you? You never used to be like this."

"No? Well, you'd better get used to the new me. They locked me up like an animal so how else am I supposed to behave? Do you expect me to roll over and play nice? The same as Dad and Steff told me to?"

"I'm not saying that."

"It's all about survival, Ames. Don't let them break you. Don't let them grind you down."

"Right."

"I've got to keep strong. And anger makes you stronger. I mean, everybody else in here hates the cops and there's a good reason for that." He sniffled and I heard him collect something at the back of his throat as if preparing to spit whatever it was onto the floor. "Hating the cops helps you survive what the Law does to you. That's the only way you can come out of the system at the other end without going mental."

I couldn't tell whether he was joking or being serious. "But it's your own fault you're in here not the police's."

He shrugged his shoulders.

"Is that what this haircut's all about? Some kind of gang you've joined?"

That's when he laughed out loud and the buzz around the room fell silent as one or two other heads looked across at us. "Jesus. D'you have to be so paranoid? I've already told you. It's part of the act."

"So you keep saying."

"As long as everybody in here thinks I knifed the guy - and I keep looking the part - no one's going to mess with me. Comprende?"

I nodded. "Suppose so. It seems a bit drastic that's all."

"Whatever." He cracked his knuckles. "So anyway, Ames. Are you missing me?"

10

I tried to blank out the journey through the outskirts of Peterhead. Traffic had been stop-start as far as the Gas Terminal. Intermittent drizzle adding to the tedium. It wasn't until we reached the dismally flat fields South of Fraserburgh that I emerged from my dream world. I began to search the misty horizon for a familiar hill or two. Anything that might signify we were nearing home. I needed fresh, clean air again. Something to take away the reek of misplaced guilt and failure that filled that wretched room. But all I could see were dark clouds grouping together for a more sustained attack.

"You're quiet. So how did it go?"

I'd barely spoken after getting into the car. My mind had shut down while I replayed the visit in my head. Now I owed my sister an explanation.

"Not good."

Nowhere near good.

"Right." A spatter of dirty water hit the windscreen as the weather finally broke. "God, that's all we need."

"Matt's changed. Nothing like I expected him to be."

"Well I could have told you that. People are going to react in all sorts of ways when you lock them up in a place like that. Don't tell me he's gone all religious and found Jesus."

"I wish." I reached into my jacket pocket for a tissue.

"Hey. I was only kidding."

"I know you were." I blew my nose and dabbed at my eyes. "He's become a completely different person. It was horrible seeing him like that."

"Never mind. He'll buck up once he's home again," she said. "Some people are better at coping than others. It probably doesn't help him being a bit student. He's not your average young offender or whatever they call them."

I wanted to laugh at the absurdity of what must have been going through Leanne's head. "Oh, he's coping fine, thanks very much. You've no idea. He's acting like some kind of hardened criminal. It's what he wants everyone to believe. And I think he's going to keep it up when he gets out."

"You think so?"

I took a deep breath and let rip. "I know so. You should have seen the state of him, Lea. His hair's all been shaved off. Apparently he gave somebody a chocolate bar in exchange for the tough-guy look. And he's got a black eye and some scrapes all down his neck. I swear he's loving every minute of it. He's even got his new buddies believing he killed some poor junkie. Stabbed him to death."

"You're joking."

"Does it sound like I'm joking?"

"But why drag you all the way across Scotland to show off his new look?"

"He didn't say."

There had been no need.

We continued in silence for the next thirty minutes or so then Leanne mentioned something about needing fuel. "We can get a snack while we're here. It'll save us having to stop at Inverness on the way home."

"OK."

The tea-room attached to a service station on the outskirts of Elgin seemed rather a crummy place for divine inspiration or whatever it was. But now everything made sense.

I stood with my back to the counter and unbuttoned my jacket while Leanne loaded a take-away baggie with paper napkins and sachets of powdered milk and sugar. Bleach, ground glass and sugar. Perhaps that had been just one more scare story doing the rounds in there. But my imagination had been fired up enough to believe every word Matt said. The same way his cronies believed he was some heartless killer with an endless supply of bravado, a fiery temper and a hot girlfriend to match.

"You sure you don't want a sandwich?"

"I'm fine. You don't have to keep fussing."

I handed her a ten pound note but she waved it away. "Keep it for later. We can get fish and chips from the Seaforth when we get back."

"Mhmm."

"Then you can have a long soak in the bath."

I ran my fingers through my hair then began sipping my tea. "Can't wait. I feel dirty."

"You're tired, that's all. An early night will do you good." Leanne knew I still had trouble sleeping. Last night had been especially difficult with the prison visit to look forward to. That's why she'd offered for me to spend the rest of the week with her and Steve. "It's his weekend off. We can maybe do something together on Sunday."

"There's no need. Honest." I needed to get home.

"So what else did Matt have to say for himself?"

"Nothing worth repeating. A lot of big talk about the screws and the block and stuff. He reckons the kitchen staff spit in the food."

"Sounds like one or two places I've worked," she laughed. "He'll be back to normal once he's out of there, you'll see."

"So how's that supposed to cheer me up?"

"What do you mean?"

"Well, we all know what Matt Neilson's like," I said. "His idea of normal is to shaft everybody. Literally or otherwise. Mum warned me often enough. The girls in school told me I was being stupid to think I could change him. I'm just surprised you haven't stuck your oar in."

"None of my business," she replied. "But that doesn't mean I'm going to stop looking out for you. If you really want to know, I think he's always been bad news - what our old granny would have called a 'bawbag'."

"Well don't worry, 'cause there's no need to look out for me anymore. It's taken a couple of hours to figure out why he wanted me there. Because his letter said one thing - how much he needed me to believe in him. I actually felt I'd be doing him a good turn. But I was kidding myself."

"What do you mean?"

"He got me there under false pretences, Lea. He'd even arranged the timing so his mates were there to watch the act."

"What act?"

"There was an audience in the visitors' room. A couple of his pals and their skanky partners. And I was the cabaret. A kiss as soon as he saw me. Groping me every chance he got. Touching my face and grabbing my hands. The usual bullshit about how much he misses me and wants me to support him once he gets outside."

"So?"

"He was using me, Lea. He dragged me across Scotland so he could show me off to his pals. Show them what a regular stud he is." I could feel the storm breaking now as the tears trickled down my face. "I can't believe he hates me enough to humiliate me like that."

11

"**SO?** What d'you reckon? Marks out of ten?"

Bubble had climbed onto the top bunk and began to rub his chin as if deep in thought. "Mhmm. Difficult to say. But I'd give her one."

"What? You crazy fucker," Matt and Barcode both laughed.

"No. I mean, I'd give her eight and a half out of ten, but I'd definitely give her one as well. I mean, the arse on her. It's a work of art."

"I told you," Matt said. "The Man from Del Monte's got nothing on me."

"Juicier than your average peach," Barcode added.

"Don't listen to him," Bubble interrupted. "He knows fuck all. He'd shag his own sister if she'd let him."

"Who says I haven't already?"

Bubble leapt off the bunk and wrapped his arms around Barcode. "You're sick, Barky. Did anybody ever tell you that?" Then he turned his attention to Matt again. "So has she been missing you, lover boy?"

"What do you think? She can't wait for when I get out of this shit-hole." Matt lowered his voice, "But I'll need to save all my energy over the next couple of weeks. The way she goes at it. Christ. She's like the fucking Duracell Bunny once she starts."

"Right. Only Barcode and me were thinking maybe she didn't seem too impressed this afternoon," Bubble said.

"I could see her eyes twitching every time you got too close. As if she couldn't wait to leave."

Matt stared at them both and his grin widened as he shook his head. "What d'you expect? This place is enough to turn anyone's stomach. It was a bit of a shock seeing me looking like this, that's all." Then he grabbed his crotch. "I'm telling you, she'll be gagging for this by the time we're out of here."

12

MARINATING in the bath with a coconut butter bomb for an hour made no difference. Half past ten and I still hadn't settled. In the end I got out of bed again, put on my dressing gown and wandered into the living room. Leanne offered to pour me a glass of wine while Steve made a discrete disappearing act.

"He's got to be up early in the morning. A load of timber to Inverness," she said.

"Right."

"Do you want to watch this?" Some re-run of a BBC costume drama filled the screen.

"Not unless you're following it," I said.

She turned the volume down to a whisper then went into the kitchen for a lighter and came back with a couple of packets of crisps and a bottle of red.

"Mind if I smoke?"

"If you have to."

My stomach was still queasy. Leanne had overdone the vinegar on the chips, so more cheap wine and salty snacks weren't going to help my digestion, but what the hell.

"So what's been happening in Lochinver? You see much of your old mates?"

I didn't mention my impromptu visit with Kay Jepson. Leanne probably knew her better than me since they'd been in the same year at school.

"Not really. I don't feel like socialising, to be honest. Getting sloshed with the same crowd every Friday night doesn't appeal at the moment."

"What about Caddy's pals? Lauren or Moolie and Sara? D'you still see them?"

"Not since the business with Paver."

"Oh my God." She relit her cigarette and pointed at the television. "That looks like Lochinver harbour."

A talking head filled the screen with banner headlines running along the bottom:

BOAT FEARED MISSING OFF THE COAST OF NORTH-WEST SCOTLAND.

She turned up the volume and we sat in silence as the lifeboat Coxswain reported the sighting of wreckage out at sea.

"We found floating debris and an oil slick about twenty miles West of Stoer Head. But so far there are no signs of survivors. No life raft. We're still trying to establish the exact identity of the vessel since we received no distress call. Weather and sea conditions were calm. A local fisherman reported evidence of a wreck which is why we attended the scene, but so far we're no nearer discovering what happened."

"Shit. I hope it's nobody we know."

"With a bit of luck it's young Paver," I said. "He's staying on his dad's boat by all accounts."

"That's a bit mean. Is he home on leave?"

I told her what little I knew. "He's out for good so his four years must be up. Got some ex-squaddie mate staying with him as well. They'd been up and down the coast every day since the end of April, following the War Games out at the Minch so Moolie's dad was telling Mum."

"Huh. So why bother packing it in if he still wants to play at being a toy soldier?"

"He was always a bit of a wannabe Action Man. I couldn't be doing with him, flashing the platinum card Daddy gave him when he finally got accepted in the Army."

"But what about Moolie's Booze Cruise?"

"What about it?"

"Didn't you and Peter have a thing going?"

A thing?

We'd had 'a thing' the previous August – almost a year after my brief encounter with a Danish girl staying at Achmelvich camp site. Keren had made me question my sexuality without exactly turning me off boys for good. Peter made the situation a little clearer

"It was nothing. I don't even know how Paver got an invite since nobody could stand being in his company for long."

The dry-run for Caddy's sixteenth birthday party had taken place at the White Shore. Invites on Facebook weeks in advance had made it clear what was expected. BYOBB - Bring Your Own Bottle and Blanket. The weather had been freakishly hot during the week leading up to it - the air growing heavier as dusk approached. Fires on the hills above Glen Canisp turned the horizon grey with smoke for days.

Caddy had already lost her virginity twelve months earlier. She'd spared me no details and I envied her attitude. Fuck and run. So the plan had been to get pissed and screwed – in that order. Peter arrived by dinghy - already blazing drunk - the 'Meera Rose' moored just beyond the breakwater. He wore denim Bermuda shorts and wraparound shades. But all I saw was the six-pack and all-over tan. There was more chance of a leatherback turtle washing up on the White Shore than a fit guy with a tan.

Seeing him and Melissa Charles together did something to my hormones. His war stories had been the last thing on my mind when she eventually wandered off to see to the five o'clock fuzz shadowing her top lip. The combination of too much sun and too much drink did its work. I couldn't even swear to what exactly happened between passing out drunk and waking up with my underwear around my ankles.

I might have struggled, put up a fight, or I might have welcomed him with open legs. I forget the finer details. But I know he disappeared once he'd completed his mission. And a couple of days later, I received a message inviting me and the rest of his Facebook friends to drinks on Daddy's boat. But I was desperate to avoid him for the rest of the time he was home on leave. He'd not bothered contacting me in person since our brief liaison - proof enough he'd been as keen as me to forget the whole affair.

"It was the vodka and raspberry juice combination that did the damage," I said. "I still can't stand the taste of raspberry milkshake."

Leanne stubbed out her cigarette in the ash tray. "I remember you throwing up all down the front of Steve's shirt as soon as you got home. Mum went mad but you couldn't stop laughing."

"I know. Steve said something about when his dad worked at the Caley they used to sacrifice a virgin on White Shore every time there was a party. Then they ran out of virgins."

13

"**SO** nothing happened between you and Peter?"
I shook my head. "Nothing worth talking about."

I'd not been able to keep my eyes off him once Melissa Charles started. She'd draped her body around him and stuck her tongue down his throat even before he hit shore. Then later there had been some truth or dare horseplay - Melissa pretending to give Paver a hand job. But when the booze ran out and she did her disappearing act Paver started to hassle me instead. No doubt he'd deciphered the signals I'd been sending out. I was looking for a summer fling that I could brag about back in school – without naming names. Something a little more romantic than the awkward fumbles I'd endured so far.

Eventually the camp fire burnt low along with most of the weed. I grabbed my blanket and suggested we find somewhere more private. Deep in the shade of the trees offered the best option, away from the midges that hovered above the scraps of barbecue leftovers. But after I laid out the blanket and got comfortable, he could hardly control himself. He was like a boy scout trying to get a fire going. I tired of his clumsy pawing and told him I needed a wee.

"I won't be long."

Once I reached the main path I decided to head back in the direction of the village. Paver would get the message.

I knew my way well enough through the Caley Woods and even though my feet kept skating from under me there were plenty of branches to hold onto. Enough trees to hug whenever the ground began to capsize. No one else seemed to be paying me any attention so I'd not be missed.

But Paver must have realised what I was up to.

I heard him close by. "Hey. D'you need any help?"

I'd stumbled to ground and could barely clamber to my feet again. "It's OK."

"No it's not. Look at the state of your trousers."

My pale yellow, low-cut hipsters were soaked in black gunge at the knees.

"Oh shit." My trainers were just as bad.

He reached out a hand, hauled me upright then led me deeper into the trees. That's when I noticed he'd picked up my blanket and brought it along. A boy scout - always prepared. I felt my stomach tighten as he stopped, turned to face me and began stroking the back of my neck. Whispering how much he wanted me. Right now. His mouth tasted over-sweet from the drink and it felt right to be wanted. To be desired. I was desperate to finish what we'd started.

He removed my t-shirt and I helped him slide down his shorts. Then I tugged off my trainers as he spread the blanket between some fallen trees. We lay there wedged inside the gap. Not exactly Babes in the Wood with him unbuttoning my trousers and both of us gasping for air and the twigs snarling my hair and his fingers digging inside my underwear.

By the time my full bladder began sending out an alarm call, the air had chilled sufficiently to sober me up. Any lingering sense of passion had disappeared along with lover boy. I retrieved my clothing and felt an unwelcome stickiness between my legs as I squatted in the undergrowth. I could smell him on my skin and my mouth tasted of iron filings. I was in two minds whether or not to wipe myself clean and bury my underwear out of sight, but then I heard someone calling my name. Caddy. I pulled on my trousers in a desperate attempt to get decent.

Yeugh.

She caught up with me as I was shaking dead leaves off the blanket. "God, look at the state of you."

"What?"

"Dad's phoned. We need to do the walk of shame before he comes looking for us."

The last thing I wanted was Mike Neilson seeing me like this. "Shit. Can you give me a minute? I need to find my trainers."

Then she must have seen the crumpled item of underwear in my hand. "Oh my God." She laughed. "What have you and Paver been up to?"

"No idea what you mean."

Caddy had said nothing more about it but I could guess what was going through her mind.

"And you haven't seen Peter since?" Leanne asked.

"No way."

But I'd thought of no one else for days after the White Shore nightmare. Then at Caddy's official sixteenth birthday barbecue I received more than enough attention to compensate for young Paver's shortcomings. Caddy's dad spent most of the evening explaining the wonders of astronomy to me while flirting outrageously whenever Steff's back was turned.

"I'm not expecting Peter to invite me round for cocktails, if that's what you mean. I'm giving evidence against his dad so I'm the last person he'll want to see."

"Have they said any more about the date?"

"For the court case? As far as I know it's still October."
"Edinburgh Sheriff Court?"
"Could be. Or Inverness or Aberdeen. It depends."
I felt something vibrate inside the pocket of my dressing gown. Incoming email alert.
"Hang on. Let me just see. . ."
I clicked the icon and there it sat in my Inbox. 1 new message.

WYWOY
ENJOY YR VISIT?

14

"**LET** me see," Leanne said.

"It's nothing. Just some junk mail."

"Amy, you're shaking. Let me have a look."

I tossed her the phone and wrapped myself up tighter inside my dressing gown. Then I watched as she scrolled through my messages.

"Who's this loner@letstalk?"

"No idea. But it must be somebody who knows me, obviously."

"Like an old boyfriend? Someone you've dumped?"

"Hardly. And they haven't exactly been hassling me or anything like that. It's like someone's watching and every couple of weeks they want to remind me they're watching. Some stupid game."

Leanne lit another cigarette and nodded, in thought rather than in agreement. "It's still creepy. I mean, we only got back a couple of hours ago but he knows where you've been."

"I know." I screwed up my face as I drained the wine glass.

"So who else have you told about visiting Peterhead?"

I'd not mentioned a thing to anyone. Not even Mum. As far as she knew we were on a girls' day out to Inverness. And I'd told Kay Jepson I intended visiting Matt sometime soon but I'd not mentioned any specific date.

"Nobody apart from you and Steve. And Matt, of course."

"Well it's definitely not me and Steve."

"Obviously."

"So that must mean it's Matt."

"But why would he bother? I went to see him like he asked, so what more does he want?"

Matt had mentioned spending time in the IT department. I couldn't imagine what he'd be getting up to in there but it seemed unlikely they'd allow prisoners to send out emails all hours of day and night.

Leanne blew a stream of smoke into the air. "It's got to be Matt. Maybe he asked somebody on the outside to send them. He's trying to wind you up so you'll turn to him for help. Manipulating you the way he always does."

"I don't know. It sounds unlikely," I said.

"Perhaps you could have a quiet word with Greg Farrell."

Greg Farrell the local bobby. He'd not even spotted what Gordon Paver and his cronies were up to right under his nose, so I wasn't holding out much hope.

"I'll leave it for now I think."

"He can nip it in the bud if it really is Matt."

"I suppose." But I wasn't convinced. If Matt was behind this he'd have wanted me to know. He could never resist admitting to a wind-up. Caddy used to reckon Matt owned up to doing stuff as regularly as the Taliban. That's how he got his kicks.

"You've not replied to any of them, have you?"

"Of course not. I'm not that bloody stupid." I eased myself up from the sofa. "Time I went to bed, I think, and thanks for today."

I bent down and kissed her cheek. She squeezed my arm then I made my way to the bathroom. Somewhere outside I heard a wheelie bin topple over. The wind had got up in the last hour. A passing storm that would hopefully head out to sea overnight.

But hours beyond dark into the grey gloom of dawn, I heard the spatter of rain on the window. I'd not slept again, and the temptation to take a second tablet was stronger than ever.

15

08:40 and I hadn't allowed for the mad dash of schoolchildren outside the block of flats. They were milling onto campus from all directions. I stood at the entrance to the stair-well for as long as possible but realised that sooner or later someone would recognise the hooded creature in grey jacket and dark trousers and maybe approach her.

Then I heard the clatter of heels behind me, the door sucked open and Kaz Cartwright appeared. A classmate and one of the few close friends who hadn't felt a need to post a meaningless comment on Facebook following Caddy's death. She seemed as shocked to see me as I was to see her.

"God, Amy Metcalf. Haven't seen you for ages. How's things?"

"Well, you know. I'm feeling better than I was. Hoping to be back at school next term."

"Right. I wasn't sure whether you'd dropped out or not. I wouldn't have blamed you. I'd have done the same, given the chance."

"No. I'll be back in August."

"So what are you doing round here this time of day?"

"I've been staying at Leanne's."

Kaz still looked a little rough around the edges. Heavy on the make-up and slutty as ever. No surprise, given her home life. Both her older brothers were trouble. Baxter

Cartwright was in prison, last I'd heard.

"You should have given me a knock. Me and some of the girls were out on the bash last night."

A door slammed shut somewhere on the upper floor and moments later Kevin Waterson appeared like another ghost from the past.

"Woohoo. Look who's come to see you, Kevin." Kaz gave a wide grin while he stood and stared at us both, as if trying to place who we were.

"Hiya," he said as he straightened his glasses.

"You OK?" she asked.

"Yeah, thanks."

"It's Amy. Remember Amy? Caddy's friend."

His face turned bright red and she laughed as he shoved his way past to join the throng heading in the direction of the school.

"Fuckin' weirdo," she said. "You've got my number. Give me a tinkle next time you're passing through to Inverstress or whatever."

"Yeah. Will do." I fumbled with the strap of my backpack. "I'll probably call round the shops before the bus leaves."

"OK." She air-kissed either side of my face. Cigarette smoke on her breath. I pulled my zip up higher and we both stepped out into the rain. Within five minutes everybody would be gone. Time to make my move. I crossed the grassed area heading for the main school gates then decided I didn't need a magazine to read on the ride home after all. It would be simpler to board the bus right here while it stood parked next to the school library. But there were more schoolchildren about than I'd been expecting. Laughing at me. Muttering about me. Watching me.

I'd forgotten all about Kevin Waterson. He'd always been a geek - a chubby kid with long, curly hair and stooped shoulders. He'd been in Caddy's class and Caddy reckoned he'd had a thing for her for ages. He'd even ridden all the way to Lochinver on the school bus one afternoon. Caddy told me how he followed her when she got off. But as soon as he saw her turn into her drive and give him the finger, he spun on his heels and headed back towards the shops.

I'd seen him at her funeral with a couple of others from Caddy's class. Nothing strange there. But he'd kept his distance from me and Matt - stalking my friend from beyond the grave maybe. I could see him lingering outside the main doors into the school now. Watching me. Bodies pushed past either side of him but he seemed to be in no rush to go inside. Then he raised his mobile phone to his eye.

My feet grew heavier and my shoulders ached as if the weight of the world was pressed down upon them. I couldn't do it. I couldn't complete the walk across to the parking area let alone get on that school bus, even if my life depended on it.

16

"I told you I don't mind driving you home," Leanne gave me a sideways glance as we followed the coast road skirting Ardmair. "But you need to sort yourself out. Talk to someone, perhaps."

"Doctor Ross, you mean? He's trying to get me to come off my meds."

"It's up to you, Amy. You're the only one who can make the situation better. But shutting yourself away from the world and getting sozzled whenever you start feeling sorry for yourself isn't going to help."

How many times had I heard this shit?

"That's easy for you to say."

"It's been three months. Time you stopped acting the victim."

I watched the ferry battling its way through the grey mizzle out across Annat Bay. Life was always going to be hard now.

"Think of all the plans you and Caddy made. Just because she died, it doesn't mean your life has to stop."

Last October Lauren and Quinn had returned from a backpacking holiday through India en route to Sri Lanka and the Maldives and we'd been so envious. But that dream was never going to happen now.

"And if you were the one who got attacked. . ."

"I'd be a victim for the rest of my life? Is that what you think?" Leanne had never been one to tread carefully on my feelings."You need to grow a pair."

We both laughed out loud.

"You're lucky Mum still puts up with all the crap you've been dishing out. Why not get off your precious backside and start doing something useful? Earn yourself a little cash. Help her out."

"Why, what's she been saying?"

"Nothing."

We continued in silence, skirting the edge of Inverpolly. Clouds swirled in angry masses above the peaks of Cul Beag and Cul Mor. On a different day than today maybe I'd put on my boots and head for the hills.

"There's stuff she'd rather you didn't know about, that's all." She gave me another sideways look. "But I keep telling her, you're not a child."

"Talking about me behind my back. Cheers."

"It's not always about you, so shut it. It's to do with me and Steve." The car slowed to a crawl as we got snarled up behind a fish wagon careening through the Elphin bends.

They'd seemed contented enough the previous night. "You and Steve? I thought things were OK between you."

"They are. But they've cut his hours again. And I'm down to half shifts. Zero hours and all that crap. There were a couple of big bills last month. The electric and the telephone. They never come when there's money in the bank to cover them."

"Right."

"I've started another part-time job but it doesn't pay that much. Mum offered to help us out until I get sorted, that's all. A couple of hundred. She knows I'll pay her back."

"OK."

"I was on my arse, Ames. I didn't know what else to

do. But it's left her short as well."

"Is that what she says?"

"She hasn't said a word. But I got a letter last Friday from some finance company threatening to come and repossess our fridge freezer and the washing machine."

"Christ."

"I know. Steve says we should get another loan, and when I mentioned it to Mum she said maybe he was right. She said she has her own bills to pay."

"So what you going to do?"

"No idea. But if you're planning on stopping off school 'til the end of August the least you can do is help out. Help out Mum I mean."

"Well there's no way I'm going back to work at the chalet park."

"No one's asking you to. It's closed down isn't it?"

"Up for sale, as far as I know."

"Right. So don't go looking for excuses. There must be something else you can find. Maybe Mum can get you some shifts at the Stag's Head. Or she could put in a word at the Boathouse."

Living under the same roof was bad enough. The idea of waiting at tables in the same bar as my mother was too much to contemplate. And working at the Boathouse would be just as dire. Tracey Macleod worked in the kitchen and judging from what Kay had told me, she and Matt still hadn't been forgiven for the night they abandoned her in the Caley and paired off together. I intended keeping well out of it.

If I was going to get a summer job it would need to be where I could keep a low profile. Some place where nobody knew me or my history.

"I'd rather help Jimmy Jump scrape around the rocks for mussels at low tide than do waitressing."

"Yeah. Right."

"I'm just saying. Everybody round here knows Amy Metcalf. The way some of them look at me is bad enough. As if it's my fault Caddy got killed and I didn't."

"That's daft talk, and you know it. If there's no work in Lochinver, you can always come and stop with me and Steve. We'll rent you our spare room." The fish wagon turned left at Ledmore Junction and Leanne put her foot down to overtake. "There's more chance of you finding something in Ullapool anyway."

"Could do."

"Just don't take all summer thinking about it."

As it turned out that wasn't necessary.

"Is a hundred and fifty enough?"

"Thanks, Mum." Leanne pocketed the cash. Then she gave me a look. "What now? The car doesn't run on fresh air, in case you hadn't noticed."

"I know. But. . ."

"So how was Peterhead?" Mum said.

They watched as the penny dropped. "You knew all along?"

"I'm not as green as I look, Amy. I knew you'd give in to him. But I hope seeing him stuck inside that place has made you realise what a loser he is. You need to get that Matthew Neilson out of your system. He's only got himself to blame for everything."

"I know, and I told him as much to his face. I honestly don't care if I never see him again."

"That's good. And I've been busy while you were away. I might have found you a part-time job. Just for a couple of weeks. But it'll get you out of your bed in the morning."

"If it's the Stag's Head you can forget it."

"It's not bar work or waitressing, if that's what you're worried about," she said. "I've been in touch with Jimmy

Jump. He's needing someone."

Leanne and I both burst out laughing at the same time.

"What's so funny?"

"Never mind."

"You won't have heard the news." Mum's face suddenly clouded over.

"What news?" I said.

"It looks like there's a boat sunk out in the Minch."

"Oh, that? Yeah, we saw it on the telly last night."

Mum seemed to stiffen. "There's rumours it might be the 'Stormy Petrel'. They're still trying to make radio contact but there's been nothing so far."

My pulse slowed and I felt by head begin to throb with the beginnings of a migraine.

"There was talk that it could be something to do with the War Games. Somebody at the pub was saying how they'd been jamming the radio frequencies and firing shells out at sea most of the day."

"Isn't that Maurice Tyrell's boat?" Leanne said.

Mum nodded. "Him and young Michael went out the back of five yesterday morning and they haven't been seen since."

Michael Tyrell – Moolie to his friends.

17

HE'D still not taken the poster down from inside the Spar.

WANTED URGENT

```
Someone to help empty a house
            Brackloch
         Good rate of pay
```

There was a mobile number at the bottom, yet the last time I'd visited Jimmy Jump he'd shown no signs of embracing twenty-first century technology. No television on view let alone a telephone.

"Paver." A much younger voice than Jimmy's answered. I kept it short.

"My mum phoned. Yesterday I think it was. It's Amy Metcalf. The job you're advertising in the Spar. Jimmy told her I should come round to see him. I was wondering when would be best."

Peter might have caught his breath when he heard my name but otherwise it didn't seem to register. "It's for my uncle, if you're still interested. Mostly packing boxes or chucking out junk. Cleaning the place once he moves out. It's a bit of a mess."

"That's OK. When should I come round?"

"It's the cottage at Luibeg. But you probably know that.

How does Saturday morning sound?"

"This Saturday?"

"Yeah. I'll tell him to expect you. I won't be there."

"Doesn't matter."

"Let's say ten o'clock, right?" he said. "And no hard feelings. Perhaps we can meet up for a drink some other time."

Seriously?

I hung up.

18

"I hate myself. I mean, I was so pathetic. I should have been honest with him when I had the chance."

"The whole thing sounds really shady," Kay Jepson said.

"You've no idea."

I'd had the perfect opportunity to do it, protected by a bunch of beefed-up security guards. Matt couldn't kick off. He'd lose face in front of his mates for one thing, and the screws would be onto him like a pack of wolves - to use his own expression. It would have been a blessing because he'd no longer be deluding himself we still had a future together.

"I should never have set foot in the place. Especially now I realise why he invited me. Some kind of trophy girlfriend to parade in front of his pals."

"Bastard."

"I feel sick just talking about it."

Kay handed me the roll-up and sank back into the sofa again. "He's not worth wasting breath over. Arsehole."

"I know." I sucked in some warmth and felt the worries recede as the empty space between my ears filled with sheer bliss.

"If I was you I'd write to him before he gets released. Tell him he's dumped. And tell him why."

"I could do. But a letter seems a shitty way out."

Kay snorted. "I can't believe you're still feeling sorry

for the guy. Honestly, he wouldn't think twice about dumping you by text. He'd not even bother telling you if he'd found himself another piece of ass. Trust me."

"That's unlikely to happen while he's locked up." I flicked some ash in the direction of the saucer on the coffee table and sucked in another hit. "I don't suppose you want to take him off my hands? We could always do a deal."

"No way. I wouldn't touch him again even if you paid me." But then the laugh dried in her throat as her own hand jerked out and released a tumble of ash onto the floor. "Anyway, I'm not into guys. Not right now."

"Not right now or not ever?" She shook her head and I realised I'd been insensitive as well as presumptuous. "Sorry, I wasn't thinking."

"That's OK. It's just, there are times when I feel if anyone came near me. Tried to do something, you know. Tried to touch me. I think I'd totally freak out. I'd fight them off like a wildcat. Probably scream my fucking head off as well."

Kay flinched as I leaned forward to stub out my spliff. "I wouldn't blame you. It's over-rated anyway," I said.

"Sex?"

"Too right."

She gave me a lop-sided grin. "Then there's other times when my hormones are screaming out for attention. You know, late at night when I'm stuck here on my own. Or waking up in an empty bed with the spare pillow squashed between my legs. Times when you need someone to snuggle up against. To touch. To go off-the-chart ape-shit with."

"Tell me about it."

I watched her toes curl inside her woolly socks and tried to clear my head of the other images I was making up. Kay Jepson sprawled out on her couch the way she was right now. Kay Jepson stripped down to her skivvies and me helping her go off-the-chart ape-shit.

"Did I say the wrong thing?" she asked.

Christ. Was she a mind reader?

I shook away the daydream. "No, nothing. Just thinking. All this guy stuff. It'll take time, that's all. Maybe ten years from now we'll be ready to trust someone. Though I'll be a virgin again by then."

"Christ, there's no way I can keep my legs crossed that long."

I smiled back. "Me neither. But Matt Neilson's had his chance and blown it. And once he's out of prison I'll tell him."

"To his face? You want that level of grief?"

"What's the worst he can do?" I said. "I'll do it somewhere public. On neutral territory. And I'll make sure I've got back-up."

"Well you can count me out." Kay twisted her body to the edge of the couch and reached out for her coffee mug.

Maybe Ullapool. Maybe Leanne or Kaz Cartwright riding shotgun.

"The trouble is, there's other stuff been going on as well and I need to sort that out first. It's complicated."

"Other stuff?"

I passed her my phone.

Matt's mum had telephoned the previous night and it struck me that things were still far from over. "I hear you've been to visit Matt. I can't thank you enough, Amy."

"Yeah, well. He wrote asking me to go and see him. I suppose I felt sorry for him."

She didn't take the hint and ask if that was the only reason. "It's still kind of you. He sounded really excited when he was on the phone. You should have told me you were going in. The least we can do is pay for the petrol."

"I never thought. But there's no need, honest."

"So how did you find him?"

Did she want the truth?

"When's the last time you saw him?"

The line went quiet for a few seconds. "About three weeks ago. Mike can't get time off work at the moment. But he telephones us whenever he can. Why? What do you mean?"

"Has he told you he's been in some kind of fight?"

"Oh, God. No."

"It's OK. He's fine, so he says. A black eye and a few scrapes." I felt like some kind of wicked messenger - the bearer of bad news that no one wants to hear.

"He's never breathed a word to me or his dad."

"Well, I suppose he didn't want to worry you. As I say, he's gotten over it. But he's made a few changes to the way he looks as well."

"What do you mean?"

"He's shaved off all his hair, that's all. But he looks a bit wild, to be honest."

I heard her gasp.

"He's going for the tough guy look. I suppose he wants to fit in. Make sure nobody else tries it on with him."

Steff gave a sniffle. "That's dreadful. I should speak to our solicitor. They can't let people attack Matt just like that and get away with it."

I almost laughed out loud. "You're best speaking to Matt first. If you cause a scene it might make things worse. He's only got another four weeks to go. And he says he's got friends in there. They watch each other's backs, I expect."

"D'you think so?"

"He said they do computer stuff together at the weekends. Play games, I suppose. And the one who attacked Matt has been shifted somewhere else anyway. I think Matt was able to stand up for himself, which is good."

"Well, yes. He's told us he's enrolled on a course as well so it's all good news, I suppose."

He'd obviously not explained the details of his rehabilitation programme to Steff.

"I'll maybe wait until he phones again before doing anything. He said how much of a boost it gave him seeing you yesterday afternoon. You've no idea how much it means to me and Mike that you're standing by him after everything that's happened."

That's when it hit me.

I was expected to continue playing the faithful girlfriend when all I really wanted was a clean break. I almost told Steff she'd got it wrong and that we were finished. But instead I asked her to do me a favour next time she got in touch.

Kay's face blanched as I mentioned our telephone conversation. "What did his mum say?"

"She said she'd talk to him, even though she doesn't think Matt's the one who's sending them."

"Well, she would say that."

"I know. But I'm starting to think the same."

"How come?" Her face straining for more information.

"Just a feeling."

The more I thought about it, the more I realised the latest message didn't have to be about my visit to Peterhead. It could just as easily be about me staying at Leanne's or even calling round to see Kay Jepson.

Mike Neilson's Honda was parked outside the Spar when I left Kay's flat and I saw Steff talking to one of the staff in the service station kiosk. She waved and I began to cross the road but then I felt a familiar vibration in my trouser pocket.

WYWOY
GOOD TO SEE U AND K TOGETHER – XX

19

I cycled the three miles to Brackloch. Everything looked the same as it had the last time I'd visited the cottage, except for a welcome warmth. Days were getting longer. The branches were already laden in green and the scent of summer and the river filled the air.

Jimmy's new pick-up stood next to the cattle grid. A black Toyota, gleaming with fresh paint. Except the wheel arches were already caked in mud and I could see one of the tail lights had a crack in its red plastic cover.

He came out to greet me. "God be praised, you're looking a picture of health again."

I doubted it.

His skin had long ago become crabbed with age and drink but his face was clean-shaven for once. He also wore a new hat by the look of it, and his shirt appeared a little less creased than usual. I'd not seen him since the incident with the Ukrainians. Of course, Matt had kept me up to date with everything I'd missed. The police turning up en masse again. The Press poking their noses everywhere. The private funeral at Inverness for Evergreen. Him and Jimmy the only two at the crematorium apart from the undertaker and a minister.

"I mind the last time I saw you. A wee thing no heavier than a new-born lamb, quivering at the world."

I rested my bike against the wall of his cottage and began to take off my helmet and gloves. "Yeah, I remember. I should have come to see you before now. To say thanks, I mean. If you hadn't been there. . ."

He shook his head. "You're not to fret yourself now. It was the Good Lord's will. You'll take a cup of tea before I show you around."

"Thanks." I followed him into the tiny, dark kitchen attached to the building and realised that nothing had changed inside despite the speculation regarding Jimmy's change of fortune.

Rumours surrounding the old man's inheritance had spread through the village like a tidal wave once the news became public. Jimmy Jump - or James Paver to give him his proper title - was rich. He always had been. But now his younger brother, Gordon, was locked up in Barlinnie awaiting trial Jimmy was to be allowed access to what was rightfully his.

"Will you take a wee dram with your tea?"

"No thanks. Just milk if you've got."

"Come through."

He led me into the living room. Matt and I had sat on that same couch less than three months ago and listened as Jimmy told us of his run in with the Klondykers. Gordon Paver's Ukrainian pals.

"Mum says you're looking for someone to help empty this place."

"Aye. It was the boy's idea to put up the poster. Young Peter."

"Right."

"Next week if you can."

"Is Peter going to be here as well?"

"Not Monday. We've an appointment at Inverness to sign the paperwork for the sale."

"So where are you moving to?"

"Let me put the kettle on."

I studied the room while he pottered about in the

kitchen. The fire had burned down to cold black embers a long time ago and I could see smuts of soot in the cobwebs suspended above the curtains.

"The milk's starting to turn," he said as he carried a mug in one hand and a cup and saucer in the other. "There was a full moon."

"That's alright. It doesn't matter."

He handed me my black tea. "You'll have heard how Luibeg has been sold."

"Peter said something about you moving out."

"Aye. I'm moving to Strathbeg House."

Shit.

I nearly dropped the cup. That was the one place I still had nightmares about.

20

STRATHBEG Holiday Park was Gordon Paver's empire. Caddy had worked there once. Then I'd taken over after she died. Jimmy had been employed as some kind of handyman-groundskeeper - when he was sober enough to find his way from one end of the village to the other. I could feel the cup rattling in the saucer as I tried to lower it to the floor.

This didn't seem like a good idea after all.

Jimmy took out his knife and began to whittle away at a fingernail. "I was never meant to be a rich man. I didn't have a head for numbers, Gordon always maintained."

"Right."

"It was Evergreen made me move here into this cottage." He looked around the cluttered room as if he'd never quite realised it was all his. Yet he'd survived here seven years or more as far as I knew.

He gestured towards the framed prints on the wall and the knick-knacks gathering dust on the shelves. "Most of these were hers. It was never a proper home. Not after she left. And it's no place for an old man on his own."

"So is that why you're selling? Only, I thought Mr Paver's place was up for sale as well."

He shook his head as if in a rage. "Strathbeg House is rightfully mine. Gordon registered it in my name years ago but never let on."

"Wow." There had been talk in the village once the

police began investigating Gordon Paver's finances more thoroughly.

"You'll have heard about my father's will. But most of the money is tied up. Gordon spent my inheritance on the chalet park. My birthright, so the boy says. And the boat is in his name."

"Peter's?"

"Aye. No one can get their hands on anything no matter what Gordon's accused of."

"So are you going to be opening the chalet park again?"

"Never." He shook his head more forcefully than before. "I'm not seeking to profit from our shame. We've already pulled down the two bunkhouses."

"You have?"

"I'm buying a static caravan to sit within the grounds."

"Right."

He put his knife away. "I'll never forget the day I first arrived there, almost thirty years ago. A fair weather crossing." As if on cue the sun broke through the rowan branches pressed against the tiny window and a chequer board of light fell across my chest.

"Of course there was nothing at Strathbeg then. Just the ruin of an abandoned sheep fank lying tight against the shore."

"No."

"We watched the waves breaking white as Waterford lace across the rocks at Inverkirkaig. And once I saw the harbour and the hotel it all came back to me. The way my father had described it."

Jimmy pulled a small cardboard box from under his chair and began rummaging inside. Then he passed me a faded photograph. A thick glossy postcard with deckled edges.

"Where's this?"

"It's the Caley Hotel."

The only part I recognised was the tall, stone frontage and the turreted tower to one side. The entire roof gaped wide open. "When was this taken?"

"More than seventy years ago. After the fire. My father would have been no older than you are now. He worked there as a bell-boy."

A tall-funnelled steam boat lay moored alongside with the sea loch virtually lapping at the hotel's front door.

"I didn't know there'd been a fire."

"Archie Paver's doing, so they said. Cursed my father to Hell and back they did but by then he'd already fled."

"Archie was your father?"

"Aye. His heart had always been across the green water. He and five brothers were raised on a croft above Kinnego Bay." He took another swig from his mug. "Archie came here to find work when times were hard at home."

"Right," I said. I took a sip from my cup.

Some frigging tea party.

"Lochinver was a fine place back in those days. Fishing boats along either side of the loch and their nets full. But there had been talk of another war against Germany. Hitler already Chancellor and looking to give his people more land. Their birthright so he claimed. Times there as hard as anywhere else."

I knew all about Hitler and the Nazis and the Holocaust from school. I could feel the heat bearing down on me, sending me under. I handed him back the photograph. "That was all a long time ago."

"My father used to tell us tales of the good fight when we were growing up."

"The war you mean?"

"No no. The Irish had no belly for fighting this time around. And the British had no cause to drag us into another war. Chamberlain, Halifax and all the other Tory warmongers. So many young men had been lost and all for nothing."

"I suppose."

"We gave them our boys' lives and got little in return except empty promises."

"Right." I could feel my eyes growing heavier as the hot sunlight folded across my shoulders like a comfort blanket.

"The Thirties were unsettled times. Perhaps with the threat of another war people chose to enjoy life despite the poverty and deprivation. There was to be a grand party at the Caley Hotel, with dignitaries from London and no expense spared."

"Here?"

"Aye." He grinned. "The management had been sworn to secrecy but the chambermaids knew all the ins and outs of the hotel and my father soon got to hear who was invited."

"Mhmm."

"The War Cabinet intended visiting Lochinver for a weekend's hunting and shooting with the Duke."

I nodded, barely able to keep up with his wandering mind.

"Archie was a young and foolish boy back then. He worshipped de Valera. The Fianna Fáil."

My head slumped back against the cushions and his words faded into the background.

". . . a bomb."

I lurched awake.

Had I heard right?

". . . left over from the Great War."

"A bomb?"

"A mortar bomb. White phosphorus. There was talk afterwards of how he'd planned to detonate it inside the boiler room once the party got under way."

God.

"Of course, the War Cabinet never arrived. They were never meant to be here. But there was a grand party and the fire began sometime in the early hours. Most of the building was destroyed. The banqueting hall. The ballroom. A fine staircase - oak and walnut veneer."

"That's awful."

"My father helped get the guests out of their beds but rumours were already spreading like wildfire even before the ashes grew cold."

"Rumours about your dad?"

"His tongue always ran away with itself the way that happens with most young boys when they first take to drink. There were many here who had their suspicions about Archie Paver long before the night of the fire. Sympathies he'd have been better keeping to himself."

Some people never change. I'd suffered my share of distrustful looks.

"They found no evidence but the stories were enough to have him seek passage on a boat across the Minch the following day with only the clothes he wore on his back. He spent the rest of his life in Donegal. Gweedore. You've heard of the Poisoned Glen maybe."

"No."

"Aye, well. It was tainted with a name that it never deserved. The same as our family, my father always said."

"That's in Ireland."

"County Donegal, aye. Gordon came along nine years after I was born. Ulster blood, though our grandparents came from these parts originally. There was a sister but she was lost when she was but a wee bairn. Sometimes I mind her in her cradle and the peat fire and a black kettle on the coals. Hissing."

"So, if you're moving into Strathbeg House why are

you buying a caravan?"

"The house is to be Peter's home for as long as he needs it while his father is in prison," he said. "I'll stay close by to keep an eye on the boy."

I laughed. "How old is Peter now? Twenty-two, twenty-three? He's not going to want you baby-sitting him."

"Maybe not." His eyes closed and his voice seemed on the point of breaking. "Peter's a fine young man, but a little impetuous. He swears now he's earned his stripes for his country he's going to finish what his grandfather started."

21

JIMMY'S refrigerator held all manner of delights. Sprouting turnips weeping with black rot. Decomposing fish part-wrapped in slimy, wet plastic bags. Bacon turned green. Various packs of butter, all part-used and stippled with toast crumbs. The smells alone were enough to turn my stomach and make my eyes water. Had there been a smoke alarm inside his kitchen I guess it would beep every time he searched for a slice of mouldy cheese or a blob of rancid lard.

Then as I prised loose a pack of greying pâté from one corner of the fridge door, the small plastic shelf used for storing bottles clattered onto the kitchen floor. An open carton of watery, yellow-green sludge that might have been milk in a previous life fell at my feet and its contents splattered all over the cracked lino. I cursed Jimmy under my breath as I stepped back from the mess. I'd already filled three of the heavy-duty rubble sacks he'd left in the porch. One held the contents of his bathroom - rusted razor blades, greasy slabs of discoloured soap with curls of grey hair still intact, and a variety of empty shampoo bottles and half-used toilet rolls.

"Don't waste time deciding what to set aside and what to throw out," he'd explained. As if that made my job any easier. I dragged the fridge away from the wall so I could wipe up the spillage and that's when I discovered the carcase complete with a wriggling mass of maggots.

I shrieked. But there wasn't a soul within miles to hear me. Mickey or Minnie had been dead a while. Months more than likely. The sudden heat-wave had presumably speeded up the decomposition process until all that remained was a lump of dried residue covered in black fluff, fine as thistledown. In the end the wriggling mass of maggots numbered less than a dozen. But they had been enough to make my skin crawl as I scooped them up with a dustpan. The mouse had become virtually welded to the floor covering but I managed to chisel it free with a spatula and give it a decent burial at the bottom of a bin bag. A sinister black stain like a patch of burnt ground was all that remained.

But I kept seeing imaginary white, wriggly shapes for the rest of the afternoon. Inside the bread bin. Under his toaster and at the back of every wall cupboard I emptied.

By three o'clock the kitchen was bare. I'd exhumed cans of fly spray, window cleaner and a box of dish-washer tablets from the darker recesses beneath his kitchen sink. No dish-washer in sight. Then as I lugged another cardboard box filled with cleaning products and crockery out into the lean-to next to his porch I heard the growl of the Toyota's engine. Peter was driving judging by the speed at which it rattled over the cattle grid then skidded to a halt.

I wiped the sweat from my face and tugged off my gloves.

Jimmy stepped out. "You're still here, God bless you. And I can see what a fine job you're doing."

I muttered explanations as I pointed to each carton stacked against the wall. "Canned food. Other bits from the kitchen. Tea towels and saucepans. Toiletries and stuff from an old medicine chest." But the old man looked shell-shocked. The thought of seeing most of his worldly goods ready to be transported to landfill maybe.

Peter slammed the door of the truck and studied his mobile phone as if poised to make an important call. But then he seemed to think better of it. "I'm going to shoot off."

"Aye, that's fine." Jimmy continued to look nervous. Almost as if he was wary of what his nephew might do next. "Can you drop off some of this rubbish at the tip on the way into the village?"

"Will do."

Jimmy turned to me. "Put your bike in the back. The boy can give you a ride home. You've done more than your duty."

"There's no need."

But Peter insisted. I'd not seen myself in a mirror but I felt totally spent.

"So how have you been?" Peter trying to make conversation.

The least I could do was be civil for the five minutes it would take him to drive me home.

"OK, I suppose."

"This business with my dad. . ."

"Don't worry. I'm getting over it. Bit by bit. I'd rather not talk about what happened, to be honest." It wasn't something I was comfortable talking about with most people. His son - never.

"The offer of a drink still stands, by the way. And what I was going to say is, it's hard to believe what the police have been saying about Dad."

Dad?

The word made Paver Senior sound almost human. Peter's eyes remained fixed on the road but I could tell he was waiting for a reaction.

"Well. You weren't around."

"No, but. . ."

"There aren't any buts." I could feel myself tensing up. Wanting him to stop the vehicle and let me out. "You've no idea what happened because you weren't here."

He smiled, nodding to himself as if he already knew what I'd say before I said it. "I'm sorry. I didn't mean to upset you. But my dad's nothing like the monster they're saying he is. Even the police are beginning to realise that now."

"Really? Well, you can believe that if you like. But it doesn't change anything, does it? He's still in prison where he belongs."

I watched as his jaw tensed up. "But it's your word against his. Right? And everybody knows you were out of your skull on drugs."

I shook my head in disbelief. "Christ, you make it sound like I took the drugs myself." I could already feel tears pricking the corners of my eyes.

"That's not what I meant." His face had turned red - but not from embarrassment. Exhilaration maybe? I couldn't begin to figure out what his game was. "But they can play funny tricks on you, drugs."

"You're as bad as your father, if you think I made any of it up."

"I'm not saying you did."

I'd had enough trying to be polite. "Whatever. Can you pull over?"

"What?"

"Just let me out. I can manage from here."

"Fine. If that's what you want." He flipped on the indicator and checked his mirrors. "Freakin' drama queen."

He pulled into the lay-by at the Inver bridge and I leapt out. Then I climbed onto the rear bumper of the pick-up to lift my bike free and I felt something touch the back of my leg. His hand began moving up and down the outside of my thigh. Caressing me through the material of my tracksuit bottoms.

Christ.

"Need any help?"

Another fucking maggot. How the hell had I ever let him touch me that time?

"No. I'm good." I fought to control my breathing. I reached for the bike and swung it over the tailgate, forcing him to move his hand away and take the bike's weight before lowering it to the ground.

"Are you sure you can manage from here?"

"Perfectly sure."

"Right." He stepped back inside the truck and waited for me to put on my helmet then he tooted his horn and signalled for me to approach the driver's door.

"What?" I mouthed, in no mood for more of his shit.

The window whirred open and he leant his elbow on the rim, face alive with unrestrained delight. "I suppose I'd better tell you before you hear about it on the Lochinver grapevine. They're letting him out."

I loosened the strap on my helmet. "What did you just say?"

"My dad." If anyone could make a smile seem ugly, it was Peter Paver. The broad grin on his face confirmed I'd heard him right the first time. "We found out this afternoon when we were in Inverness. We saw Dad's solicitor while we were there and it's official. That's why I'm borrowing the truck. I'm picking Dad up from the railway station this time tomorrow."

22

I couldn't speak. Couldn't even connect the dots of my life into a recognisable shape. My place in this universe made no sense based on what Peter Paver was saying. Mum must have noticed the stunned look on my face because she didn't scurry in my wake, retrieving my trainers from inside the front door or hanging up my back-pack before suggesting I take a shower. Instead she followed me into the kitchen and closed the door behind us.

"You look like you could do with a cup of tea."

I nodded.

Give Mum her dues, she said nothing until I was ready. Maybe she could sense my distress, some kind of maternal instinct.

"How did it go? Bad day?"

I shook my head, trying to wipe away the tears before they betrayed my distress. "No. It was OK." I snivelled. "Just emptying Jimmy's bathroom and kitchen. It was worse than I'd expected but it's no big deal."

"And does he want you back again tomorrow?"

I raised the cup to my mouth and froze. I could already feel tears trickling down my cheeks but I didn't even have the will to wipe my face dry now.

"Amy, love. What's happened?"

She reached out a hand and helped me lower the cup.

I began sobbing, and once I'd started it seemed I might

never stop. Mum got up from her chair and stood behind me then she wrapped her arms around my chest and began to rock me gently. "Ssh. It's OK."

But it wasn't OK. How could it be OK?

I tugged one of my sleeves down over my hand and used it to wipe my eyes.

"I'm sorry."

"Hey, it's alright." She released her grip and I felt her fingers comb through my hair, pulling it away from my face. "Shall I go and run you a bath or do you want to tell me what's wrong?"

I leant my head back against her, closed my eyes and took a deep breath. "It's Paver. Gordon Paver. They're saying he's about to be released from prison."

Mum stepped from behind my stool and sat next to me. "That's nonsense. Who'd say such a thing?"

I snivelled again. "It's Peter. He reckons the case has fallen through or whatever."

She took hold of my left hand. "How's that possible? Listen, Amy. Peter's only saying that because he can't believe his dad would do the things he's being accused of. He doesn't know what he's talking about."

"They went to see his solicitor this afternoon. Him and Jimmy."

"He must have got it wrong. We'll ring Victim Support first thing in the morning."

"And what are they going to do?"

"It's what they're there for."

"To do what? To tell me there's nothing to worry about like everyone else keeps reminding me?" I wiped my cheeks dry of tears. "His dad'll be home this time tomorrow."

She let go of my hand and swept back a stray lock of hair from my eyes. "Remember what they said? To ring if there was anything bothering us?"

"I know, but I can't handle even thinking about it right now. If it turns out Peter's right and his dad's going to be let out, I don't know how I'll cope. You've no idea what that feels like."

Nobody could possibly know how it felt.

"Let me speak to them. Perhaps they can send someone round. Get this sorted."

"Oh, I don't know. Leave it for now. I need the loo." I got to my feet and took my bearings.

"OK, love. But don't let it get on top of you. Peter's trying to unsettle you, that's all."

I sat on the toilet and felt my insides empty. But still I didn't feel empty enough. All those bad feelings that had festered inside me for weeks began bubbling up again. I needed a temazepan. I needed wine. I needed dope. But most of all I needed to escape somewhere. I pulled my mobile from the pocket of the jeans pooled around my feet and tapped out the number I'd stored there twelve days earlier.

"Hello, yous," I whispered.

"Hey. How's it going?"

23

"**GOD,** that didn't take you long. I haven't even put the kettle on."

"I came on the bike." I barged past her and headed down the passageway in the direction of her living room.

"What's your hurry?"

"I just need something. Anything you've got." I danced from one foot to the other and fought to catch my breath; digging my fingernails into the palms of my hands while Kay stood next to me and reached for my shoulder.

"Hey. Maybe we need to calm down first. Yeah? You look like shit."

I slumped onto the sofa and felt my underwear sticking to me as I tried to get comfortable. I'd not bothered changing from my sweaty work clothes and my hair was a total mess.

"Can I at least have a glass of wine? Or something stronger, if you've got it."

Kay gave my shoulder a squeeze. "Give me a couple of minutes."

I heard her pottering about in the next room. A clink of glasses. A tap turned on and water pouring into a kettle. My nose was running worse than ever and I tugged the end of a sleeve over my hand to swipe my top lip dry. Then I gave my eyes a wipe to erase the worst of the evidence. Mum had asked where I was off to in such a hurry but I'd been in no fit state to reply. The cycle ride here a blur as my eyes teared up at the very thought of Gordon Paver strutting his stuff on the streets of Lochinver once more.

"I've made us some herbal tea." Kay passed me a mug half filled with a steaming concoction smelling of hay and flowers and spices.

"Shit. Is that all you've got? I'm desperate here."

"It's Mexican goldenrod, with ginger and liquorice and dried lemongrass."

I took an exploratory sip before pulling a face. "Christ."

"It's guaranteed to settle your nerves and restore harmony. At least, that's what it's supposed to do, so stop whingeing."

"It tastes like potpourri."

"I'm still working on it but at least show some gratitude."

"OK. But you didn't need to go to all this trouble. Gin and weed would have done."

"I'm not giving you anything stronger until you tell me what the hell's going on." Kay sat across from me and took a sip from her own mug.

I gave her the short version. Peter Paver's suggestion that I'd dreamt the whole thing up while in some drug-induced haze didn't seem to surprise her that much. But the news that his father was being released made her laugh out loud.

"That's total bullshit," she said as my voice began to falter. "I know what Peter's like. All talk. And once he gets an idea in his head, there's no stopping him. He'll have got hold of the wrong end of the stick, you'll see."

But I wasn't convinced. "Not according to his solicitor."

"Is that what he's told you?"

I sniffled and gave a nod. "You should have seen him. He called me a freaking drama queen."

"It'll be a wind-up. He's hardly going to go around saying his old man's the complete bastard we all know he is." She stared me out as I began figuring out how to argue with her logic. "He's got a lot of issues. So much pent-up anger. And it's not helping when he hears what people are saying about darling daddy."

"I know, but still. . ."

"No buts. He's talking bollocks." She pulled out a tobacco tin and began to build a spliff. I watched as she wet the edge of the paper with her tongue then rolled the contents into a tight tube. Then she got to her feet. "Budge up."

I placed my mug on the coffee table and slid to one end of the sofa. Kay settled next to me then she took hold of my left arm. "Lie yourself down."

She helped me half turn until my legs were resting on the arm of the sofa then I lowered my head and shoulders onto her knees.

"Let me do this first."

She slid a cushion under my head then pulled a stray hair from the corner of my mouth, lowered the spliff to my lips and picked up her lighter from the low table.

"Slow breaths. There's no rush."

The flame flared between our faces and I inhaled. One breath, and another; desperate to allow the weed to do its work.

Time seemed to slip past in chunks. We talked about our mutual dislike of Matt Neilson. We talked about school. The teachers Kay and I remembered best. Her colourful reputation and dropping out when she was threatened with expulsion.

"I was a bit of a handful, but it was an act. School bored me to death. So playing up was my idea of entertainment - having fun at everybody else's expense. That time I offered to do a split roast with Johnny

Burrows and that Harvey kid. Paul was it? I just wanted to see the look on everyone's faces."

"So you never?"

"Christ no. I hadn't even slept with anybody until my last term in school."

"Baxter Cartwright?"

"Barcode. Yeah."

"Wasn't there some story about his Organ Donor card?"

"How the hell did you hear about that?"

"I know his sister. She told me."

Kay blew out a spurt of smoke and passed the joint back. "He handed it over by mistake in the FBI one night when they asked him for ID. Then he offered to donate one of his organs to me if I wanted."

"Kaz said. He was offering you his dick rather than one of his kidneys."

"Yeah."

"God, you're so alike. You and Matt."

I felt her hips reposition themselves under my head before taking back the spliff. "Don't say that."

"The way you both put on an act, I mean. Trying to impress everybody. But none of it's real."

Kay opened her mouth wide - a silent yawn to let a curl of white smoke drift free. "If you say so." Then she closed her eyes and I saw the dark circles surrounding them. Sunshine through the part-closed curtains highlighting her pale face. Her lips pouted as she raised the spliff to her mouth for one more hit.

"Don't worry. It fooled the girls in S2 and S3," I continued. "They thought you were so cool."

"Whatever."

"But they did."

She handed me the stub of the joint and I sucked in what little was left before placing it in the ash-tray next to my empty mug.

"And what about you? Did you think I was so cool?" she asked, stretching out the last two words.

Our eyes met and I didn't need to reply. I gulped as she lowered her face to mine and our mouths met.

I don't know what I'd been expecting. A peck on the forehead maybe, or a long lingering kiss before she pulled away and wiped her mouth clear of the memory. But instead her tongue probed between my lips and I tasted her breath, then her fingers began moulding my head, combing through my hair and I could feel her stomach clenching beneath my head and I wanted more. And then the buzz of someone's telephone broke the spell.

"Shit! That's me." I fumbled in my jeans pocket for my mobile and sat up to read the incoming text.

Damn.

"It's only my mum. It won't be urgent."

Kay's expression changed as she leant further back against the cushions. "That's OK. I've got my own calls to make anyway."

It felt as if I'd woken from a dream. A fantasy dream. And now bang back to earth. I swung my legs down and sat up. "Right. I didn't realise I was intruding."

"You're not. Another time."

"Yeah, right. I should be off anyway. I'm needing a shower 'cause I must stink like road-kill after the day I've had."

She placed her hand on my stomach as I made to rise. "No. I mean it. Another time. You can stay the night if you want."

24

IF I'd been asked to choose two telephone calls that changed my life - the best then the worst - I don't suppose Mum's text would qualify as one of the worst. But for a time I hated her for the intrusion.

```
Amy. You need to get home asap. It's
important.
```

Important enough to cut short our romantic interlude - if that's what it was? Hardly. But it left me feeling more upset than I'd dare admit. My emotions had run away with themselves and I'd read more into the situation than perhaps Kay intended. She hadn't seemed too bothered when our kiss broke off. Maybe she had a hot date lined up – one of the more pressing calls - inviting some mystery man round, once I left. The offer to stay the night another time could simply be her way of letting me down gently. But she needn't have gone to the trouble. I was a big girl after all.

When I walked in, Mum was on the phone to Mrs Neilson and I was reminded of another telephone call. The one telling us Dad had been killed offshore, somewhere out in the North Sea half way between Shetland and Norway. He might as well have been working on the moon for all the sense it made. I couldn't begin to understand why he kept leaving home to spend weeks underwater or living on a flimsy metal platform with accommodation attached - surrounded by thousands of miles of open sea. An oil rig battered by storms and constantly sprayed by saltwater until its metal corroded to nothing.

That had been seven years ago, yet I remember the exact moment the telephone rang as if it was yesterday. Despite all their tears and cursing, I felt the loss more than Leanne or Mum. I'd never got the chance to know Dad properly so I didn't have enough memories to soften the blow. He was away at sea so much. Losing him left a hole in our lives. We lost Mum for a time as well.

"I know, it's terrible. I don't know what we're going to do. Oh, here she is now." I'd barely had time to unfasten my trainers. "It's Matt's mum. For you."

She passed over the phone.

Steff explained how she'd been in touch with Matt. "He says he knows nothing about the emails you've been getting. But you're not to upset yourself."

"That's easy for him to say."

"He says he's going to sort it."

Huh?

"How can he sort it when he's in prison?"

"He doesn't want you worrying yourself, that's all. As soon as he finds out who's been sending them he'll take care of it."

"How the hell can he do that?"

I could tell she'd been expecting a more gracious response. "I'm just telling you what Matt's told me. I've no reason to disbelieve him."

"No. Well, thanks for letting me know. Shall I put you back onto Mum?"

She said not. The pair of them had obviously been discussing the situation in my absence.

"Why didn't you tell me? These messages you've been getting?" Mum said as she replaced the phone in its cradle.

"There was no point. Anyway, what's so bloody important that you had to text me? I don't see the house burning down."

"We need to talk. What we discussed earlier."

Paver?

"There's nothing to talk about. I'm going for a shower."

But there was. When I wandered back into the kitchen, looking for a nightcap, Mum was standing at the table waiting for me. She pulled out one of the stools.

"You'd better sit down, love."

"I told you, I don't want to talk about it. Not now. Not ever."

"I phoned that Cathy. You know. The lady from . . ."

"Victim Support? God, I told you to leave it."

Mum patted my hand as if I was about to throw a tantrum. "She was very understanding."

"What d'you mean? Understanding about what?"

"The stuff Peter said."

"What the hell did you tell her about him for?"

"I didn't. I just asked if there was any news."

The guilty look on her face suggested she'd done more than that but I let it pass.

"I don't want to hear it. I'm shattered so I'm going to have an early night, OK?"

But there was no escape. She took hold of my hand. Another show of unexpected physical affection.

Christ.

"I rang her at home but she promised to get back to me as soon as she found out more."

"And has she?"

"Yes. I'd just come off the telephone with her when Mrs Neilson rang."

I could tell from the tone of Mum's voice that the news wasn't good.

"She got in touch with one of the investigating officers." Her grip on my hand grew tighter. "I'm so sorry, love. It looks like Peter was telling the truth. The Crown Office are dropping all charges against Mr Paver."

25

I'D long lost count of the number of times the build-up to my death replayed inside my head. From the moment that hypodermic first pierced the vein - a tiny pin-prick of hurt snagging the crook of my arm. Then cold wine coursing through my body. Numbing. Warming. Chilling. Cold turning to liquid fire and eyes smarting and sounds amplified beyond all reason and the realisation that for sure this is how my life would end.

The dream seemed to be just as real no matter how many times I relived it. Muffled voices. Someone removing my jacket and bobble hat. Hands taking hold. Lifting. Dark. Light. Dark. Silence. Then the touch of the cold zipper against my bare skin and the ache in my stomach from the retching. The stench of vomit inside the dark cocoon of my sleeping bag and my bladder letting go. The sensation of both arms clamped behind my back.

Then the bed itself seemed to rattle in tune with the topography of the twisting road we were driving along. I squirmed and twisted, never quite managing to roll onto my back. Maybe that was a blessing because when my mouth finally coughed up vomit I was on my side. Not choking on it but feeling it caked on the fabric pressed against my face. Except I was coughing up air. Foul air and choking smoke that filled the back of the vehicle. The floor hot beneath my body despite my being sodden with cold piss from the waist down. Then I caught a whirl of yellow flame somewhere close by followed by the sounds of snarling and snapping and screeching.

As I struggled to emerge from the cloak of yet another nightmare, the flapping shape flew in from nowhere and I was pulled away into the darkness. I touched the ground, cold as deepest winter, and opened my eyes. There was no face. Just a shadowy outline with a familiar wide-brimmed hat obscuring its head.

"You'll live, lassie."

I began to heave once more as my lungs ejected strands of soot-darkened mucus. Jimmy was already pulling at the zip of the sleeping bag but it had snagged tight from my twisting. In the end he sat me upright, encased like a mummy, my legs screaming in pain as each muscle cramped.

"Can you breathe?"

I felt his fingers parting my hair and a calloused palm smeared my lips, wiping away the vomit. The scent of his rough skin, of peat and salt water, was like being reborn.

"Cold." I shivered and my head felt off-balance, as if it belonged to a different body. Snow was drifting all around us and the chill had already soaked through the sleeping bag into my wet clothes.

"Cold," I whispered again.

He attempted to wrap his arms around me but seemed clumsy as a young boy on his first date. "It's Jimmy."

26

THERE was no sign of Jimmy or his truck when I arrived but the porch door was wide open and I could see someone had continued where I'd left off. The refrigerator, an old, collapsed sofa, two threadbare armchairs and a roll of dusty carpet sat out on the yard. Time for a bonfire, maybe.

I rested my bike against one of the rowan trees propping up the lean-to and approached the house.

"Jimmy?"

The sun was dazzling and it was too dark inside to see through the windows. But I could hear movement.

Stepping into the shaded kitchen was like entering a freezer. Refreshing after the furnace heat outside. I could see the small gas cooker had been disconnected as well. More garbage ready for the tip.

"Hello?" I called out before venturing further into the cottage. "Anybody there?"

Jimmy stood with his back to me in the centre of the sitting room, empty apart from a large sideboard still decorated with tiny photo frames and knick-knacks. The kind of stuff I remember seeing at my granny's house when we used to visit.

"You've been busy."

"Aye." He held a framed photograph in one hand. "It takes my mind off things."

"I thought I'd come and see you instead of phoning." I

paused to swallow the lump in my throat. "I'm sorry, but I'm not going to be able to carry on helping you."

He didn't seem to have heard me. Instead he turned and held out the picture as if seeking an explanation. Whose photograph? It was Evgenia. His Evergreen. Looking as if she didn't have a single care in the world. I couldn't bring myself to touch it.

"It was Gordon turned her against me."

"I know. Matt told me everything. It's awful."

He placed it back on top of the sideboard. A tiny strip of clean wood showed where it had resided in the dust. "She was no bigger than you. A slip of a girl."

"I remember."

"You'll have heard about Gordon?"

"Peter told me yesterday afternoon. He couldn't wait to pass on the good news."

"I got to hear about it on our way to Inverness. Gordon's solicitor had phoned. And now Peter's away to collect his father from the railway station. I didn't have the stomach to go with him. I'm not wanting to see my brother's face again in a hurry."

"That's how I feel. I'm going to Ullapool for the summer."

He nodded. Then he reached into his jacket pocket and pulled out a wallet, worn away almost to the lining. "You'll still need paying for your trouble."

"I'm sorry I couldn't have done more to help."

"There's no need to apologise." He handed me three twenties and a ten.

"That's too much."

"No." He took my hand and folded my fingers around the money. "You worked hard yesterday. It's the least I can do. My plans have changed, as you can imagine."

"Does that mean Gordon is moving back into Strathbeg House?" I said.

"Oh, no. It's my home fair and square." He led me back to the kitchen and fumbled with the kettle. Three mugs sat on the worktop along with a packet of tea bags. "When the solicitor said the police were letting my brother go, I couldn't make sense of it. I still can't."

"We got a phone call last night. Well, Mum spoke to them. I was out."

"They're saying he did nothing wrong." I thought the quaver in his voice was relief at his brother's innocence but instead I could see tears on his cheeks.

"Not necessarily. They can't prove anything. There's a difference."

He turned to face me. "He betrayed everyone's trust to line his pockets."

Cathy had explained everything to Mum. The Polish girls had disappeared. The police were convinced they'd fled back to Poland. No doubt threats had been made. There were also CCTV images that showed me walking out of Paver's house and heading off in the direction of the bunkhouse. I couldn't possibly have been sedated inside the house as I claimed. The falling snow made it difficult to pick out the detail but they were able to identify my woolly hat and jacket.

"They're saying if it went to court now, it would be my word against his," I said.

"Your word? But why would anybody doubt your word?"

The drugs they found in my bloodstream had been the clincher: ketamine and some kind of opiate. Probably heroin. Ketamine - an anaesthetic and hallucinogen, renowned for causing short-term amnesia and false memory. I didn't have a prayer of convincing anyone I could remember every single detail of what Paver had done to me. His legal team would have a field day pulling apart my testimony word by word. Coupled with the fact that the police had been unable to find any physical evidence connecting the Polish girls to Paver's boat, they had no case.

"I'm a nobody. Your brother's a successful businessman." I almost gagged at the words. "A highly-respected member of the community."

Jimmy poured boiling water into two mugs then dropped a tea bag in each. "But you're going to be alright? Whatever happens?"

"Leanne, my sister, says I can stay with her as long as I want. I don't want to be around when Gordon comes home. Sorry."

"He'll not be welcome in the village."

"But if the police are dropping all charges, nobody can stop him."

"I've already spoken to Peter. He's to take his father back to Portrush."

"Huh." Back to where it all began. "D'you think Gordon's going to leave just like that?"

Jimmy took a sip from his mug. "There's nowhere else for him to go. I'll be setting up home in the house instead of the caravan."

"Right."

"And I have good friends here. Stalkers. Men with guns."

"What's that supposed to mean?"

"I'll never forgive him for Evergreen's death. He'll not want to risk setting foot back in these parts while I'm still breathing."

27

LEANNE had told us to let ourselves in. Steve was away on the East coast until Saturday afternoon and my sister was covering a full shift at the care home, for once.

"Can you manage?"

"Yeah." A rucksack and a Tesco 'Bag for Life' held all my summer essentials. I planned to survive the next couple of months on the bare minimum.

"You go and sort your room out while I make us a coffee."

Mum set off to the kitchen, no doubt desperate to do what she did best. Tidying up after her daughters. I could hear the clatter of crockery and the sound of running water. If I took long enough unpacking, there'd be no need to help out.

By the time I'd freshened up she'd stacked the kitchen drainer with clean dishes, cutlery, a frying pan, spatula and a couple of empty plastic containers.

"I'll let Leanne put them away. She knows where everything goes."

"Yeah."

"She must have been running late this morning."

Either that or she knew Mum was coming round and wouldn't be able to resist clearing up the mess.

"Where do the bin bags go? This needs emptying." She flipped open the kitchen bin. God, it stank as bad as Jimmy's old fridge. Empty cans - baked beans and tuna and spaghetti hoops. Crisp packets. Egg shells. Banana peel. Used tea bags. Cigarette stubs.

"Let me do it." I heaved it free of its moorings and fastened the loops together. "I'll take it down to the communal bins on the way out."

Leanne kept the empty bin liners underneath the kitchen sink. I could see two grey flexible pipes snaking from the plumbing into the parking space where their washing machine had stood.

"She's lucky there's a launderette," Mum said.

I closed the double cupboard doors under the sink. "Yeah. I can take our washing round there if she wants. Give me something useful to do."

Leanne had laughed it off. "Steve managed to get an advance on his wages. Enough to pay the bailiffs for another month. But we still had to decide what to keep. Fridge or washing machine."

Mum offered to drop me off outside the Post Office afterwards - my first port of call in search of a notice board advertising local job vacancies. Someone out at Lochside was looking for a gardener. No thanks. Weekend changeovers at Ardmair or up on the Braes. Waitressing at the Royal Hotel. I'd done my share of both in the past. Maybe bar work would suit me better. Leanne had worked at a couple of places in Ullapool before she met Steve.

"Serve them their drinks and show them some cleavage and they're no trouble." That might prove problematic.

The Arches Wine Bar was advertising for someone to work Friday and Saturday nights. Two eight-hour shifts. £6.50 an hour plus tips. It would do for a start.

I rang and left a message with the young guy who answered the telephone. He sounded foreign.

"Beth will call you back after six o'clock. Tonight or

tomorrow."

Then I wandered down to the newsagent's on Shore Street but there didn't seem to be anything else on offer. The foreshore was buzzing. Crowds of visitors paraded along the sea front - paired off or herded together. Some stopped to lean against the railings and watch the hobby sailors out for an afternoon's splash around Loch Broom. No breeze and barely a ripple on the water. I thought about Moolie and his dad lost at sea, and Gordon Paver and son crossing the wide stretch of sea further West. Sometimes it seemed the sun shone more brightly on the guilty than the innocent.

I wandered as far as the picnic tables above the campsite and drank in the view. A solitary seagull hovered overhead, fishing for scraps. No chance. Across the water a small white boat left a lazy trail of ripples in its wake as it trawled the far side of the loch. This was as good as it got. Or maybe life was getting better and I'd not noticed. All the loose ends finally tied up. All the incriminating evidence swept under the carpet.

Mum and I had sat transfixed the previous evening as Gordon Paver faced the cameras on *Reporting Scotland*. Or more accurately as a lone cameraman and a toothy red-head with a microphone attempted to mob him as he emerged between the platform barriers at Inverness railway station.

". . . away to Northern Ireland for a while to collect my thoughts. But I shall return once the situation has been resolved. I have nothing to hide. Nothing to be ashamed of. The past few weeks have been a testing time for myself and my loved ones but I would still like to express my gratitude to the police and the Procurator Fiscal's office for the professional manner in which they handled the accusations levelled against me. I was treated with respect at all times which reflects well on this country's judicial system.

"My sympathies are now extended to all those individuals who became innocent victims of this heinous crime, directly or indirectly. Rest assured that I shall continue to cooperate with the authorities in every way possible to ensure the perpetrators are brought to justice. Until that happens I would ask that we are now allowed some privacy to come to terms with the events of the past two months. Thank you."

The entire speech looked too rehearsed to be genuine.

"Bastard," I muttered.

"He manages to make Donald Trump look humble," Mum said. "I can't believe the nerve of the man."

Paver's tan had faded; his hair a millimetre or two longer and less groomed than usual. He also wore a navy blue sweatshirt and jeans rather than the customary crisp white shirt, sober tie and pin-striped suit. But the voice and demeanour were unchanged.

"He'll be loving every minute of it. Playing the martyr."

"But it's wrong, Amy. People like him always seem to get away with things."

"That's karma for you," I said.

Yet in some ways it was a relief the entire business was

now over. I'd not be asked to testify in court. Cathy had explained everything when she telephoned again that afternoon to check how we were coping. The COPFS were now going to concentrate on Stuart Coleman and John Fleming: Gordon Paver's alleged co-conspirators when the offences first came to light. The investigating officers had more than enough evidence linking that pair with the caravan site in Rosehall and a number of flats in Aberdeen that were being run as brothels.

There had been nothing to tie Paver to that part of the operation - or so it appeared. He even denied all knowledge of the Ukrainians' criminal activities. Maybe it was time for everyone else to get used to the idea that he was a free man with his honour and reputation intact.

Mum had given me seventy-five pounds to be going on with.

"That's all I can spare so don't spend it all at once. You'll need to find yourself a job - start paying your way and help your sister out a little bit."

Leanne had agreed to let me sleep in their spare room - rent negotiable, depending on how soon I found work. In the meantime I'd offered to do my bit around the flat. Cooking. Cleaning. Anything to pull my weight. Tonight I'd planned on making omelettes for supper. I already had a list prepared after a cursory inspection of the contents of her fridge. We'd need eggs, mushrooms, peppers, milk, butter, cooking oil and a loaf. I also decided to splurge on a couple of bottles of cheap wine. My treat. While Steve was away Leanne and I could maybe celebrate.

But when she got in from work just after ten she looked frazzled. Eight hours without a break feeding a bunch of oldies then putting them to bed. I didn't know how she did it.

"Supper's ready whenever you want. It's something quick."

"Thanks."

"There's a bottle of wine in the fridge as well," I said.

"I was planning on having an early night but I could definitely go for a glass or two. Let me freshen up first. Steve always says he can smell that place on my uniform."

I followed her into her bedroom and told her about the job at the Arches while she unbuttoned her blouse then pulled off her tights.

"I did a couple of shifts there before they changed hands."

"They said they were going to ring back but they haven't yet."

"Did you give them this number?" She gave me an accusing look as if I'd done something wrong.

"No. They've got my mobile. Why?"

She went into the bathroom and I stood in the doorway as she turned on the shower. "Oh, nothing. Just asking. We've had a fault on the line, that's all."

"They haven't cut your phone off as well, have they?"

She unhooked her bra and made a face. "How did you know?"

"An educated guess."

28

I heard no more from the Arches until the following morning. I'd been making haphazard attempts to keep busy while Leanne had a lie-in. Cleaning the kitchen window, wiping down the tiles in the bathroom, taking out the empty bottles to the recycling bin.

"Come around later and we can have a proper chat. Just ask for Beth."

She'd suggested I turn up between five and six, before things got too busy. Then on my way there I bumped into Kaz and a couple of girls I'd been kind of friends with at school.

"We're on the prowl Friday night if you're up for it. Woohoo."

That seemed like a plan.

My so-called interview didn't take long. It seemed that all I'd needed to do to get taken on as temporary staff was turn up, produce proof that I was over eighteen and look eager.

"Pop in tomorrow after six and we can sort out your National Insurance details and so on. I'll introduce you to Lukas as well. He's from Lithuania."

As if that made a difference.

Kaz, Terri Frazer and Donna Grey huddled around the bar the following evening while I completed my induction. Beth showed me the ropes - the till, the credit card reader, the ice-making machine in the cellar, the stock sheets and the plastic container for the staff tips.

"You'll soon get the hang," she said. "Let me get you and your friends a drink."

I joined them at one of the window seats and we chatted about the job for all of two minutes.

"So when do you start?"

"Next Friday, officially."

"Does that mean we get freebies whenever you're on?" Kaz asked.

"No chance," I said. "They've asked me to do next Monday afternoon as well. Two 'til five. Just to get used to being behind the bar."

"God. You wouldn't catch me working on a Bank Holiday," Donna said.

"I need the hours," I said and left it at that,

The three girls seemed to be in a party mood but I was still feeling out of place. "We're not staying here all night, are we?" Kaz asked. "It's a bit blah."

So we moved on. The Frigate. Then the FBI further along the sea front. Then the Argyll, Caledonian Hotel and the Seaforth. By the fourth round of drinks I'd switched from cider to vodka shots with cranberry juice. I could feel my head buzzing and I soon realised I'd not be able to keep up with the other three.

I'd ordered a gin and tonic at the FBI but Kaz told me that wasn't on, and I saw her pals give me a pitying look. "It's what my granny drinks, Ames. We're all on voddies and Red Bull."

Somewhere in the back of my mind I could remember reading about the effects of too much caffeine. Cranberry juice seemed the healthier option, given that I was still on medication.

By ten o'clock the Seaforth had filled up. Tourists. Locals. One or two lads I recognised from High School.

The sound level progressively rising until we had to shout at each other to be heard.

"What about you and Matt Neilson? You still together?" Donna asked.

"How can they be?" Kaz laughed. "He's inside with Baxter and all the other neds."

"She's going to wait for him, though. Right?" Terri said. "I mean, it's so romantic."

That's when I told them about the Peterhead visit and how I intended dumping Matt once he was out of prison.

"Did you just say 'hump him'?" Donna screeched and one or two faces turned our way.

My jaw had already become numb from trying to speak and smile at the same time so I just shook my head. Then I felt the floor tilt fractionally and I grabbed the nearest high-backed chair.

"You still with us, Ames?" Terri said.

"Yeah." But I was and I wasn't.

The lights were too bright. My gaze flitted from someone's lipstick-smeared teeth to a bendy straw and a glass of melting ice cubes and a blonde woman's ear studs. I straightened up and gave another wobble, trying to steer clear of the louder voices to my right as a red-faced girl gave her boyfriend grief about where to go next and a bunch of boring old farts dissected their latest round of golf. Then I gave another lurch as someone pushed past.

"Can I just get through?" I spun round to face the girls. Words slurring like I'd copied and pasted them from someone else's mouth.

An old guy sat perched next to us nursing a pint of whatever and I caught his lecher's eyes latch onto mine before switching attention back to all the other young flesh parading in off the street.

"Shit. Are you OK?" Kaz said, her wide grin suggesting

she was loving every minute of my rapid decline.

"I need the loo, that's all."

"I'll come with you." She picked up her handbag and guided me away from the crowd. But what I really needed was fresh air.

"I'm OK, honest." But I was as far from OK as it's possible to get while still upright. "I'd better go outside. Clear my head."

"Hope you're not going to hurl, girl."

I didn't. The night air hit me like a drench of cold water, and panic replaced the nausea. I could remember only too clearly the last time I'd thrown up. I breathed in, swallowing the bile. Sweat grew cold on my bare skin. I sucked more air and tried to get my bearings.

"What's the time?"

"You bailing out already?" Kaz asked. "I thought Lochinver girls could handle the pace better than that."

"I'm just not used to it, that's all." I straightened my top. "It was too hot in there. I'm feeling better, but I think I'm going to call it a night."

"If you're sure."

"Next time maybe."

The four of us linked arms and they steered me home. I could hear them debate where to go next but all I wanted was my bed. Someone offered me a cigarette and I declined. Then once we reached the entrance to the flats I disengaged myself from them and fumbled for my keys. "I'll be fine from here."

I muttered a prayer to myself as someone screamed further up the road.

Let Mum be in bed and not see me in this state.

There was an unfamiliar key-ring in my bag - the keyhole as impenetrable as something impenetrable. "Let me give you a hand," Kaz offered. The door opened and she helped me shuffle inside. "Can you manage?"

I shushed her and she took the hint and left me to it.

Light switch? Someone had moved it. No TV sounds. Nothing. God knows what time it was. I kicked off my shoes and managed to find my way to the bathroom. That's when it struck me where I was. This was my sister's flat. My buttons seemed too large to unbutton and there was a desperate struggle to pull my underwear down to my knees. Then I filled the pan with loo paper before taking a long, drawn out wee. The less noise the better. I didn't bother flushing. But I rinsed my face and scrubbed my teeth with cold water and a worn-out toothbrush. Mine? Probably not.

Then I used the door frame to help manoeuvre my body in the direction of the spare room. Except I'd turned right instead of left. The mental map of home taking over once more. That's how I finished up on my knees outside Leanne's bedroom door; face pressed against the woodwork and too disorientated and dazed to care whether she found me here next morning or not.

My brain had already turned to mush as I stretched out on the carpet, but I could hear a voice close by. Muffled yet distinct enough to identify Leanne and to make out the occasional word.

"I already know. Want me to make some noise? Like this?"

Then she started to moan and ask for more and I tried to cover my ears and crawl away and pretend none of it was happening. But I couldn't move a muscle.

29

THE sleeping bag had twisted tight around my body as I'd slept. Tight enough to suffocate.

I tried to fight my way free, on the point of screaming out for help before the flames took hold. Then my eyes opened and I figured out I was safe. They were caked with gunge, and unfamiliar sunlight scorched my pillow, but I was no longer where my dreams had taken me. I unravelled the top sheet and realised I was naked but thankfully alone.

So where the hell was I?

Green curtains. We had the same at home but this was a single bed with pillows that smelled of stale sweat. Something bad curdled inside my mouth like sour milk and I gave an involuntary belch. Acid rising at the back of my throat. Dry lips. I needed a drink. Something to rinse away the taste. I rolled onto my side and planted a foot on the floor.

Shit. I was dying here.

My rucksack sat on the chair where I'd left it after unpacking. And the trousers and top I'd worn the previous evening lay folded on the back of it. I studied the decor for more clues. This was Leanne's spare room, looking exactly the same as every other time I'd slept here. Except now an apocalyptic hangover kept me company. Not just alcohol-related but also from the sick feeling of how I'd behaved the previous night. What I'd done. What I'd said. And what I'd overheard that I maybe wasn't meant to.

I'd managed to make my way to bed after all and get undressed, but how could I have been so stupid and drunk so much? I remembered cursing Matt Neilson to everyone who'd listen. Telling them over and over how much of a shit he was - the way he'd treated me during the prison visit. The dodgy emails that he'd got someone to send on his behalf.

"You're well rid," Donna said finally. To be fair, she'd warned me off him when I first mentioned we'd spent the night together. But the look on the other two girls' faces seemed to signal as much embarrassment as sympathy.

Their reactions made no difference. I needed to purge myself of every single memory. The party at Achmelvich. The attempted kiss on Quinag. The Valentine's Day card. It seemed everyone knew our entire history anyway. When we finally slept together, he was forgiven everything - the sheer bliss of being so close to someone made up for all that had happened. And it seemed he knew exactly what words to say.

"You've got to give Matt his dues," Kaz said eventually. "He didn't do his usual trick of jumping on you the first chance he got then doing a runner."

"That's his normal tactic," Terri continued. "But it sounds like he's given you the full treatment, girl."

"I suppose so, but none of that matters now," I muttered. "He's blown it as far as I'm concerned. We're finished. And I'll tell him to his face next time I see him."

Kaz had slammed her empty glass on the table. "I don't get it. You share a candle-lit supper in your own wee love nest out in the middle of nowhere followed by some morning-after sweet talk and you're still feeling hard done by? Shit, Ames, he even tried to save your life didn't he?"

"So?"

"You got a fuck-load more action than I've had in the last six months."

"I don't believe that," I said.

"One poxy Valentine card from that geek Waterson. I even saw him sneak off after shoving it under our doormat."

"Kevin Waterson sent you a Valentine card?"

Her face creased with laughter. "Some kind of gay bullshit, telling me how he'd rather watch me than a hundred sunsets."

JUNE

30

NINE days and counting. Matt could almost taste freedom. The other guys had already started giving him sly looks. Respect masked by envy. No more piss tests. No more random cell searches. Those with months ahead of them only needed to watch the way Matt swaggered about the block to realise how it would feel to have no more than a few days' sentence left to serve.

"You'll be back," one of the longer-term residents joked. "You love this place so much you won't be able to stay away."

"No fucking way."

"That's what they all say. But what d'you think it's going to be like once you're outside? You can't pick up where you left off and carry on as if nothing happened."

"I'll be OK."

"Yeah, sure. You'll go back to college or get yourself a nice cosy office job. Then you'll marry some tart, settle down with a family and live happily ever after."

"Or none of the above," someone else said. "Everyone treats you no better than a lump of shite on their shoe once they know you've done time."

Matt's head had dipped when he heard these words. He knew they were right. He'd not given his immediate future much thought until a small group of them due for release were invited to a session with someone from Social Services and various charity group representatives. Suddenly it was real.

They handed out lists of addresses. Agencies specialising in rehabilitation and reintegration into the community. The benefits he could claim if he needed support and the emergency funds available for shoes and clothing or even bedding. Drop-in centres where he could use a computer to print out his CV or borrow a telephone to enquire about accommodation - or job vacancies, assuming there was someone out there prepared to give an ex-con the chance to work for buttons. There were even helplines for dealing with drugs, alcoholism and depression.

Shit.

Matt had planned no further ahead than release day when he could pack up his meagre belongings and kiss goodbye to Peterhead. What happened once he was outside hadn't needed much more strategic thinking than that.

Steff had hinted his dad had money set aside for a rainy day. A few thousand that would allow Matt to do his own thing until the dust settled and he could start rebuilding his life. Get a job. Earn some respect. Mr Fix-it taking control.

But all Matt could focus on was getting the hell out of Dodge. He'd take a taxi to the nearest railway station, grab some cannies and get quietly pissed en route to Inverness. Then Steff could pick him up and he'd be home in time for tea. He might even catch the latest episode of *Stash in the Attic*. Except, the more he thought about it, the more he could see it not working. It would be exactly the same as when he'd come home from Raigmore hospital following his breakdown. Dad huffing and puffing every time their paths crossed – alternating between Mr Fix-it and Mr Angry on steroids. And Steff stressing out, walking on eggshells from room to room as she tried to make an empty house into a happy home. There was only one solution. Once Dad handed over the cash, Matt would take the money and run.

Barcode got out on the 10th - three days before Matt - and he had no such worries.

"It's going to be fuckin' ace, I'm telling you," he'd said. "It'll be party party party. We might still be at it on Friday when you're passing through Ullapool."

"I bet."

"Give me a bell when you're leaving Inverness. We can meet up for a pint at the Seaforth."

"Could do, I suppose."

"You're a fucking legend, man. Some of the lads already know all about you. If you need anything - a place to crash or a little earner on the side."

"That would be good. I'll have to think about it though. Don't know what my plans are yet."

"Well soon as you know, give me a buzz. I'm serious, Mattie boy. I've got contacts coming out of my arse. All desperate to help people like you and me who keep their mouths shut whenever they get lifted."

He nodded, but most of what Barcode said was not registering. Matt had a home to go to regardless of the shit he'd have to put up with, and earning his keep wasn't going to be an issue if Dad was going to hand over a nice, fat cheque. His first priority once he got back to Lochinver was to make things right with Amy Metcalf. He still had feelings for her. Not necessarily love, but he wanted more from their relationship than just the occasional shag. And he knew Amy felt the same. Even Steff had told him how Amy was prepared to forgive him everything and stick by him.

But then less than a week before his release, Barcode was on the telephone and he waved Matt across, handing him the receiver. Some of those waiting in line to make their own calls had started muttering threats but Barcode put them straight.

"It's family. Somebody wants to say hello, that's all."

The voice at the other end of the telephone quickly brought Matt up to speed with events back home.

"Amy's staying at her sister's. Did you know?"

"No." He hadn't a clue about any of that. He hadn't heard about Amy's drunken decision to finish with him either.

"You're kidding me."

"She swears she's going to tell you first chance she gets."

He'd not believed a word of it until Kaz described Amy's visit to Peterhead in more detail and her determination to end things.

Barcode had been eager to find out everything once the cell lights dimmed and they climbed onto their bunks.

"So what's happenin' bro? Is your wee bit of skirt giving you grief again?"

"Nah." Matt pulled up the blanket to his shoulders and buried his face in the pillow. "I'll get it sorted once I'm out of here."

"I'm telling you, man. I love my wee sister to bits, and I know what you're like when it comes to fanny. But if that stuck-up cow is messing you about, maybe you and Kaz should get together. I wouldn't stand in your way."

"Cheers for pimping your sister."

"I'm serious, bro. I can put a good word in for you."

Maybe Matt had been too full of himself to spot the signs. Maybe Amy had kept quiet to spare his feelings - only agreeing to visit because she felt sorry for him.

She'd not even bothered mentioning the creepy messages she'd been getting because she realised he couldn't do anything about them.

Fuck.

Prison had taken away everything - his dignity, his self-respect. When Steff mentioned how Amy was getting hassle, he'd promised to sort it out. But that had been all talk. He'd not been able to do a single thing even when Kaz told him who was responsible.

31

LEANNE and I didn't get around to discussing my drunken meltdown in detail until the day of the funeral. The Tyrrells. Whispers that Moolie and his dad had been killed instantly didn't make the pain of their loss any easier to bear. Nor did assertions by the Navy that they were in no way responsible for the explosion that destroyed the 'Petrel'.

The entire village had turned out to pay its respects. Traffic cones lined both sides of the road from the newsagent's to the RBS. We walked from Inver Park and stood at the roadside opposite the kirk as both coffins were carried out to the hearse. I'd passed on the offer of a lift to the cemetery. A double burial – father and son - too much to handle. I crossed the road with Mum and Leanne to pass on my commiserations to Sara then made a hasty exit. The cemetery at Stoer was the last place I wanted to spend a summer's afternoon. Too many memories.

On the way back to Ullapool Leanne decided it was time for the big-sister-knows-best talk. She'd been appalled at the state I'd arrived home in on Friday but had the good grace to let me recover in my own time. In return I'd said nothing about what I'd overheard. But now she warned me in no uncertain terms. She'd had to get up in the night to use the toilet and that's when she found me laid out face-down on the floor, my dishevelled underwear barely covering my modesty.

Leanne was the one who undressed me and put me to bed.

"I don't want you turning up here pissed and half naked on a regular basis. It's not fair on Steve."

"I won't."

"Just as long as we're clear."

We were.

Maybe she'd been Skyping her boyfriend on her laptop. Maybe I really had drunk way too much and imagined it all. Either way, I decided what my big sister got up to in her own bedroom was none of my business.

By the following weekend I was coherent and fully functional. I'd been out for a drink with Kaz Cartwright the Thursday night and realised I could get used to this lifestyle if I had the funds. But I didn't, and the Arches beckoned.

Working such a busy bar was no holiday but Beth had a system. I coped with it, and by the second weekend I felt I could hold my own while Lukas took his half hour break. He told me he usually waited until things got quieter. That meant us each taking our rest period after the kitchen closed up for the night. As long as we both kept the drinks flowing and I made sure there was a regular supply of clean glasses and ice, there might even be time to chat. Or in Lukas's case, flirt. The worst part was wrapping up after closing time. Most customers were in no hurry to leave.

Sunday morning I didn't surface until noon. One look in the bathroom mirror and the bags under my eyes told their own story. I'd need to pace myself better or I'd never survive the summer.

"So how did last night go?"

I opened one of the kitchen cupboards and took out a pack of muesli. "I'm knackered but the shift goes quick enough. There were a lot of foreign tourists in off that cruise ship so we got loads of tips."

"The 'Artania'? Well, make the most of that. It won't last once the kids break up and the place is full of campers."

"Suppose not." I searched for a clean cereal bowl.

"We had a bit of trouble here last night," Leanne said after she switched the kettle on. "Just after Steve got home from work."

"What d'you mean? In the flats?"

"Out in our stairwell. Steve and me heard the ambulance about seven o'clock. And the police have been round again this morning while you were asleep, asking if we'd seen or heard anything."

"God. What happened?"

"Well, you know Mr and Mrs Waterson? Third floor?"

"Yeah, of course."

"Somebody attacked their son last night."

"Kevin?"

"The police think whoever it was must have been waiting for him at the top of the stairs. As soon as he came in through the outside door, they threw a jug of boiling water over him. It's burnt all down one side of his neck."

"That's awful."

"I know. The police are no nearer finding who did it."

"God." I sat down and began munching.

"We could hear him hammering on poor Mrs Bradshaw's door across the passage but Steve thought it was just some idiot messing about."

"Christ."

"And it wasn't just boiling water they'd used."

"What d'you mean?"

"Someone at the paper shop told Steve they added sugar to the boiling water. It's one of the mean tricks you pick up in prison."

Jesus.

"It sticks to the skin," she continued. "Makes the scalds ten times worse."

I pretended to look horrified but I'd already heard about napalming.

32

KAY sounded surprised to hear from me. A little miffed even. But understandable, given how I'd left Lochinver without a word of explanation.

"I thought I'd done something wrong. Or scared you off for good."

"Nothing like that." I could feel myself blushing like a stupid, love-sick teen. "It was Paver being released without charge. I didn't want to stick around and have to see his ugly face."

"He was on the local News for about five minutes."

"I know. I thought there'd be banners everywhere. Bunting and a pipe band and people lining the streets."

"In Lochinver?" Kay said. "Well if there was I never noticed."

"I was joking." The thought had crossed my mind that it might be exactly the kind of welcome Matt would be expecting when he came out of prison.

"As far as I know Paver's on his way back to Northern Ireland. Peter's taken him across in the boat." Then Kay paused, taking a drag from her spliff no doubt. "I still don't understand how he got away with it."

"I'll tell you when I see you."

"Are you back home?" I sensed a shift in the tone of her voice. Or maybe I was reading too much into everything as usual.

"I'm still at Leanne's."

"Oh." There it was again. Delight then disappointment.

"I was just thinking. How about if you come here for a couple of days?"

Silence at the other end of the line.

"You can stay at Leanne's. I can show you the sights of Ullapool."

"Huh. And how long's that going to take? A couple of hours?" This wasn't going the way I'd anticipated.

"We can go out for a meal together if you like. I get staff discount at the Arches."

"I don't know." An awkward silence again.

"It's OK," I said, hating every word. "You don't have to come if you don't want to."

"It's not that. I do want to see you, of course I do. But I'm a bit of a home bird."

"I just thought it would be a nice change."

Why was it so hard?

"While the weather's fine."

But no matter how much I tried, Kay refused to budge an inch. Excuses or explanations, they both served the same purpose. Kay Jepson was terrified of setting foot outside her door. In the end I decided I'd have to visit Lochinver if I seriously wanted to have what I thought I wanted. I asked Leanne to say nothing to Mum. Everything was going to be fine. I'd be staying with a friend. A girl friend. Leanne didn't comment.

"I know I get under your feet at times," I said.

"Not really. But go if you want to go, I'm not going to stop you."

"It'll only be for a couple of nights."

"Listen, Ames. You don't have to explain anything to me. I'm not your mother."

"I know. I just thought you'd be glad of some privacy. If you want to chat with Steve in the evenings while he's working away you don't have to go into the other room."

She laughed. "Fat chance. He doesn't even bother sending me a text unless he's after something."

I stored that information for later.

The only other passenger on the late bus to Lochinver was Donna Grey. She was visiting her grandparents who were holidaying at Badnaban.

"So how's it going at the Arches? I suppose you've recovered from your night out by now."

"Yeah." I spared her the details.

"We'd all had a few."

"More than a few," I said. "I can't ever remember being so bladdered."

"You were steaming."

"So where did you finish up?"

Kaz had mentioned a party they'd gate-crashed but she'd kept the details vague.

"It was up the Braes. Cindy O'Connor had the run of the house while her mum and dad were away."

"You and Terri got chucked out or something, so Kaz said."

"Terri gave Robin Kerr a mouthful so her and me ended up having to get a taxi back to the village. I think Kaz stayed on, but you know what she's like when there's booze and guys going spare."

"So Robin Kerr's seeing Cindy O'Connor now."

"Looks like it."

"I hope he keeps it in his pants or Cyrus'll be after him with his gutting knife."

Everyone in Ullapool knew Cindy's father by reputation. Cyrus O'Connor aka Slippy - a small-time gangster who'd got his heavies to give Matt a going-over once upon a time. Cyrus was a fisherman who netted more than fish by all accounts.

As we passed through Elphin I watched layers of mist

cloak the hunchback ridge of Suilven, waiting to wrap us in a veil. Next minute the bus driver switched on her wipers.

"Shit. So much for summer."

"They live in the most amazing house," Donna continued prattling on. "There's under-floor heating and a sauna."

"Yeah, well. There's a lot of money to be made from herring."

We sat in silence for most of the rest of the way, rain spattering the windows as the clouds closed in. I looked for signs of Jimmy's truck out towards Brackloch but the place already appeared abandoned. Then Donna leant her head towards mine as if she had a secret to share.

"I probably shouldn't tell you this. It's Kaz."

"What?"

"You need to watch your back, that's all."

"What d'you mean?"

The bus trundled down past the Glac. Two more minutes and we'd be getting off.

"She's the one who spiked your drink."

"Spiked my drink? When was this?"

"That night we were on the razzle. I thought you'd already guessed. She poured vodka into your cider when you weren't looking."

"You mean at the Frigate."

She nodded. "Every round she bought. But it wasn't that much."

"And you didn't think to try and stop her or warn me?"

"She wanted to help you chill - let your hair down. You're too up-tight for your own good sometimes."

Bitch.

"Thanks for nothing. I don't need anyone's help to chill out."

"It could have been worse. When we dropped you off at

your sister's flat she said we should have stayed and helped you get rioted."

The bus reversed next to the recycling bins and Donna waved at the occupants of a red saloon car parked nearby. I was done with her. But once we stepped off the bus she took hold of my arm and steered me towards the bus shelter.

"Do you know about her and Matt?"

"Who?"

"Kaz and Matt. Apparently he's been phoning her."

"Since when?"

"After she heard you were finishing with him. He knows everything - what you said about dumping him."

"Right."

"I wouldn't trust either of them." Donna pulled up the collar of her jacket and turned her back on the squalls of rain blowing in off the sea. "She says she can't wait to see your face when Matt gets out. He doesn't seem that bothered you two are finished, so she reckons. Just thought you should know."

33

"GOD, you're soaked through. And look at the face. Somebody's in a grumpy mood."

"More of the usual crap. Nothing to do with you."

"Sorry for asking." Kay fumbled with the sleeves of her sweatshirt. She had the hood pulled up over her head, looking as if she was about to leave.

"That's not what I meant." I gave her an awkward peck on the cheek. "Were you on your way out?"

"No."

"Only you look like you're not stopping." I unslung the rucksack from my shoulder and tossed it onto the couch.

"Give me your jacket and I'll hang it up."

"Thanks."

"I saw the bus go past, that's all. Then I waited but there was no sign of you so I thought perhaps you'd. . ."

"Aw. You were going to come looking for me."

"Not really." She took my wet coat and offered to fetch me a towel so I could dry my hair. "I'm cooking us a veggie thing. A North African recipe my dad's girlfriend makes."

I'd smelt something spicy as soon as she opened the door.

"Cool."

"So what's in the bag?"

"Just a few bits. Toothbrush, meds in case I can't sleep, spare undies and a bottle of wine."

"Why didn't you say anything earlier? I'll get the glasses."

She told me to make myself at home. Except this wasn't home. Nothing like home. I'd not thought far enough ahead to figure out where this was leading but my body was already tingling with apprehension. Or anticipation. I'd hung around the bus shelter for an age after Donna left, absorbing the information I'd just been given and waiting for the rain to ease off.

It didn't.

While watching the cars hiss by I took out my phone, opened my Facebook page, posted a snarky comment on Kaz's wall then defriended her.

Bitch.

We sat in the kitchen, each savouring the silence while we ate, and once the wine ran out Kay opened a couple of cans of cider. "So. Come on. Enough of the sulks. Who's upset you?"

We clinked cans together and I took a swig from mine. "Nobody you know. One of the girls from school. A mate, or so I thought."

"Somebody being a cunt?"

"Yep. You could say."

I meandered around the topic of Kaz Cartwright, how she'd come across as my bezzie mate before stabbing me in the back.

"I just found out about an hour ago that she'd gone and spiked my drinks a couple of weeks ago. And now her and Matt are phoning each other."

"Matt?"

"I'd got pissed and started mouthing off to everybody about how much of a wanker he'd been. Building up the courage to dump him as soon as he gets out, I suppose. But Kaz obviously beat me to it. Sounds like she wants to grab him for herself."

"So he already knows he's dumped."

"Saves me the trouble. I think I must have mentioned those dodgy emails to her as well. We figured out who's been sending them and it looks like she's gone and done something about that as well."

Her face seemed to sag. "Was it Matt?"

"No." I passed her my phone and let her scroll through them as I explained about the attack on Kevin Waterson.

"He must have been watching me for weeks."

"So who's K?"

"It's Kaz. Baxter's sister. The girl I was telling you about. He'd seen us talking together and he's a bit of a stalker. Caddy had her share of trouble with him last summer."

"And he lives in Ullapool?"

"In the same block as Leanne." I mentioned the napalming.

"Sounds awful."

"I know."

I'd thought about nothing else as I made my way from the bus shelter to Kay's flat. Matt had been in contact with Kaz. She'd no doubt mentioned Kevin. So it didn't take a genius to work out how they organised the attack between them.

34

"WHEN'S Matt supposed to be getting out?"
"This Friday. Why?"
"Just something somebody said."
"I can't believe it's come round so quick."
"You're going back to Ullapool."
"Yeah," I said. "I don't want to be anywhere near Lochinver when he turns up. Mike and Steff will probably have something planned. Back in March his mum had mentioned taking us out to the Albannach if he got away with a slap on the wrist. Thank goodness that came to nothing."
"But just think - fine dining in a Michelin star restaurant," she laughed. "You'd have been guest of honour."
"Exactly," I said. "I'll have to speak to him sooner or later, but it won't be such a big deal now he knows we're finished."
"I'll drink to that." We clinked cans again then Kay grabbed the remains of the six-pack from the fridge and we retired to the living room. We chose opposing chairs and lay back, listening to the rain drum against her lounge window.
"I told Leanne I'll be back sometime Thursday. I mean, if you're OK with me staying here two nights."
"Sure." I caught the twinkle in her eye but then her smile disappeared and for a moment I didn't know

whether to believe her or not.

"What are you thinking?"

Kay seemed to come to her senses. She leant forward and put her can down on the coffee table. "We need to talk."

"If you say so." I'd not thought of the ground rules regarding what we were getting ourselves into, but maybe that's how these things worked. "I'm not expecting anything to happen, just so you know?"

I swear I saw pity in her face as soon as the words were out of my mouth. "It's not about that. I mean, that's not what I want to talk about. Not right now."

"So what?"

"These messages," she said. "I think I might be K."

"But you can't be."

"Why not? They could have seen you coming out of my flat, whoever it is who's watching you."

My heart gave an involuntary skip. "But Kevin. . . I mean, how could he?"

"I'm not on about Kevin." The temperature seemed to drop a few degrees as she continued. "I'm fairly sure Peter Paver's the one who sent them. He knows you've been calling here. And he knows exactly why."

My whole body seemed to shut down as each individual bone slipped free of its moorings and sank to impossible depths. I needed to somehow clamber to my feet and leave. But there was about as much chance of my getting off this sofa as a jellyfish has of standing on dry land.

"Peter Paver knows I'm staying here tonight?"

"Christ, no. You're off his radar now, as far as I know. But he's been hanging round since when this all started. Since his dad got arrested." Kay stood and fumbled in her pockets. "Sorry. I need something. Can I roll you one?"

"No thanks."

I had to keep my head clear to focus on what Kay was telling me and work out how Paver fitted into her story. I could already picture the look on his face if he ever found out exactly why I was planning on sleeping here when my own bed was less than half a mile away.

Kay lit her joint and after a couple of puffs she began to explain. "I've known Paver since when we were at the High School. He never really got on with the rest of the Lochinver crowd because he lived outside the village, I suppose. He didn't seem to want to mix with any of them."

"So what?"

"I felt sorry for him. Maybe I could see a bit of myself in him. A loner. Somebody else who didn't quite fit in."

"Like a freak."

"If you say so," she muttered. "Anyway, we became friends. That's all we ever were. I mean, I've never fancied anyone in uniform. And long before he left school he was into combat knives and guns and all that macho shit. He kept going on about joining the Army once he was old enough. Said he wanted to train to be a professional killer."

"Christ, what a joke." I could remember how they used to tease him on the school bus. Calling him 'Peepee'. Moolie and Matt were the worst. "He used to run home to Daddy like a cry-baby whenever we called him names. Threatening to kill us. The guy's a total wanker."

She gave a smirk. "I thought you had a thing going last summer?"

"What?"

Kay took a long hit from her spliff. "I know all about the party at White Shore. And before you get all defensive, I don't give a shit how many guys you've screwed or who they were, just so we're clear. It's all water under the bridge."

I felt sick to the stomach. "What exactly did he tell you?

"It wasn't him. It was Caddy. Me and Peter had lost touch long before she mentioned anything. He'd joined up and gone to Afghanistan or wherever."

"Right."

"She said something one night but I couldn't have cared less. I didn't even know you that well so the name meant nothing. And it was before I got mixed up with Rick and Rooster."

"But you and Rooster ended up together. Before he drowned," I said.

"We had this intense relationship for a couple of months and I kind of went a bit mental. That's how it is with me."

I thought back to the photo Matt had shown me of the party at the chalet park. A spaced-out look on Kay's face. Red eye – from the flash or from something else.

"There was this TV programme about the ten most addictive drugs and Rooster reckoned he'd done nine of them. The only one he'd never tried was methadone. It's like he was proud of the fact."

"Fuck."

"Exactly. He was a bit wild but it was never boring."

"I bet."

"Whatever we tried was never enough. Everything we did - I wanted more. Dad always said I've got an addictive personality and I suppose Rooster could see that. He brought out the worst in me."

"Really?"

"Even when I was a wee kid I was never satisfied. I always wanted one more push on the swings or one more bedtime story or five more minutes out in the canoe with my cousin Finlay. They blamed it on my ADHD."

"But what's Paver got to do with all this?" I drained the

can and waited as she composed herself.

"I'm getting to that."

"OK," I said.

"It was about three weeks after the attack. Everything had kicked off by then. I wasn't long out of hospital. Doped up on pain killers for most of the time. And I'd been smoking more of this shit than was good for me. Dad wanted me to go and live with him and Lucy Links out at Reiff until everything blew over."

"Is that your dad's girlfriend?"

"She's from Lincolnshire. She said it was too flat and the mountains were calling her. No idea how they got hold of her number. But she's fine, if you like vegan hippies who believe in healing crystals and all that shit. She tried it on with me but I told her to do one."

"Is that why you didn't go? 'Cause you two don't get on?"

"It's not that, Christ. Who wants to live out on Fraggle Rock?"

"I suppose."

"And every time Dad looks at me I know exactly what's going through his mind. He feels guilty. Guilty as fuck. He can't hide it no matter how hard he tries."

"Why would your dad feel guilty?"

"Why do you think? He'd watched me go off the rails from when I was about fourteen and yet he'd never said a word. He knew I was into all kinds of heavy stuff but he kept telling everybody it's my life. I can do what I want as long as I don't hurt anyone along the way."

I nodded.

"I hardly spent a night at home from one week to the next. Most of the time I'd be crashed out at a mate's in Ullapool. It was easier sofa surfing than having to get up every morning at seven o'clock in time to catch the bus to school."

"I suppose."

"But then I'm the one who ends up getting hurt and Dad reckoned he should have seen it coming."

"So it's all his fault?"

"He knows what they did to me," she gave a shudder. "Everything. All the medical details. And whenever he sees his precious little princess I know exactly what's going through his mind. There are times when he can't even look at me."

"Shame on him. You're still his flesh and blood."

"I know. But it's not me he's judging. He blames himself for giving me too much freedom."

"You were twenty-one when they raped you, not fourteen."

"That's what I keep telling him. I don't expect him to look after me for the rest of my life. I brought this on myself. Those two Ukrainians turned up on my doorstep because I had their drugs."

I swept my fingers through my hair, looking at the despair in her face and seeing she meant every word. "But it's not all your fault."

"I'm not saying it is." I'd never seen Kay as tense as this. She stared me out and I felt like I was the one being interrogated.

"So what are you saying?"

"I'm saying it's all Matt Neilson's fault. He's the fucking jinx who got me in this mess."

35

KAY'S bloodshot eyes bulged from her head as if she was mainlining on anger. "Just think about all the bad choices he keeps making. First he gets himself involved with Rick's dodgy dealings and Caddy gets murdered. Then when he gets his hands on Rick's stash instead of going to the police he brings the gear round my place 'cause he knows what I'm like. I thought all my Christmases had come at once."

"But he wasn't to know what would happen."

"Huh," she spat out a spurt of smoke. "He already knew somebody had been after Rick and Rooster the day he went disappearing to Ullapool. He knew somebody was bound to come looking."

"But still. . ."

"No, Amy." She took another hit from her spliff and it seemed to calm her nerves. "I'm not making excuses for the way I handled things but Matt's the one who gave me the drugs. It's Matt's fault they turned up here looking for their stash and the money Rick Tyler owed them. Money Matt kept for himself, in case you forgot. He knew they were up to no good yet he still did nothing about it until it was almost too late. He could have got you killed as well, for Christ's sake."

"It's not that simple," I said.

"When I was on the kitchen floor, my face battered to a pulp and my body torn apart with blood coming out of both ends, I hated Matt Neilson enough to wish him dead. They didn't just want the drugs. They were after the name of the person who'd stolen their money."

"But you didn't let on," I said.

Her gaze seemed to impale me against the back of the armchair. "What d'you think? Of course I didn't. I had no idea, but I don't think it would have made any difference if I'd given them Matt's name. They enjoyed hurting me. Even when the police grilled me about the drugs I never mentioned Matt. But if I'd known how he'd turn his back on me and let someone else clear up this mess I'd have dropped him in it with pleasure. He didn't even have the decency to text me or phone to find out how I was."

"Why am I not surprised by that?"

"Exactly. The more I thought about Matt, the more I loathed him. I wanted him to suffer the same way I had, if you must know. I was praying he'd get raped in the prison showers by some psychotic thug."

"So what's this got to do with Peter Paver?"

"Like I was saying. The doorbell rang one morning, about eleven o'clock, and there he was."

"And you let him in after what his dad had done?"

"Why wouldn't I? I wasn't thinking about his dad, to be honest. And we'd been good pals in a previous lifetime. One friendly face was better than none, I suppose. Apart from Dad and Lucy, I'd not seen a soul for almost a month except for Doctor Ross and the nurse who came to change my dressings."

"So what was he after?"

"Paver?" She grinned. "Same as you. He came here looking to score."

The irony of what Kay had just said wasn't lost on either of us and we both managed a smile for all of a split second.

"I don't mean that. He knew I was dealing."

"Right." It still wasn't making much sense.

"He had a wad of cash and some story about his medical discharge from the Army."

"Medical discharge? First I've heard of it," I said.

"It must have been about three months ago. His dad managed to keep it quiet, I suppose. Peter ended up in some kind of rehab centre."

"What? You mean he was on drugs?"

"I'm not sure. He gave me this story about being given a malaria vaccine before they were due to fly back to Helmand or wherever. Some of them suffered a bad reaction."

"And you believed him?"

"No reason not to. A few of his mates went a bit loopy. Suicidal. The Army shipped him out pretty quick once they could see he wasn't cut out for combat. Though I think there's more to it. You've only got to look at his eyes when he starts going off on one."

"What d'you mean?"

"Just some of the stuff he said. His plans for the summer."

"Coming home and getting high? Sounds like a wonderful plan. Can I just use your loo?"

When I came back Kay had lit another joint.

"Peter guessed I was still self-medicating. There's no way I'd have been able to stay here on my own otherwise. Not after, you know."

"But I'm not seeing the full picture. If Peter only came here to buy hash why would he start sending me those messages?"

"We got talking and I must have said something about how much I hated Matt Neilson. And that's when we realised we both felt the same way."

"About Matt?"

"He was raging. He reckoned Matt was the one who got

his dad in bother with the law. With everything else that had happened, he was burning up inside."

She let the words sink in and I reached for the joint. "Let me have just a drag."

"None of this was meant to hurt you, Amy."

I passed the spliff back and let her take a couple of drags.

"None of what?"

"What Peter was doing. Those messages. He'd heard you and Matt were together. Through his dad maybe, 'cause I never mentioned anything. So there was probably a bit of jealousy after what happened last summer. But it was Matt he wanted to pay back, and he couldn't get to him while he was locked away."

"So he thought he'd get at Matt through me?"

"He probably worked out he could kill two birds with one stone by hassling you."

"I don't get it."

"Peter was terrified you'd testify in court and get his dad sent down for years."

"But I was telling the truth."

"I don't doubt it. And the more I think about it, the more certain I am that Peter knew what his dad had been up to."

"Bastards."

"But he figured out the police wouldn't have enough to go on without your testimony. There was nothing else to link his dad with the Ukrainians."

"So he needed to shut me up? Is that what you're saying?"

"Nothing quite as dramatic." She stubbed the dead joint out in a saucer and sat back against her chair. "I reckon the emails were meant to scare you off."

"Christ."

"That sounds worse than it really was. He wanted to

make you feel uncomfortable. And because he's ex-Army, everything ends up like a fucking campaign. He had it all planned out. You and Matt were the enemy and he was going to put the wind up the pair of you by making you think there was somebody after you. Somebody who'd get you worried enough to maybe retract your statement."

"Like who?"

"Who knows? Some of those involved with Paver's dodgy dealings have never been caught. But they'd be losing business with the police sniffing around. People in Lochinver, Rosehall and Ullapool as well as in Aberdeen."

"You mean people like Slippy?" He'd been the last person on my mind when I started receiving the emails.

"Peter never said. And I didn't think he'd take things any further because he's all talk."

"But he did," I said.

"Sounds like he decided it was time for action. I'm not sure what would have happened if they hadn't let his dad out of prison, but some of the stuff he talked about used to scare me."

"So he's been here more than once?"

Kay nodded. "Weekends mostly. We'd get high. Share a drink - just like this, but nothing more."

"Sounds very cosy."

Her face flushed red. "He knows better than to try anything on. I'd warned him right at the start."

"So when exactly did he decide to target me?"

"He must have seen you that first time you called round."

"How do you know?"

"He phoned about ten minutes after you left. Wanting to know what you were doing here," she said. "He must have been watching you."

"Watching you watching over you."

"Exactly."

"And what did you tell him? That I'd come round here to buy weed?"

Kay shook her head. "I had no reason to. He was fishing, that's all. I mentioned something about Matt's letter and you going in to see him. We both thought you were out of your mind."

"What else did he say?"

"He went on about how Matt didn't deserve you and how he'd make him pay once his dad was proved innocent."

"Shit," I laughed. "If Peter thinks I'm better off with him than Matt after all this crap he's put me through, he really must be crazy."

"It's not just Matt he was gunning for. He was saying all kinds of stuff about people in the village turning against him and his dad. The local councillors and businesses. The police. He said he'd make them all pay."

"Christ!" I thought back to what Jimmy Jump had told me about Peter's promise to finish what his granddad had started.

"The next time he came round he was already high. And not just weed."

No surprises there.

"I tried to calm him down. I told him you and Matt weren't a threat any more. Matt was going through hell in prison and you were on medication for your nerves. That's when I mentioned you coming round to buy some weed - to help you cope. I thought he'd get the message - to stop obsessing about you both."

"But he didn't."

"No. He went hyper. Said I'd given him this brilliant idea. He'd pass on everything I'd said to his dad's solicitor. You were unhinged and nobody would believe a word you said in court once they heard you were a dope head."

"Bastard." The ground kept shifting under my feet as I tried to make sense of this information overload.

"I felt awful."

"So why didn't you tell me about all this sooner?"

"I haven't seen you for nearly three weeks, Amy. And now Gordon's out of prison, he's stopped sending them. Right?"

Theoretically.

"I never even realised it was Paver who'd sent you those messages until you mentioned K."

"Right."

"So we're still cool, yeah?"

Cool? We're ice fucking cold.

36

KAY disappeared for a moment then returned with a couple of shot glasses and a bottle of spiced rum.

"You going to have one?"

I nodded.

"It's a mess. But I never realised he was so twisted."

"Paver?" I said.

"I probably made things worse, encouraging him."

"But you didn't have to tell me any of this."

"Suppose not."

She handed me a half-filled glass and raised her own.

"Cheers."

I drained mine in one.

"I don't want there to be any secrets between us," she continued.

"Us?" I could feel tears at the corner of my eyes but I was determined to sit this out without breaking down. "What else have you told Paver?"

"What do you mean?"

"Kissy kiss? What did he mean?"

Suddenly there were tears running down Kay's face and she put down her glass. Then it struck me: the ultimate deception.

"Oh, God. It was all an act." I needed to get out of here. Now. I staggered to my feet, blind with embarrassment.

"No, wait."

"You get me round here, all loved up on some herbal

tea and super-strength weed, and then what? Photos of me on your Facebook page? Like the one of you and Matt? Is that what tonight's supposed to be about?"

"It's nothing like that."

"I suppose Paver thought a photograph of us in bed together would be enough to shut me up."

"Check your fucking phone," she said.

"What?"

"The dates. Check when he sent that email about you coming round here. It was before any of this - before I kissed you."

I didn't need to check anything. I knew she was right.

"He sent it the same night you came round in a state, after going to see Matt in prison. Remember?"

"I just thought. . ."

"What?"

"I didn't know about you and him back then."

"Me and him? There is no me and him. There never was." Her face flushed again. "We need to calm down. The pair of us."

I slumped back onto the couch and held my head in my hands, hoping the doubts would stop spinning around inside my skull. "I suppose I'm being stupid."

"If there's anything else you want to know you'd better ask me now and get it done with."

I pulled a tissue out of my jeans pocket and blew my nose. "That night we kissed. When you said you had to telephone somebody."

"You think I was phoning Peter to let him know we'd just snogged? Christ, you haven't got a clue have you?"

My own eyes were wet now and I wiped them dry with my sleeve. "I'm sorry. I don't know what to believe any more."

"If you must know, I did phone him. Not then, but later. And only to ask if it was true about his dad getting out.

That's when I told him he'd got what he wanted so he had no reason to keep up his stupid threats."

I snivelled and tried to steady my trembling voice. "And what did he say?"

"He laughed. He reckoned I didn't know what I was talking about. He said he hadn't even started. There's unfinished business and a world of pain coming once Matt's out of prison."

I could hear the occasional car passing in the street below; the hiss of tyres on wet tarmac. But otherwise the world seemed to have stopped turning.

"So what do we do?" she asked eventually.

"About what?"

"About all this. I know you'll probably never trust me again, and I deserve it. But that means everything else has changed as well."

"Not really." I was still snivelling like a pathetic dishrag. "I trust you, but maybe it would have been better if you'd said nothing. You're scaring me, Kay."

"I had to let you know after that poor kid got the blame for something he hasn't done."

"I still can't stop thinking about it."

She picked up her quarter-empty glass and drained it. "Like I said, if Paver's got unfinished business where Matt's concerned, you should warn him when you next see him."

"Why is it always me?"

"Whatever." She laid her glass on the coffee table. "I was going to suggest we get pissed together, but maybe it's best we both sleep on it."

"Yeah."

From the look on her face I was already locked out of her life for the rest of the night. "It's been one of them fucking days," she continued. "Let's write off this date or whatever it was supposed to be and pretend it never happened."

I could see it was already dark outside and the sensible thing to do would be to retreat with my tail between my legs and maybe have a cry on Mum's shoulder if she was still up.

"You're right." I could hear the rain spattering on the window but what the hell? "It's going to take a while for all this to sink in. I still don't know who I can trust."

"I know."

"Sorry." I got to my feet and made my way to the corridor where she'd hung up my jacket and rucksack.

"Will you be alright?"

"If I go home you mean?"

Kay nodded.

"I've got my key and Mum always keeps the bed made up for me."

She gave me a hug and I almost gave in. I was aching to stay with her, despite it all. "I hope you manage to get some sleep."

"You too," I said. "See you later."

"I'll ring you."

37

THE film of my life was never meant to be a disaster movie - jump-cutting from one car crash relationship to the next. Mum had still been at work when I got home so I left her a cryptic note on the kitchen table and hauled my body off to bed. Then shortly after midnight I heard someone open my bedroom door to look in on me. I held my breath and waited. The last thing I wanted was a mother-daughter chat with my heart in pieces.

Hours later, I woke in pitch darkness imagining something warm and soft moulded against my back. One arm lay draped across my belly and the slow rhythm of her breathing told me Kay was sound asleep. I turned onto my back and manoeuvred myself so I could place my own hand on top of hers. Then I pushed both hands further down my body. But then she was gone again. Another dream that left me crying into my pillow until I felt empty - like everything I'd ever hoped for had been taken away from me.

When I got up I still felt washed out and dizzy with indecisiveness. There was barely time to grab a coffee before stepping out into a new day. 06:38 on the microwave clock. The overnight rain had cleared. Ground wet with dew, wall to wall blue sky and the sea loch a flawless mirror.

Only two vehicles passed me between Kirk Road and

Cruamer: a white BT van with a rattling exhaust and an anonymous, metallic grey hatchback. A solitary fish wagon with its side-lights on stood next to the harbour sheds. All the shutter doors were closed. No movement other than a large fishing boat wallowing in the oily water alongside the ice plant; its radar antenna lazily spinning high above the wheelhouse.

I counted the small craft moored at the marina as I walked past. Eleven boats - not a sign of the 'Meera Rose'. Had it been there, I might have turned round and abandoned my mission. I'd felt the same when passing the shops in the village, desperate for a sign in an upstairs window. One twitch of Kay's bedroom curtain and I'd have been outside her door, hammering to be let inside. Desperate to tell her how empty life was going to be without her.

Nothing much had changed since I'd last followed the coastal path beyond the breakwater. The same bone-white boulders and overhanging crags hemmed me in as I picked my way along the foreshore. The same sting of rotting seaweed and fresh salt water hung on the air. Heather bloomed on the higher reaches of the headland and here and there a spray of yellow ragwort and flush of green fern signalled summer days but otherwise everything here brought back memories of winter.

I still missed Caddy.

I'd not visited the White Shore since the day after Matt's trial. In certain light, the trees that bordered the narrow curve of beach gave the place a sinister look. But I knew every branch, every skeletal finger of exposed root, every patch of bare rock and dense shadow. It had always been a special place.

Dad had brought me and Leanne here often enough. Teaching us both to swim, pointing out the silver fish, almost transparent in the clear water, and the dreadlocks of seaweed swaying on the currents as the tide exposed then covered each boulder. I remember the taste of salt on my tongue; the rasp of grit between my clenched teeth. I'd worn a turquoise bathing costume with ruffles and Dad had said I looked just like a little mermaid.

I stopped to rest on a length of tree trunk, sawn down and laid across a low trestle to form a makeshift bench. Close by, the shimmer of water revealed a familiar world beneath the waves. But the deeper I searched the less certain I became. If I peered any closer into the past I knew I'd never find the courage to continue along the narrow track South.

Finally I made my move. Every step felt as if I was wading against the tide of panic swelling inside me. The last time I'd followed the path to Strathbeg, there had been hailstones and a biting wind off the sea. Grey snow clouds racing inland and dusk less than an hour away. But now it felt like part of someone else's past.

The chalet park lay in silence - the silence of abandonment rather than absence. Driftwood and strips of kelp littered the barren shoreline adjacent to the nearest cabin where Matt and I had spent a night together a lifetime ago. I tested the door but it was locked tight as expected. I'm still not sure what I'd have done if I'd gained entry.

Two rectangles of bare concrete marked where the bunkhouses had stood. Jimmy had already told me they'd been pulled down. His truck looked like a discarded shoe below the steep incline leading up to the house. I could see no movement behind any of the windows. No smoke from the chimney. There were no sounds other than a bird chittering to itself somewhere close by and the random buzz of insects. But I sensed I was being watched. And as I approached the front door, it opened a crack. The crack widened and Jimmy stepped outside, the braces of his trousers hanging down to his knees and his sleeves rolled up to his elbows.

"You're here at last."

38

WE sat on the steps and gazed out to sea, eating rounds of thick toast and marmalade and drinking cups of over-sweetened tea, watching the haze grow impenetrable then evaporate. The scent of wild garlic everywhere around us.

"Have you heard from anybody? Your brother or Peter?"

"Not a word," he said.

"I don't suppose you're too bothered."

"I know there'll be unfinished business where Peter's concerned. I'll hear from him soon enough."

An echo of Kay's warning made me hold back the question on my lips.

"Evergreen always used to tell me. Don't praise the day until the sun is set."

"What d'you mean by unfinished business?"

"It's his birthright. When you're used to having nothing, you consider yourself rich. But to have your inheritance snatched away from you."

"You mean Gordon's?"

"His money made him greedy. And my share was never meant to bring me joy."

"But legally Strathbeg was always yours," I said. "Gordon can't ask for it back now."

The old man shook his head. "I'm not talking about Gordon."

"You mean Peter?"

"Peter says I've taken what's rightfully his. That's how he sees it. And I'm feared he's going to come and claim it."

I laughed. "That's crazy. He's got the boat. And I bet his dad's got plenty more money hidden away where nobody can get their hands on it."

"Maybe. But I managed well enough without any of this." Jimmy raised his hands to his face and wiped each eye with the ball of each palm. "My father warned me when I told him I was coming over here in search of work. No honest man gets rich quickly."

"What d'you mean?"

"My brother and his son. There's things you don't know. Things that went on here last winter. And maybe it's best you're kept in the dark."

"Last winter?"

"Whatever I say now won't change what happened. The past is the past and sometimes it doesn't do to turn over a stone that's lain undisturbed for so long. But I ken how Peter won't let things lie."

"So he thinks he should have the house as well as everything else?"

"I could read it in his face when we left the solicitor's office." Jimmy began to blink furiously as if desperate to stem the tears welling at the surface. "There'll be hard decisions to make the day he returns from Portrush."

"What d'you think he's going to do?" I already had an inkling.

The old man tapped a finger against his right temple. "In here he counts the days as if they're loose change. Scheming how long he has to wait."

"Wait for what?"

"For the day I pass on to my Maker. He helped me make a will when we decided to sell Luibeg. He wanted me to make everything official. So when I die there'll be a fortune enough to tempt any young man to recklessness."

I let the thought of Peter's recklessness settle before relaying what Kay had told me the previous night. Then I handed him my phone and showed him how to scroll his way through the list of messages, but he passed it back to me.

"I've no time for that nonsense."

"OK."

"I can choose to believe what I hear with my own ears or see with my own eyes without needing proof from that contraption," he said.

"So will you try to talk some sense into Peter when you see him? I think he's going to go after Matt and try to harm him somehow."

"Good counsel never comes cheap. The boy's not for changing once he gets a notion in his head. My words could well drive him in search of more vengeance. And there's no comfort to be found in vengeance."

39

JIMMY insisted on driving me to Ullapool. He said he had people there to see. Things to do.

"You don't have to. Leanne isn't expecting me back until sometime tomorrow so there's no hurry. I can get the bus."

"Your sister."

"Yeah."

"I mind when she came to Luibeg one time a while ago. A wee lassie with nut brown skin and hair as fair as barley. She was walking her dog. A lurcher with a coat the colour of mustard."

We'd never owned a dog and I could never imagine my sister traipsing all the way out as far as Brackloch.

"A lurcher?"

"It was a while ago. Almost twenty years or more. It set off my Jem and I had to close her up inside the barn."

Leanne would have been three or four years old. And, to the best of my knowledge, Jimmy had still been in his caravan at Clachtoll twenty years ago.

"Some days sit as fresh in the memory as yesterday," he continued. "The first time I set eyes on Evergreen. And the day we spent hay-making over on the MacLeod's croft."

I fumbled with my phone. "I need to send my mum a message so she knows I'm OK. Then I'd better text Leanne and let her know I'm going to be back early if you're sure you don't mind taking me."

The list of emails from Peter Paver was still displayed on the screen. Taunting me.

"That's fine. I'll find my jacket then we'll make tracks."

I waited until he went back inside the house then walked down towards the chalets in search of a better signal. Once I had three bars on my phone I pressed the Reply button and swiftly typed in my message.

WYWOY
I KNOW EXACTLY WHAT YOU'RE TRYING TO DO
BUT ME AND MATT ARE FINISHED
HE'S USED ME
HE USES EVERYBODY
AND I HATE HIM NOW MORE THAN EVER
SO LEAVE ME ALONE

I pressed *SEND* then made my way back up the drive towards Jimmy's truck.

40

PLAN A came to nothing - the jumping into a taxi and getting bladdered on a train en route to Inverness bit. For one thing, the nearest railway station to Peterhead was over thirty miles away at Inverurie. And those who'd gone through the joyless procedure of release day several times before were only too happy to spell out what it would be like stepping outside the prison gates at ten o'clock on a Friday morning.

"It's like a fucking punch in the guts that you don't see coming. Cars everywhere. Drivers rubber-necking whenever another body walks out. Young mammies with their buggies, eyeing you while you hang around at the bus shelter, your black hold-all at your feet. And the look they give you."

"The look?" Matt said.

"Like you're going to murder them and their bairns first chance you get, 'cause you're a psycho killer and you shouldn't even be out on the streets. They all know where you've just come out of. They're no stupid. There's even a fucking primary school a couple of hundred yards down the road to crank up the communal paranoia."

In the end, Steff promised to pick up Matt. He spotted her little red Clio parked next to the pillar box on Towerhill as arranged. But even then the walk of shame across the main road to freedom was almost too much to handle.

"How are you?"

"Sound." Matt was nowhere near feeling sound.

"You look cold."

"No, I'm OK. Nice to have some fresh air for a change."

"Good."

"So what time did you have to leave?" he said.

"Just after five. The roads were quiet until I got to Nairn."

"Thanks. For this I mean."

"Matt, you don't have to thank me," she said. "It's what I'm here for. Your dad hasn't said a lot during the last few days but I know he's looking forward to seeing you back home."

"Dad is?"

"Well, you know what he's like. We both thought we'd lost you."

"Yeah."

Matt knew what his dad was like. No matter what financial incentives might be on offer, Dad would have plans in place to handle things his own way – to bring his delinquent son back in line, make the black sheep of the family pay for his sins, etcetera, etcetera. The slightest misstep and Mike Neilson would kick off. More so now he could play the prison card.

"Have you decided what you're going to do?"

Matt began drumming his fingers on the dashboard. "Oh, yeah. First priority, get out of these clothes and have a long, hot soak in the bath. Then a proper cup of coffee and a decent meal."

"We thought we could go out to the Albannach tomorrow night."

"Right."

"We haven't booked, but maybe you could ask Amy if she'd like to come as well."

Maybe. Maybe not. Matt gazed at the familiar landscape unfolding all about him. So much open space. Cul Mor, Suilven, Canisp and Quinag like toy mountains - each in its own corner of the playground, exactly where he'd left them before his three months' detention for being a naughty boy.

"We haven't heard from her for a while but I'm sure you're looking forward to catching up with each other."

Matt reflected on the day she'd dragged him to the top of Quinag – desperate to drop her pants yet blowing hot and cold all the way there and back.

Silly bitch.

"I'll have to see. She's living in Ullapool now."

"What? She's written to you?"

"No," he said. "Somebody I know said something about her staying at her sister's over the summer. She's working in a bar. That's only until she goes back to school, I expect."

"I had no idea."

"I'll maybe take a trip down there tomorrow. I've got a couple of mates I can stay with overnight if I need to."

"You'll be careful won't you, Matt?"

And so it began. The whining and the whingeing and the controlling freakishness of being back home.

"I'll pop in to see her if she's working. Maybe give her a surprise."

"That'll be nice. I know how much she's been missing you."

41

SOME weekends are like sticks of dynamite. You light the fuse, stand back and wait for all Hell to break loose. This one began with a text from Kay even before I got out of bed.

```
WTF. Are u crazy?
```

No kisses. I figured that was an oversight. I plumped up my pillow and thumbed in her number. Time to speak. I'd already wasted two days before finding the courage the previous afternoon to press the *SEND* button.

```
Hope u r OK. Thought I'd better let u
know  I've  finally  replied  to  P's
emails. Told him I know exactly what
he's been up to. No reaction so far.
Watch this space ☺ xx
```

Paver hadn't bothered replying to my original email. That fact had been playing on my mind since I'd got back to Ullapool. What if he turned up at Kay's and gave her a hard time? It wouldn't take him long to work out how I'd discovered he was the one behind the anonymous threats.

Kay had promised to phone me as well. That was the last thing she'd said before I left on Tuesday night, so it gave me another reason to call her. I was desperate to hear her voice even if she wasn't feeling particularly chirpy.

"Hi."

"Where are you?"

"I'm still in bed. I was working 'til God knows when last night. Got in about three o'clock."

"So you're back in Ullapool."

She almost sounded relieved.

"Looks like it. So how about you?"

"Yeah. I'm OK, though you managed to freak me out a bit."

"My text?"

Her voice seemed to slide off its tracks as if she was high. "Not just that."

"Oh."

"The way things ended up Tuesday. I went and did something really stupid."

"What's happened?" She was managing to freak me out now.

"After you'd gone, I got off my face. Totally ripped."

"Pissed?"

"Rat-arsed." A pause. "I finished off the rum – the whole bottle. But then I took some other stuff to help me stay awake. I had a lot of thinking to do."

"What other stuff?"

"A little white powder that happened to be lying around."

My grip tightened on the phone. "God. You mean coke?"

"Well it wasn't fucking Fairy Snow."

"OK."

The silence that followed seemed to crackle like static before a thunderstorm.

"But you're fine now."

"Yeah. All mended." I heard the snip of a lighter and

pictured her lying in bed with a roll-up in her hand and her hair messed up and the scent of sleep still on her skin.

"Look. I'm sorry if it was my fault. I admit things got a little heavy."

"It's no big deal." I heard her take in a deep breath. Getting high maybe.

"You sure?"

"I said so, didn't I?"

Christ. Why did she make it so hard to be civil?

"OK. It's just, I wanted to hear a friendly voice that's all. Sounds stupid, I know."

The line went quiet again.

"You still there?"

"You could always try ringing the Samaritans," she said finally.

"What?"

"Well, if you're needing to offload or whatever. That's what they're there for."

I curled up tight and pressed the phone against my ear. "Have I pissed you off or something?"

She seemed to ignore my question. "'Cause I have people I can ring. Monday night at seven o'clock. Regular as clockwork. I tell them my troubles and they tell me to take one day at a time, even though they have no fucking idea how hard that can be."

She sounded more than high.

"Are you talking about Alcoholics Anonymous?"

"No. I'm talking about Screw-ups Anonymous. For those freakin' losers who take drugs because it's what you do when there's nothing else."

"Kay. Are you on something now?"

"Shit, you're starting to sound like my dad. I'm fine, OK? Just tired? You wake me up on a Saturday morning and it's not even half ten. How do you expect me to sound?"

The fact that she was the one who had texted me half an hour earlier seemed to have been overlooked.

"So maybe I should let you get back to sleep and we can talk later."

"Whatever."

Silence hung in the air again and I sensed there was more she wasn't telling me. "Look. I'm going to try to get to Lochinver again next week for a night. No strings, but it would be good to see you again."

"Why? So you can fuck with my head again?"

"I don't know what you're going on about. Just because you got ripped and want someone else to blame for your so-called problems, it doesn't mean you have to take it out on me. I thought we were friends." I was shaking and when she laughed I honestly thought she was losing her mind. "Just tell me what I've done."

"It's not you, OK? It's me. I seem to attract damaged goods so maybe you're better off on your own," she said. "I'm no friend of yours."

"What?"

I heard her take another long breath. "You shouldn't get involved with someone like me 'cause you'll only end up getting hurt. I promise you, I'm bad news."

"That's not true."

"Oh, but it is. I lie. I hurt people. I do stupid stuff whenever I'm bored. Bored, bored, bored."

"We all do stupid stuff. Look at me and Matt?"

"I lied to you big style on Tuesday."

"What d'you mean?"

"There's things I didn't tell you. About me and Peter."

Suddenly I felt the gorge rising at the back of my throat. "What sort of things?"

"Ending up in bed every time he comes round to see me. Getting off our heads on cocaine and screwing like polecats."

"Oh, fuck no." I'm not even sure if she heard my reaction because her voice seemed to tumble out of the phone like loose change from a slot machine. The sound tinny and artificial.

"You think I'm trashy? Well get used to it, 'cause I'm not the sorry little victim you think I am. I'm not someone who needs saving. And if I was, you're the last person I'd fucking call."

"Why are you being such a cunt?"

I ended the call as soon as the words were out of my mouth. Then I turned and buried my face in the pillow, desperate to erase the image from my mind.

Kay didn't ring back. I didn't expect her to. And when Leanne tapped my bedroom door fifteen minutes or so later with a mug of tea and some tissues, I could tell she'd heard some of the conversation.

"These walls. Steve says they're like rice paper."

I wiped my eyes and took the mug. "It's OK. I'm just being stupid as usual."

"No you're not. Blow your nose."

She gave me another tissue. "Ta."

"Boy trouble?"

I nodded. "Yeah. But nobody you know and I'm already over it."

42

LEANNE had suggested I ring in sick but I needed the cash, and besides, a busy Saturday night behind the bar would help take my mind off things.

I kept seeing them together. The pair of them stretched out on her red, silk sheets. Kay squirming as his fingers touched her breasts and every other place when she'd sworn she'd scream if anyone went near. His mouth on hers. His lips on her flesh. His body pressing against her, pressing inside her.

"Two pints of dark when you're ready, darling." The guy's fingers clicked as if trying to bring me out of my trance.

"OK, OK."

Lukas looked on but said nothing.

Wise choice.

Kay had already told me how they worked their way through a bottle of wine and a spliff or two whenever Peter called round. It seemed they took something stronger as well. Something guaranteed to cut her inhibitions loose maybe and allow her to forget everything else in her screwed-up life.

"Can we settle our bill please?" The couple who had complimented me on the amazing weather I'd managed to personally arrange for them when they first came in now stood waiting for me to respond. "Miss?"

Lukas took me by the elbow. "Amy?"

"I'm onto it, OK?" I totted up their account and waited while the husband searched in his wallet for a credit card.
Jesus.

I'd come so close to letting Kay touch me that time we kissed. Lifting my butt off the couch, hips raised, inviting her to slide her hand inside my tracksuit bottoms and touch me the same way I longed to touch her.

He took two attempts to type in his PIN then I handed him his card and receipt and turned to put the print-off in the till. No polite goodbye. No enjoy the rest of your evening. No tip.

"What's the matter with you tonight?" Lukas in my face again.

"Nothing."

I heard him mutter about it being that time of the month and as I spun round to set him straight I saw a familiar face. Two familiar faces. Kaz Cartwright and the shaven-headed yob from Peterhead who'd kept giving me the eye. Flicking his tongue out, winking at me. They both looked well pleased to see me.

I did my best to keep control of my shaking hands as Baxter slapped a fifty pound note on the bar. Slow breaths. In. Out. One. Two. Two pints of lager, two Glenlivet chasers and a vodka and Red Bull.

"Fine."

"Hi, Ames." Kaz pressed up against his shoulder like a vampire getting ready to bite. "D'you know my big brother?"

I sneered and continued drawing the lager.

"I seen what you put on Facebook and I don't give a shit, girlfriend. But the least you could have done was say thanks."

I parked the two pint glasses on the bar and took Baxter's money.

"Have one yourself, doll."

"No thank you."

"I got that fucking freak off your back for you," Kaz said. "Shit. Show some respect why don't you?"

But before I could spit fire in their direction, someone came out of the Gents and there was Matt Neilson standing at the bar with a grin on his face as wide as the Pentland Firth. I didn't give him the opportunity to say anything. The first pint caught him chest high but the second hit him square in the face. If it had been boiling water I'd have reacted no differently.

"Fucking Hell, Amy." Lukas grabbed both my arms and steered me into the passageway leading to the kitchens.

"Let me go."

"Just calm the fuck down first."

By now the racket in the bar had become loud enough to drown out the piped music. I could hear cheering, and someone screeching with laughter. Probably Kaz.

I shrugged myself loose. "Tell Beth I'm taking an early break."

"No need," he said. "Tell her yourself."

Beth had come out of the kitchen and one look was enough to suggest my bar-tending days were over.

I was tempted to call at one of the other pubs for last orders. To drink myself stupid. I needed something to calm my nerves. Something to drown the flames as fury welled up inside me. Kaz was no better than the rest of her family. And Matt already best pals with the pair of them.

I couldn't square it in my head. What was he thinking, walking in on me like that?

It was obvious.

He wanted to humiliate me one more time in front of his new buddies. The chances were they'd be on their own pub crawl en route back to the flats. He might even be staying the night with the Cartwrights. Cozying up to Baxter or Barcode or whatever he called himself these days. Screwing Kaz now I was off his playlist.

In the end, I continued walking along the sea front then up past the tiny cemetery. I could see a light inside Leanne's flat. Steve was away at some football match. It looked like Leanne was still up but I'd sneak in, get to bed and pray for the day to come to an end. I could hear music as I eased the front door closed. Then the warble of her telephone almost made me jump out of my skin. Someone turned down the volume and I heard Leanne's voice.

Her words seemed to slur into each other.

"34D. . . . black silk. I'm already wet. So are you rock hard?"

43

07:55 Monday morning and the flat remained blissfully silent. I'd had an entire day to plan my escape. Curtains drawn. Comfort blanket wrapped tight around my body. A tightrope walk between fevered sleep and snivelling self-pity.

God. Why was I so pathetic?

And now, for the past half hour I'd been sneaking around as if I was the one in the wrong. Removing the evidence. Stuffing everything into my rucksack. Clean clothes. Dirty laundry. Shoes. Phone charger and Kindle. Toiletries. Not caring what went where. What got creased. What got stained in the process.

Then I stripped my bed and bundled the sheets and pillow cases inside the duvet cover. I'd drop everything off at the launderette and save Leanne the trouble. I shut my bedroom door behind me and tip-toed into the kitchen. I had time for a glass of juice before heading into the village. My sister rarely got out of bed before nine, unless she was working. The last I'd heard she was back in on Wednesday and Saturday this coming week.

I scribbled a note of apology and placed it under the pepper mill along with £25. That was all I could spare. The chances were I'd not get the wages I was owed for the weekend just gone. The Arches was the last place I wanted to visit. This flat the last place I wanted to stay after a weekend to forget.

Then I hoisted my bag onto my shoulder and headed for the front door. The fleeting thought that I should have left my spare key on Leanne's kitchen table to prove I was never coming back got somehow forgotten as I felt my phone vibrate in my back pocket.

Shit.

I reached for it, desperate to cut the sound off. Who was trying to get hold of me at this ungodly hour?

I stared at the screen.

Inbox - 1.

I clicked on the icon.

To : Amy Metcalf
From : loner@letstalk.co.uk

NO SURPRISES RE MATT
TIME FOR PAYBACK
LETS MEET UP SOON.

Then I heard a voice behind me. "Where the hell are you sneaking off to?"

44

LEANNE gave me no choice. Confess my sins or she'd drive me home and we would have it out with Mum.

"You threw a glass of beer over Matt Neilson?"

"Two pints actually. And it was Stella Artois not beer."

She laughed but I could see a hint of disapproval lurking on standby. "That's a stupid thing to do, even by your standards."

"You should have seen the way he looked at me. I couldn't bear it with Kaz Cartwright there in the front row seats loving every minute of it."

"What's she got to do with it?"

I brought Leanne up to speed with the latest detour my life had taken. I spared her the details of who attacked Kevin Waterson and the fact that Peter Paver and Kay Jepson had been sharing the same bed. But by the end I couldn't hold back the tears.

"Why didn't you tell me any of this yesterday?"

Yesterday the wounds had been raw and I'd spent most of the day deciding how far I needed to run to escape a world where I couldn't trust a single soul.

"So Peter Paver's been sending you these stupid messages," she continued.

"That was him just now. He wants us to meet up."

"But you're not going to, surely."

It seemed pointless now. If Paver wanted to wipe Matt Neilson off the face of the earth, I couldn't stop him. I might even give him my blessing. Jimmy Jump had promised he'd speak to his nephew as well. My only knight in shining armour.

"Whether I do or not, I need to get away from Ullapool."

"Because of Matt."

I nodded. "And this place. It's been really kind of you and Steve putting me up, but I don't know who to trust. Don't know where it's safe."

Leanne reached out to grip my hand. Just like Mum. "You're safe here, Ames. And you can trust me, you know that."

I felt something cold and hard form inside me. Bone turning to steel. Blood to antifreeze. Tears suddenly drying up as I stared her out. "Can I?"

"Of course you can." Hands reaching out for me again.

"Only, I heard the phone ringing Saturday night. When I came in."

"So?"

"Your landline. You told me they'd cut it off."

She shook her head. "Did I? I can't remember. We only use it for in-coming calls. It's handy for work, that's all. I might have said something because I didn't want you thinking you could use it whenever you feel like - ringing your mates or whatever."

"So who was on the phone last night?"

Her face dropped a fraction. "Work, that's all."

"At ten to eleven?" I laughed in her face. "I heard every word. How hard his cock was and you telling him how wet he makes you."

Her gaze hardened.

"Are you shagging someone behind Steve's back? Is that why he spends so much time away from home?"

If she'd slapped me I'd have felt better, but instead she reached for my hand.

"It's not what you think."

"You weren't talking to Steve, were you?"

"If you shut up a minute."

"And you've got more than one on the go. I heard every word," I said. "Three calls. I counted three calls in half an hour."

"OK. OK. So you know what I get up to when you're not here." Her grip slackened. "You don't have to rub it in."

"All the same sick stuff over and over," I said.

"I know. But you have to promise me you won't tell Mum. And don't dare judge me until you've heard it all."

In the end I felt too weary to argue as the ground shifted beneath me once again.

"A chat line?"

"There's nothing sleazy about it. We're all grown-ups," she said.

"Christ."

I got to my feet, reached for an empty glass off the drainer and filled it at the tap.

"You alright?"

"What d'you think?" I said. "My sister's no better than a cheap tart, giving blow-jobs over the phone, and I'm supposed to keep calm?"

"Yeah, and I can do it while I'm catching up with the soaps on my iPlayer if I want to." She pulled a pack of cigarettes from her dressing gown pocket.

"And Steve's away with his mates, not a clue what you're doing."

Leanne let the smoke drift between us. Letting the seconds pass while I drained my glass.

"You need to get off your soap box and ask yourself why I'm doing it. How do you think we manage to cover the rent and all the other bills we've got coming in? I'm left with less than a hundred and fifty quid a month after

Steve makes his repayments?"

"Don't tell me Steve knows about this." It got better and better.

"He doesn't know everything. But yeah."

"What d'you mean?"

"He knows there's money going in the bank every week. Enough to help pay off the debts and keep our heads above water. He thinks I'm giving tarot readings, if you must know. I'm only on call when he's away from home."

"Tarot readings? What the hell do you know about tarot cards?"

"Nothing. And anyway, I didn't feel comfortable taking money from some poor sod who wants a stranger to reassure them their shitty life is going to get better because it's all written in the cards. There's enough misery out there without me adding to it."

"So you're saying it's better listening to some sad old git while he has a wank at the other end of the phone."

"Yes." She straightened her shoulders and looked me square in the face. "That's exactly what I'm saying."

"It's pathetic and you know it is."

"I'm providing a service, whether you like it or not. And when they get home pissed from the pub, I'd rather they talk dirty to me than make a random call to some poor old biddy asking her what colour drawers she's wearing."

I couldn't argue with that, much as I wanted to. "So most of them are pissed when they phone you?"

I could see the shake in her hands and I wanted to take her in my arms and apologise for putting her through it all. "Some of them can be really obnoxious. But I get to hang up if they give me abuse."

"Christ."

"Most of them are polite. Just normal guys. And it's not

all about getting their rocks off. Some just want to talk. To hear a woman's voice on the other end of the phone who's not giving them grief 24/7."

"Normal?"

"Yeah. Sad. Lonely. Some are on their own. Widowed. Divorced. Or with a wife upstairs in bed who doesn't understand them."

"You're beginning to sound like Mother Teresa."

She smirked and stubbed out her cigarette.

"God, I don't know how you do it."

"If you were desperate, Ames, it's surprising what you'd do. I'm trying to earn a little extra cash, that's all. But don't let on to Steve I've told you. He'd be gutted." Leanne's gaze dropped a fraction. "He's the one who got us in this mess in the first place - borrowing to pay back money we already owed someone else."

"How much?"

"Thousands, so don't breathe a word to Mum. She'll freak."

"Maybe not. I'm sure she'd offer to help if she knew."

"This is different," she said.

"If you say so. I'm going to drop off this washing at the laundrette and get the nine o'clock bus. I'll probably keep my head down for the next few days."

"Matt Neilson's pulling your strings again."

"There's people queuing up to pull them," I said. "I don't know where I am from one day to the next."

"You mean this business with Paver?"

"That's the least of my problems. I'm already on it."

I spent most of the journey back to Lochinver sorting that one out.

IF YOU INSIST
HOW ABOUT TOMORROW AFTERNOON?

I lost my signal until we got to the outskirts of Elphin but then. . .

OK U SAY WHERE AND WHEN

I typed in my reply, pressed the *SEND* button and prayed for an end to it.

1400 WHITE SHORE

45

AS crises go, I got off lightly. Leanne no doubt phoned Mum as soon as I left to warn her I was on my way home. When I walked in there were no questions. No interrogation. No thumbscrews.

"Your sister's told me about this business with Matt."

"What's she been saying now?"

"How he's got himself in with a bad crowd by the look of things. He's spending a lot of time with the Cartwrights."

"Right."

"Maybe he's better staying there than hanging around this village. People are fast losing patience with him."

"I suppose."

"Anyway, it's as well you're keeping out of his way. He's nothing but trouble."

"You don't have to keep going on."

"I'm just saying, you deserve so much better."

"Thanks, Mum."

"Ach, I don't tell you often enough what a fine girl you are, do I? I've got two special daughters and I'm so proud of you both."

"Right." I had to bite my tongue.

"By this time next year it'll all be forgotten."

"Probably."

I had enough to keep me on my toes without looking that far into the future. I couldn't help wondering how things would go with Peter next day.

I took a stroll down as far as the breakwater later in the afternoon. There was still no sign of the 'Meera Rose' but that meant nothing. He could be moored in Strathbeg Bay. Or he might have even flown in to Inverness from Belfast and got someone to pick him up.

I glanced up at Kay Jepson's windows as I walked past. Both sets of curtains were drawn but I guessed she was hard at work inside. Leanne wasn't the only one who was strapped for funds, I was guessing, and presumably Kay made enough from her home-grown hash enterprise to earn a living. Maybe she dealt with other illegal substances as well. I was better out of it.

The weather held fast for our appointment. I'd not mentioned a word to anyone. The chances were that Paver would have plenty to say for himself. He might even kick off, but he'd not dare do anything stupid. Crazy or not, it was Matt he had his sights fixed on, not me. But as insurance I took the pepper spray Steve had given me the week I arrived home from Raigmore. He'd got the same for Leanne from one of his contacts on the pier. No bigger than a lipstick. Perfectly effective at less than three feet – perfectly illegal but what the hell.

"It'll fit in your purse. Make you feel safer."

It didn't at the time. My long-term plans hadn't included ever setting foot outside the house. I would become a recluse: content to vegetate for the rest of my days with weed, cheap Shiraz, the occasional bag of marshmallows and Netflix to see me through until Judgement Day. Yet deep down I knew there was more to life. Kay Jepson might have withdrawn into a shell but I still had some fight left in me.

Bring it on.

I got to the White Shore half an hour early. There was

no way of knowing where Peter was holed up so it was pointless trying to hide and watch out for him at the same time. Instead, I stood at the water's edge, arms crossed, heart thumping behind my rib cage, and waited. The sea was calm and the sky virtually cloud-free. Air balmy and spiced with baking rock and saltwater. On any other day I'd have been tempted to strip down to my underwear and wade into the waves. Rocks sharp as flints under my bare feet until the water became deep enough to sink into and let go. Caddy and I had floated in this tiny cove countless times.

"There you are."

Sneaky. I'd been so preoccupied, I'd not heard his footsteps on the shingle.

"What are you doing here?" I asked, conscious that time had somehow slipped through my fingers.

A brief flash of confusion crossed his face. "Don't be like that. It's what we agreed. Two o'clock."

I stared into his piercing blue eyes and shook my head in defeat. "I was expecting somebody else, that's all."

46

"YOU'RE the last person I expected to see."

"Yeah, well. I don't give up easily," I said. "And there's still some unfinished business."

Kay unhooked the chain. "You'd better come in. Though I don't know what you're after."

"Information."

She snorted. "I'm making coffee if you want one."

I followed her into the kitchen. "So when's the last time you went roller-blading?"

"What? Is that why you're here?"

"I remember the pink pair I saw lying round first time I called, that's all."

"Oh, God. I got rid of them to eBay. I hardly used them once I left school. Rooster used to do a lot of snow boarding at Aviemore. He took me out there for a weekend last November but I never managed to get the hang of it."

"Right."

"You don't need to keep your feet so close together when you're roller-blading. It's easier to keep balance, that's all," she said.

"And we all know you have problems keeping your legs close together whenever Peter Paver's around."

She threw a stare across the room poisonous enough to floor me at twenty paces. "Is that what all this is about?" I could hear the stress in her voice, and her lips had become compressed into a narrow, bloodless slit of white. "There's nothing going on between us. How many times?"

I laughed. "I don't know where to start. I mean, I'm told one thing one day and the complete opposite the next. So-called friends go out of their way to do the dirty on me or tell me a pack of lies because I'm so frigging gullible. And all the time I'm shitting bricks about these stupid emails Peter Paver's supposed to have sent me when it wasn't even him."

That got her attention.

"What d'you mean?"

We retreated to her living room and I told her. But I held back the juiciest bits. My bad.

"Mike Neilson?"

"That's right."

I let the information sink in, watching Kay Jepson readjust her thoughts while she tried to figure out what else I knew but wasn't telling.

"So what was he playing at, threatening you like that?"

"He was doing what he said he was doing. Watching me while Matt was inside. Watching over me."

"But what about all the other stuff?"

"I kind of misread everything. Because he didn't identify himself, I assumed I had a weirdo stalking me."

"And you don't think it was creepy when he didn't leave his name?" she said.

"He was trying to let me know he was there if I ever needed someone to talk to. But without the baggage of being Caddy's dad and so on."

"Sounds a bit off to me. So what about the visit?"

"He knew I'd been to Peterhead before I even got back to Leanne's. Matt had phoned Steff and she tells Mike everything, obviously. Why wouldn't she?"

"In which case he also knew you were freaking out

about the emails. Yet he kept sending them."

"He pretty much stopped. And like I said, I misinterpreted what he was really saying."

"And K and the kisses and all that?" she said.

"He saw me coming out of here the second time I called round. I'm not the only one he was watching over. But you probably already know that."

For once Kay didn't deny the truth or appear to be ashamed at withholding information from me.

"I didn't think it mattered. It had nothing to do with everything else that was going on."

"How much did he give you?"

Her head swayed to one side as if I'd landed a punch strong enough to at least daze her for a moment or two.

"I didn't ask him for a penny, if that's what you're getting at."

"How much?" I waved the cheque in front of her face. "He handed me this less than an hour ago. So I'm wondering how much he paid you."

She closed her eyes and took a breath. "Exactly the same."

Now it was my turn to flinch. "Mike gave you ten thousand pounds."

"Two instalments, each for five grand."

"Right," I said, totting up the massive hole that must have made in his bank account.

"He called round with the first cheque the day after I got out of hospital," she continued.

"Nice coming home present."

"Yeah. He must have been waiting outside because as soon as Dad and Lucy left he was at my door."

"And you let him in."

"I thought Dad had come back for something."

"So what exactly did Mike say when he gave you the money?" This was like building a new version of reality brick by brick.

"He said I was due something for the way Matt had treated me. And he said nobody had to know."

"Right."

"The police had already mentioned something about compensation for my injuries," she continued. "Some government scheme for victims of violent crimes. But it takes forever."

"And the second cheque arrived shortly after Matt's court appearance, I'm guessing."

"A couple of days after."

"A little thank you for keeping your mouth shut when the police came round fishing for evidence against his precious son."

"Kind of, I suppose. But I've got nothing to hide."

"If you say so."

"I do," she laughed. "What the hell did he pay you for?"

"Same thing I suppose. Guilt money," I said.

"Yeah, sure."

"He'd intended for Matt to have it, but he thought twice once he saw the new look."

"The radical haircut not going down so well."

"And the attitude," I added. "Matt virtually threatened his dad to hand over the cash."

"So Daddy sends him packing without a penny pocket money. God, I can just imagine the look on Matt's face."

"He wanted me to have the fresh start he'd intended offering Matt."

We both paused for breath, winded by the fact that the distance between us was shrinking.

"So what are you going to do with it?" she asked.

I'd been tempted to screw up the cheque and throw it back in Mike's face. But he told me it wouldn't burn my fingers if I held on to it. Then I thought of Leanne and what she was going through, and the likes of Matt and

Gordon Paver snow boarding through life without a care for anyone else.

"Same as you."

"How did you know I'd kept mine?" she asked.

"How else you gonna pay the rent, sistah?"

The frowns were gone along with the grey bags under her eyes. The girl I was falling in love with returning from wherever she'd wandered off to.

"If I'd been thinking straight, I'd have realised it wasn't Peter Paver or Kevin Waterson. They don't have my email address."

"So how come Mike Neilson's got it?"

I side-stepped the truth. "Simple. It's still on Caddy's laptop. Along with whatever else she has on there." I cursed under my breath, imagining all the private stuff that might have come to light. Caddy's mum and dad privy to their daughter's most personal secrets.

"What you thinking?"

"I'm thinking all sorts," I said. "What else Mike might have found. Did you know Matt got his hands on the photo of you, Caddy and Rick Tyler at the chalet park party?"

"No."

"So how many more are there like that floating round in cyberspace? Because the chances are Caddy transferred them all onto her computer as soon as she got home."

Kay shook her head. "Peter only took the one. He asked to borrow my phone so that's how I know."

I thought she'd got the names mixed up, given the stress I'd put her under. "You mean Rooster."

Then I saw a flicker of realisation cross her face. "Rooster wasn't even there. He'd had to go to Ullapool and meet up with Slippy. Why?"

Matt and I had assumed Rooster had been there with the rest of his buddies.

"The whole party thing was Peter's idea. His dad was away, and he was on leave before they shipped back out to Afghanistan."

"So you were shagging Paver back then."

"I already told you. We've never."

"It all makes sense now," I said. "Why he keeps coming round for more."

Kay shook her head. "It was all about getting high together, that's all."

"Always?"

"He's never touched me once." She couldn't get her story straight from one minute to the next.

"But you admitted it less than two days ago. At it like polecats."

Her blank stare made my words dry up. "I only said that to get you to stay away from me. It was for your own good."

"Really? How does that work?"

"When you texted me, I realised if Paver found out about you and me he'd make a big deal of it. Another excuse to continue hassling you."

"Right."

"So I thought if you kept away I'd be able to divert the flak onto Matt and nobody else. The last thing I wanted was for you to get hurt."

The tears burst free and there was nothing I could do to stop them. I'd been doubled up in love. When a guy breaks a girl's heart it's expected because that's what guys do. But when a girl breaks a girl's heart that's betrayal of the lowest order.

"Hurt?" I could hardly get the words out. "God, you've no fucking idea how much you hurt me."

Kay came and sat next to me on the arm of the couch. "Aw, honey. You don't understand the first thing about me, do you?"

She combed her fingers through my hair and kissed my forehead. Butterfly kisses on my eyelids. My cheek bones. The corner of my mouth.

"Fucking phone!"

Before I could beg her to let it keep ringing - beg her not to stop – she flipped the cover open and raised it to her ear.

"Yeah. . .

"Where are you. . .

"Don't be stupid. . ."

She snapped the phone shut. "For fuck's sake."

"What is it?"

"It's Peter Paver. He's on his way back from Ireland," she muttered.

"Shit."

"He'll be here late Wednesday night or early Thursday. He says war has just been declared."

47

"YOU awake?"

The dream where he got to remove Kaz Cartwright's pyjama bottoms right there in her bed disintegrated as Matt felt someone shake him by the shoulders.

"Shift your arse. Now!"

Matt sat up on the couch and rubbed the sleep from his eyes. "What's the hurry?"

"They're waiting for us," Barcode snarled. "We've got to go and pick up a van from Bonar."

He pulled on his jeans and began to fold up the duvet and pillows.

"Leave that. They're outside now so make it quick."

Matt peed away the dregs of the previous night's six pints, splashed cold water on his face and wiped the crud from his eyes. Then he made his way back to the living room and searched for a clean t-shirt in the blue plastic bag he'd brought with him for the weekend. A weekend stretching to five days and counting.

Matt heard the impatient blasts of a car horn.

"Alright. Alright."

He stepped back into the corridor after checking he had his mobile phone and wallet. Kaz's bedroom door remained shut tight. No time for a farewell hug.

He took the staircase two steps at a time and let the outside door slam shut as he searched the car park for signs of Barcode. Headlights flashed twice. A maroon

Mondeo, its bonnet discoloured by a large splash of rusted, bare metal. Napalmed by a can of brake fluid some time in its past, presumably.

"About fucking time." Barcode had one of the back doors open waiting for him. "Get in."

Matt knew better than to ask again why they were in such a hurry. He'd recognised the two sitting in the front of the car.

"This is Matt. The one I was telling you about."

The introductions ended there but Matt had already met Tommy and Ken before. The last time he'd been in their company, he'd ended up requiring major dental work. He figured it might be best to keep his mouth shut this time and enjoy the scenery.

Tendrils of early morning mist marked the damper reaches of Strath Canaird, otherwise the air was clear - the light razor sharp. Fields either side of the broad valley glistened under a coating of fresh dew. By the time they gained higher ground and the backdrop of Coigach and Inverpolly opened up on their left it had all the makings of another perfect summer's day. Matt's heart had been known to soar more than once at this view, regardless of the number of times he'd made the same journey.

"You got any cash with you?" Barcode whispered as they swung right at Ledmore and followed the single track road into the wilderness.

"About thirty five quid left over from last night. Why?"

"That's good. Breakfast's on you when we get to Dingwall."

"Thought you said we were going to Bonar Bridge," Matt said.

"Ssh. We are."

Within forty minutes they hit civilisation again. Tommy feathered the brakes as they entered the 30 limit.

Like most Highland villages, Bonar Bridge welcomed careful drivers. Then he took the first left and slowed down some more as Ken began to scan the row of nondescript white houses lining one side of the street.

"D'you know which house?" Tommy asked.

"It'll be the one with a white van parked outside," Barcode suggested.

They continued a hundred yards along the road before coming to a set of red-roofed, timber-clad properties in various stages of modernisation.

"There. The third one," Barcode said.

A white Peugeot with a 54 plate was parked with its nose angled onto the pavement. The words TECHNIX DOMESTICS printed in blue across its rear doors had almost faded away.

"I'll go." Ken got out and made his way up the garden path. He carried a baseball bat in one hand.

"Neat," Matt muttered.

Barcode raised his eyebrows in reply and lit a cigarette.

They were obviously expected. Before Ken reached for the door bell, a downstairs window opened and someone threw out a set of keys onto the lawn.

Tommy gave the horn a blast. "You two, out now."

"Who's driving?" Matt asked.

"Just get the keys."

Barcode scooped them up, climbed behind the wheel, and as he coaxed the van's engine into life all Matt could hear was the sound of splintering wood and breaking glass. Ken was busy trying to demolish the front porch of the house. They headed off in the direction of the village centre while Ken and Tommy left their calling card.

"What the fuck was that all about?"

"It's called repossession, Mattie boy."

"Repossession?"

"White van man doesn't keep up his repayments so

Slippy takes back what he's owed."

"Along with some interest."

"You got it."

Barcode wound down his window and flicked out the cigarette stub.

"Christ," Matt said.

"You're only coming along for the ride. You can get your head down until we get to Dingwall."

"No. It's OK. I'm awake now."

Barcode grinned. "You sure you don't need to catch up on your beauty sleep? 'Cause it sounded like the pair of you gave each other a good time last night long after we'd gone to bed, even though it's a school night."

"What d'you mean?" Matt couldn't hide the satisfaction from his voice.

"I'm just saying, you might want to turn the volume down next time you decide to give my sister one on our fucking sofa. I could hear you, so the chances are Mum and Dad could as well."

"Shit. I haven't. I mean, we weren't," Matt said.

"I don't care what you do. I mean, you're free to fuck her any time you like - as long as you don't fuck her about."

"I won't."

"Just so we're clear. Kaz reckons that stupid blonde bitch has gone back home to Mummy."

"Yeah."

"Good riddance."

Matt tightened his seat belt as the van took the steep, twisting back-road up Struie Hill. "So why exactly are we going to Dingwall?"

"We're picking up some gear for Slippy."

"Gear?" Matt hissed.

"Yeah. Gear gear not drugs gear, so don't wet your panties. It's a two man job and I told him you were up for it. Am I right?"

"Well, yeah."

"Good. 'Cause if you behave you might be invited on another wee jaunt."

"Yeah?"

"Defo. We've got ourselves a set of wheels, Mattie boy. Slippy's investing in our future."

"Shit." Matt had no wish to reacquaint himself with Slippy or his two pet Minions.

"No need to sound so grateful."

"It's just, I wasn't expecting things to happen so quick. I'm still out on license so I need to keep my nose clean."

"I hear you, bro. It's all legit."

"You mean this Technix Domestics stuff?"

"We're in business, like I'm telling you. There's a couple of boiler suits and a box of tools in the back. There'll probably be some spare parts as well. Hoses, copper pipe, spools of cable," Barcode replied.

"I still don't get it."

"In case we get pulled over. The coppers only stop unmarked vans that travel up the A-fucking-9, but you can't be too careful. It's like every dodgy dealer North of Glasgow drives a white van now."

"So what we're doing is dodgy?"

"Course not. It's insured. I've got a clean driving licence. And we're not even running on red Diesel so stop being such a fanny."

"That's not what I meant."

"Let's just say we're not going to be fixing anybody's washing machine any time soon."

48

SOMETIME during the night, the floorboards rattled beneath the bed as another heavy truck rumbled past Kay's flat. A fish wagon maybe, or an oil tanker en route to the harbour. I let out a silent yawn, stretched my legs then twisted onto my side and buried my head in the pit of the pillow.

Something warm and soft moulded against my back. One arm lay draped across my belly and the slow rhythm of her breathing told me Kay was sound asleep. I turned onto my back again and manoeuvred myself so I could place my own hand on top of hers. Then I pushed both hands further down my body. It was no dream this time and Kay's fingers needed no further guidance.

Hours later, with the snarl of street sounds filtering up into the bedroom, we lay awake next to each other and fantasised how we might spend Mike Neilson's money. A party first, then a holiday in the sun. Or a second-hand car so I could finish taking driving lessons and pass my test.

But once I told Kay all about my sister's double life, I knew what I should do with the money.

"You've got to admire her," she said.

I hadn't looked at it that way.

"Does she use a webcam as well?"

"Christ, no." I didn't even want to imagine Leanne going down that route. "She just takes telephone calls and talks dirty. She gets paid for how long each one lasts. It's like a call centre. She tells them when she's logging on and off. They divert calls to her landline as soon as someone rings her private number."

"It must pay."

"Don't know," I said, "She reckons she was desperate because they're in so much debt. Steve took out a payday loan last winter and most of his wages go to paying back the interest. It's like a fucking bad joke."

Kay slid out of bed and padded across to the window. She drew back the curtains just enough to let in a shaft of weak, washed-out sunlight, and I held my breath. One side of her body seemed to glow, but her skin was soft as suede rather than silky smooth and glossy like Keren's. I could make out the faint stubble of dark hair in her armpit as she raised a hand to adjust the curtain.

"Are you flashing your boobs at the tourists now?"

She turned to face me and I felt a flush of heat rise to my face and chest. How could something so tiny and waif-like turn me on when all I could make out was her silhouette against the morning light?

"Stay there. I'll make us some coffee."

"Not yet," I managed to say. I unfurled her half of the duvet and stared into her face.

She stepped closer. Her breasts took shape as the light changed and her mouth twisted into a knowing smile. "What d'you want?"

The feral scent of her body swamped my senses and I felt my bones turn to liquid as I stretched out an arm. "Come back to bed. It's my turn to play nice."

49

"I never know when you're going to turn up from one day to the next," Mum said when I reported back shortly after three. "You're worse than a stray cat."

"Don't keep fussing. It was just one night. And I stayed at a mate's."

"Anybody I know?"

"I doubt it. I'm going for a shower."

I could still smell Kay's sex on my fingers. Taste her on my lips. How could Mum not notice?

"Never mind all this dashing about. You need to think about getting yourself another job for the summer if you're not going back to stay with Leanne."

"Yeah, I know."

"I was thinking, I can put a word in for you at the Stag's Head if you like. It doesn't have to be more than three or four shifts a week. They're always looking for waitresses."

"Whatever. If it makes you happy."

"Really?"

Anything to get her off my case.

"Really. Just leave it until after the weekend. I need to pop to Ullapool on Monday. I left my phone charger at Leanne's."

"There you go again. We never get a chance to have a proper chat."

What about?

"It's only going to be a flying visit. There and back."

"Let me give you some magazines to give her."

My head was still overflowing with the memory of how Kay's skin felt: the texture, the taste, the scent. I needed to be alone – somewhere more private than our kitchen.

"Can we talk about this later? 'Cause I really need that shower."

50

"**HE** says there'll be somebody waiting for you in the lay-by. Look out for a Land Rover."

"I know. Seven o'clock," Matt said. "I got it so there's no need to tell me more than once."

"I'm just telling you what Tommy said. Leave the packages in the back of the truck underneath the tarpaulin."

"A black Hilux. Yeah. I got that too. As long as you're sure I'm not going to be carrying anything dodgy. If I get caught with drugs again, I'll be back inside before they even finish redecorating my cell."

"Matt, Slippy's already told you. It's nothing like that."

"It's OK for him."

"He's giving you the chance to earn some extra. You should be thanking me for putting out the word."

"Whatever."

"And once you've done the drop, get the hell out of there. Slippy doesn't want you seen hanging around. There's a traffic camera just past the hotel and God knows who's watching, so use your head."

"I thought I'd call for a pint while I was there."

"Fuck's sake, Matt," Barcode said.

"I'm kidding. Christ, you'd think I'd never done this sort of thing before."

"Don't screw this up because I'm sticking my neck out for you here."

"Gotcha." Matt planted a kiss on Barcode's cheek, rattled the keys in his face and left the flat.

An hour to kill. Time enough for him and Kaz to have some fun on the way. She was still in her school uniform. Black tights, short black skirt and white, long-sleeved shirt.

"Don't bother getting changed. We're only going for a spin."

"In the van? I hope you're not expecting me to get in the back of that thing."

"We can do, if you've got a car blanket or a spare mattress."

"Fuck off."

"Lighten up."

"So where are you taking me?" she said as the van rattled down the steep hill between the top of Morefield and the Rhue turn-off.

"Ledmore Junction."

"You what?"

"I'm meeting someone there at seven. Got some stuff to pick up and take to the Aultguish."

"Sounds like fun. Not."

"It's OK. We can stop off on the way."

"I've already told you, Matt. I'm not some Pikey princess ready to drop her knickers whenever you fancy a feel."

Matt indicated left and pulled off the road just past the row of holiday cottages at Ardmair. "You don't have to. We can just chill."

"Define chill?"

"God, Kaz. We never get a chance to do anything at your place with your mum and dad watching every move I make."

"Is it any wonder?" she said. "The way you start

drooling whenever I'm in the room."

"Drool? I don't drool."

"You should see yourself. Mum's warned me not to get any bright ideas about us sharing my bed."

"Huh."

"She's only looking out for me."

"What about Baxter? Is he looking out for you as well, 'cause he sits up all night with his ear pressed to his bedroom wall."

"Why? What's he said?"

Matt shrugged.

"Come on. Tell me," she sniggered.

"He heard us. It must have been Monday night."

"Monday? God."

"When you got up in the night for a glass of water."

"But that was the back of two."

"I know. He reckons he heard everything."

"Oh, fuck. Poor Baxter."

"Don't worry. I told him it wasn't what it sounded like."

"It doesn't matter." She took out a lipstick from her bag and tilted the mirror so she could see her reflection. "He probably gets off on it."

"Could be."

"So what are we supposed to be doing here?" She wound down the window a fraction. "God, smell that rotting seaweed. It's gross. And the same view every time I come past here gets on my tits. Can't we park somewhere else?"

"Wherever you want," Matt said.

"Well I'm not giving you a hand job with all these people about."

"That's not why I brought you out here, for God's sake."

Down along the crescent of shoreline an elderly woman walked her dog, and a military-style campervan and a blue hatch-back were already parked in the same lay-by, perfectly in place for a photo opportunity.

"Pick up a tink from Dingwall if that's all you're wanting."

"I never said. I thought we could just talk. Decide what we're going to do once the school holidays start."

"Talk?"

"Well, yeah. But if you've got any tissues in your bag, they might come in useful."

A battered Land Rover with a trailer hitched behind it stood in the lay-by just beyond Ledmore Junction.

"Who is it you're meeting?"

"No idea. Just keep your gob shut and your head down."

Matt swung the van round to face the way they'd come and reversed up close to the trailer's rear end. Then he got out and opened the van's back doors. The driver stayed inside his cab, reading a newspaper and making no attempt to acknowledge Matt's arrival.

"Hi, there," he said as he walked up to the open window at the passenger side of the Land Rover.

The driver signalled with his thumb. "In the trailer. Forty-eight cardboard boxes. And if anybody drives past wait for them to be gone."

"Gotcha."

Then as he made to walk away the driver shouted across. "Don't fucking drop them."

"I won't. You going to give me a hand?"

"What do you think? You're being paid to do a fucking job so get on with it."

When Matt had loaded the last carton into the van, he walked round to the driver's door. "If that's everything, can I go now?"

"Just a friendly warning. Take it steady. It's old gear

long past its sell-by date, if you know what I mean. It hasn't started to crystallise yet but you'd best be careful."

Matt turned to look at his van then stepped closer to the driver's window. "Why? What d'you mean?"

"Haven't they told you what you're carrying?" The driver smirked.

Matt shook his head.

"Shit."

"Come on. Tell me."

The driver laughed. "It's dynamite. A ton and a half of old stock that got condemned months ago."

"Condemned?"

"It's still OK. I know a guy who knows a guy. He sells it off dirt cheap. There's crofters use it when they want a bit of ground clearing or a trench digging."

"And it's safe?"

"You can pretty much do anything you want with it and it won't go pop. It's only when it starts to weep you have to watch what you're doing."

"Right."

"So if anybody stops you."

"I know the drill. Don't say a word."

"Good lad."

Matt took his time driving back to Ullapool.

"You've gone quiet all of a sudden."

"It's alright," he said. "I'd better drop you off, 'cause I don't know how long this is going to take."

"Oh yeah, fine. As long as you got what you wanted."

"Don't be like that. I didn't hear you complaining."

Kaz smirked. "Yeah, well. You need to up your act if we're going to be seeing each on a regular basis."

Matt leant across and gave her a kiss. "Don't stay up on my account. School night and all that."

He could taste the chewing gum on her tongue as she

gave him another deep kiss before getting out of the van. "One more week, and we can do what the hell we want."

"I know," he said. "See you tomorrow."

He watched Kaz straighten the strap of her shoulder bag before opening the door to the block of flats. She turned to wave then disappeared inside.

Three months in prison and all he'd thought about for much of that time was getting laid. There had been other items on his to-do list once he got out as well. A cup of decent coffee and a long soak in the bath followed by a pint or two and a good night's sleep.

But overriding everything was the thought of spending quality time with Amy Metcalf. Picking up where they'd left off before all that nonsense with the Ukrainians and Gordon Paver. They'd only managed one cosy weekend at the chalet park. But that had been more than enough for Matt to realise Amy was in a different league to all the other girls he'd slept with. The way she looked. The way she moved. Her skin. Her eyes. The way she left him wanting it never to stop.

Normally, Matt would have overtaken everything in sight once he got past Braemore Junction. It was like a race track between there and the dam below Glascarnoch. He knew every bend and most days he managed to beat the queue of traffic heading East, even when the Stornoway ferry had just landed and convoys of HGVs took to the road between Ullapool and Inverness. Tonight traffic was light, but as soon as he heard the boxes slide in the back of the van when he hit the bumps past Lochdrum he slowed right down. A couple of motorbikes screamed past, otherwise the road ahead remained empty.

Only five vehicles occupied the car park of the Aultguish Inn. The black pick-up sat facing the road, mud spattering its sills and its windscreen smeared with death-wish insects. Matt got out of the van and checked the truck's tailgate was open before starting to unload his cargo. The back of the pick-up was empty apart from a spare wheel, a hessian sack and a coil of orange, nylon rope. The tarpaulin covering the load area was strapped down tight.

Almost fifty boxes. Each heavy enough to make Matt catch his breath as he hoisted them out of the van then slid them gently along the bed of the Toyota. No one had mentioned tying them down securely. Not his problem any longer.

He snatched a glance through the windows of the hotel bar before climbing back inside the van. The light was too dim to make out any faces he might recognise. Anyone could be inside having one more pint of Guinness for the road, watching Matt's every move before he drove off.

51

KAY was on the phone when I turned up just before seven. She unlatched the door then wandered into the living room while I unpacked my supplies. Pizza. Stuffed-olives. Some left-over salad and a bottle of red wine.

I waited and eventually she came into the kitchen and gave me a hug. "It's good you're here. I'll give you a hand to unpack."

"Mhmm, thanks. You OK, hon?"

"So-so. What kind of pizza did you bring?" Kay looked preoccupied. Eyes glazed and her lips twitching.

"Pepperoni. Has something happened?"

She turned to face the sink, rearranging the dishes in the drainer and wiping away crumbs from the worktop with a dish-cloth.

"Oh, it was Dad on the phone. He says the police have been round."

"To his place? What for?"

"I thought it was something to do with the poly-tunnel. Somebody new to the neighbourhood with a big nose or an even bigger mouth."

"You mean the weed he's growing?"

"Yeah, but it wasn't that," she said. "It was Greg Farrell and one of the uniforms from Ullapool. They were wanting to talk with Lucy."

"Why? What's happened?"

Kay hung the tea towel back on its rail and took a corkscrew out of the cutlery drawer. "Get the glasses."

"I'm on it. What's this about Lucy? Is it bad news or something?"

She uncorked the bottle and began to pour. "Last April she got involved with one of those wind farm action groups. About a dozen tree-huggers ended up chaining themselves to the front doors of some big fancy office block in Aberdeen. It was in all the papers."

"Right."

"One of those big power suppliers. They threw red paint all over the windows as well."

"So she's got to go to court."

"No no. That was over and done with months ago," Kay said. "I think they got fined."

"OK."

"They were protesting about the new wind farm up by the Aultguish. Said it was an eyesore and would drive the visitors away."

"Corriemoillie you mean?" We'd been invited by the company involved to do a project about it in school. Environmental impact and all that. All to justify their decision.

"Farrell wanted to know where her and Dad had been for the last twenty-four hours. Said they'd been given some information and he was acting on it."

"Information?"

"Aye, well. That's what he said. But he was obviously fishing. It looks like someone's tried to blow up a couple of wind turbines out on the hill above the dam and they haven't got a clue who did it."

52

"YOU know what we should do?"

"Have an early night?" I swear Kay was purring like an alley cat – not exactly hissing and spitting, but with claws extended. To tease rather than draw blood.

"Can do. But I was thinking we could get up early tomorrow and watch the sunrise."

I was rinsing the suds from the last of the cutlery and Kay stopped midway through wiping the dining plate in her hand.

"Why the fuck would we want to do that?"

"It's Midsummer. The longest day."

"So what?"

"I just thought it would be special." I turned off the taps and wiped my hands on the seat of my jeans. "The weather's supposed to change by the afternoon."

"Christ," she said. "Lucy Links pulled the same stunt when I was twelve, thirteen. A sleepover at the bothy then a tramp up Suilven to watch the sun come up."

"But it would be so cool."

"Well, trust me. It wasn't. I got eaten alive – fleas or midges. Don't know what. And by the time we got to the top, the sky had clouded over and we couldn't see a fucking thing."

"Right. But what about the life-enhancing experience?"

She flipped me the finger. "Enhance this."

I grabbed the tea towel and flapped it against her

backside.

"OK, OK!" she yelled. "Don't let me stop you. We're not the Olsen Twins - joined at the hip."

"Mhmm. That would be something."

"I'll be thinking of you when I'm in my bed."

"You better had," I said. "Always."

In the end bed won.

"But there is something else I need to run by you," I said. "Something more important."

53

"**IT** would drive me crazy being stuck in here all that time."

"You get used to it," Kay said.

"But it's been nearly four months. At least come with me for a walk. White Shore or somewhere."

"Yeah, well. I stopped counting after the first few days. Dad brings my shopping round once a week, and whatever else I need. My meds."

"Meds?"

"He picks up my prescription, if you must know."

"And a little extra, I expect."

"Christ, Amy. Get off your fucking high horse. I don't see you refusing the odd spliff when there's one going spare. And you know how hard I'm trying to do the right thing, coming off it at my own pace."

"Herbal teas and cocaine. Yeah."

The problem was, I didn't know what Kay got up to half the time. I'd accepted that her relationship with Peter Paver had been purely platonic, despite all the bullshit she'd given me on the telephone days earlier. She'd made it clear Peter slept on the couch whenever he passed out drunk and spent the night here.

But despite her coming on to me, it hadn't been any easier getting closer to Kay once we got under the sheets. She was allowed to touch me. But there were trust issues when it came to paying back the compliment. No man would be allowed anything more than a hug. Not even her dad. And that rule was set in stone for the foreseeable future.

"I went through the same shit," I said. "When I came out of Raigmore, the last thing I wanted was to get close to anybody, pick up my life where I left off and continue as normal."

"Normal doesn't exist anymore."

"That's exactly how I felt."

"But you're fine now," she said.

"It's what I'm trying to tell you. You need a change of scene. We both do. But we can get through this together if you'll let me help you."

Kay clenched her eyes closed. "Help me or fix me?"

"It's the same thing." I reached an arm across and pulled her in for a kiss.

Kay's skin felt clammy with sweat and I could sense the shine disappearing from her smile. "I don't know why you even bother."

"Kay, of course I'm going to bother. I love you."

There it was out in the open. But if she heard my confession it didn't register. Kay pulled free of my arms and announced she would shower first. Then when I finally came back into her bedroom to dry my hair she was already dressed.

"Rooster used to take me to the White Shore on my days off. We'd get high and cuddle up in one of those fishing net hammocks they had hanging from the trees. We'd search the shingle for mermaid's purses and shells."

"So come with me there now."

"Nah. It wouldn't be the same. I haven't been back since the night of the party. Hard to think that they're all gone now: Rooster, Rick and Caddy. It's kind of creepy, don't you think?"

"How?"

"Like they're all there, watching over us."

"Where d'you mean? White Shore?"

"Hmm," she muttered.

I wasn't sure whether that was a comforting thought or not. "I always used to go there when I needed space."

"Space?"

"When my dad died, and after we lost Caddy. It's one of the few places near to the village where I know I'll always be safe." I said. "I can't imagine anything bad ever happening there."

54

WHEN I let myself into the flat, Leanne was still in her pyjamas.

"That you, Steve?"

"It's Amy."

The front room stank of curry and cigarettes and I could see a couple of empty wine glasses on the low table next to a stack of takeaway food trays.

"Home alone?" I said.

"Steve's gone out for some tobacco. He won't be long. You should have let us know you were coming round."

"I'm not stopping,"

"I must look a sight." Leanne clambered onto the couch and wiped her eyes with the ball of her hand. "We had a late night and I've only just got out of bed in case you hadn't noticed."

I dropped my rucksack on the floor, squashed myself next to her and took her in my arms.

As soon as she noticed the look on my face she gave me a tight embrace in return. "God's sake, Ames. What's wrong?"

"Nothing."

"Is it Mum?"

"No," I snivelled and pulled my head away from her shoulder so she could see the broad smile on my face. "It's nothing like that. I just wanted to see you again, that's all."

"Wow! What's brought this on?"

"I've been a right cow, I know. I shouldn't have said some of the stuff I said."

"Aw, hon. It's only to be expected - you finding out the way you did.."

"No excuses."

"If you insist."

"Anyway, I've got something for you," I said. "Just to say sorry."

Her gaze shifted to the rucksack. "You don't have to. I mean, it's all forgotten with."

I reached into the pocket of my jacket and pulled out the cheque, folded in two like a love letter. "I wish it was more. But if it makes a difference."

Her face stiffened when she read the amount. "Five thousand pounds? I can't take this, it's crazy money."

"I've dated it tomorrow - the 24th. But it won't bounce if you pay it in later today, so don't look so worried."

"It's not that. Where did you get it? Has Mum given it you to give me?"

"No. She doesn't know a thing so you have to promise not to tell her. She thinks I've come here to pick up my phone charger."

"I'm not being ungrateful," she said. "But it's too much. I mean, how did you get your hands on so much cash?"

"If I tell you, you have to promise."

"Promise what?"

"Don't go blabbing to Steve or anybody else."

"Now you've really got me worried. What the hell's been going on?"

"Matt and his dad had a fight?"

"One almighty row, so Mike said. Matt hadn't been home two hours before he started going on about how it was worse than being stuck in prison."

"No wonder there was a falling out."

"I know," I said. "Steff thought Mike was being unfair when he said the cheque came with conditions attached. She told him he should let me and Matt spend some quality time together and leave the lecture until later."

"You and Matt? What did she mean?"

"Matt had said nothing about being dumped. Steff mentioned his plans to visit me at the Arches. She'd said it would be a lovely surprise and that's when Mike laughed in her face."

"He knew Matt was lying," Leanne said.

"Yeah. I'd already emailed Mike, thinking it was Peter I was in touch with, letting him know me and Matt were finished. When Mike warned him to stay away from me Matt went off on one. Accusing us of all sorts."

"What? You and Mike?"

"It's nothing. All in Matt's head."

"So why exactly has Mike Neilson given you five grand?" she said. "Are you sure there's nothing going on between you two?"

"Of course I am. And it was ten grand not five."

55

ANY residual awkwardness had vanished once Mike reached out and took me in his arms. "You're looking tired, love. How've you been keeping?"

"Oh, you know," I said.

It was as if he knew exactly what I meant without me having to explain. Sometimes having someone hold you is more about receiving comfort than sharing passion.

The last time anything like this happened between me and Mike, it had ended with a not-so-innocent kiss. Enough to set my heart trembling. Enough to make me believe I was experiencing more than a stupid crush. It had been a bitter day with grey waves piling against the rocks and the wind carrying in fresh snowstorms off the Minch. Caddy's body had been found twenty-four hours earlier and we were both in pieces. Mike had hugged me for an age and I felt safe. Then he pulled my woolly cap down over my ears the same way any father would.

But then reality took over within a matter of days. Things had been painful for a while but I became preoccupied with other matters and Mike Neilson faded into the past.

Had I known I was to meet with him once more in such a special place, I might have worn more than a flimsy t-shirt and tight jeans, torn at the knees. No little girl lost anymore. Mike knew all about my on-off relationship with his son, yet there had been no attempt to treat me any differently than before. An innocent peck on the cheek then he took my hand and we sat side by side on the rocks.

"He talked about Caddy mostly," I continued. "He hadn't known the first thing about the trouble she'd got herself into."

"Was he digging around for more info?" Leanne asked.

"More info? Not really." I cleared my throat. "He realised I had nothing to hide. I'd never been involved with Rick and Rooster - all the drugs and so on."

"Right."

"He kept saying what a good friend I'd been to Caddy, though I still feel guilty as hell. Then he started going on about Matt. What an embarrassment he's turning out to be."

"That's the understatement of the century," she said.

"He said I deserved better. All the times I went round to see Matt when he came out of hospital. Being with him at the funeral. All the other stuff. Even going to see him in prison. Mike said he wanted to make amends for all the upset. To fix things."

Leanne laughed. "It's a bit late for that."

"Probably, but if he hadn't given me the cheque I wouldn't be able to give you a share, would I? I'm trying to help you the same way he was trying to help me."

"Help me or fix me?"

Christ. Kay all over again.

"You know what I mean," I said.

"Yeah. I know exactly what you mean. But you're not my mother. It's not your job." She grabbed a cushion and nursed it against her breast, wrapping her arms tight against it as if it was in need of comfort. "Some things can't be fixed, Amy. Don't even try."

"That's not what I'm doing. Can't I look out for my big

sister once in a while? When I'm flush?"

"God, you sound just like Mum when you start interfering."

"Me like Mum?" I laughed in her face.

"It doesn't feel right me taking your money like this. Not all this. You're going to need more than your share of the ten grand for when you go to uni."

University had been Plan A. Plan B was more romantic and the five thousand would make things easier. Kay and I would move away from Lochinver and set up home together in Inverness. I'd continue my studies and she could play at being a housewife or whatever.

"I know it's a bit hasty," I said. "But you don't have to make your mind up right now." I'd tried every angle to convince Kay it would be for the best. A clean break. A fresh start. A change of scene. But Kay had killed the idea stone dead.

"It's never going to work," she said.

"What d'you mean?"

"You and me in the big, bad city."

"How come? I thought you felt the same way about me as I do about you."

"It's not that. It's the level of temptation. Pubs. Clubs. Dealers hanging round the railway station and the back of the Legion. That's how all this business with Rooster started."

"But I'll be there. I can look out for you."

"And what am I supposed to do all day while you're in class?" Kay said. "Watch daytime TV and do the hoovering? Or get off my head 'cause I'm bored senseless? If you're set on going then don't let me stop you. You have my blessing, of course you do. But I'm staying here."

We'd agreed to disagree and I'd packed my bag then

wandered home, shattered dreams in my wake. Not a falling out, as such. But we'd not been in touch since.

"Yeah, well university's a long way away," I said. "Not for another twelve months at least. And I know you'll pay me back when you can."

"When?" she said. "When we win the lottery?"

"I'm just saying, there's no rush. Five days ago I had twenty-eight quid in the bank and I'd just blown my job prospects for the summer holidays."

"Even so." She took out another cigarette and fumbled with her lighter.

"I love you to bits, Lea. But I hate what you're having to do – and what it's doing to you."

"Don't say that." Her eyes screwed up as the first hit of nicotine hit the mark.

"I can't help it. I'd rather die than do that stuff, honest." I got to my feet and pulled the hem of my jacket below my waist.

"You're not going already. You've only just got here."

"Best had. It was only meant to be a quick hello," I said. "I'll phone you later in the week, make sure the cheque clears."

I picked up my rucksack, took out Mum's magazines, dumped them on the table and headed for the door. I could hear Leanne at my heels as I fumbled for the latch; her bare feet slapping against the laminated flooring.

"You could at least stay for a coffee. Steve won't be long."

"Next time, OK?" I turned and gave her a kiss on the cheek. "I don't want to hang around in case I bump into Matt."

"He's still at the Cartwrights, last I heard," Leanne said. "Him and Baxter have got hold of a van, according to Steve."

"A van?"

"God knows what they're up to, but he saw them offloading crates of wine at the back of one of the hotels late Saturday night."

"Right."

"You can bet they hadn't just got back from the cash and carry."

"What d'you mean?"

"I mean they were probably nicked. Fallen off the back of a wagon, or been smuggled in from the continent. Cheap knock-off booze."

"Ah."

"That's how Steve gets his baccy, to be honest. But don't let on I told you."

"I won't," I said. "See you soon."

I closed the door behind me and battled my way through the clutter of discarded shopping trolleys and kiddies' bikes at the bottom of the stairwell. Then I dashed down the outside steps two at a time, breath clutching at my throat. I needed to clear my head. I needed to get away before Steve got back and I had to look him in the eye and pretend I knew nothing.

Rain was spitting and I fumbled for my hood. A white van sat next to the recycling bins; wipers scraping streaks of greasy rainwater across its screen. I heard it give a toot then the passenger window rolled down and I saw a familiar face.

56

"CALMED down yet?"

"Fuck off."

"I take it that's a no."

I heard the passenger door of the van creak open and turned my back on him, pulling at the straps of my rucksack as I lowered my head and prepared to complete my escape.

"Amy! Give me a couple of minutes. I can explain everything."

I spun round to face him. "I don't want to hear it."

Matt's hair had started to grow back but his face was still unshaven. He looked the part. Ex-crim back on the streets or whatever. More at home in Ill Manors than Ullapool.

Steve was crossing the road ahead of us, heading in my direction.

Christ.

"Hi, Ames. You OK?"

"Yeah, fine."

"What's the hurry?"

Then he must have noticed Matt lurking close by.

"It's nothing, Steve. Honest."

But Steve knew Matt's reputation as well as anyone. "You giving this wee lassie here some grief? 'Cause if you are I'll cut your balls off and hang them round your fucking neck."

I waited and watched Matt back off.

"I was only wanting a quiet word," he shouted as he turned on his heels and wandered back towards the van. "Forget it."

The driver opened his door and leant out. I recognized Kaz's brother – Matt's new BFF. "What was that all about?"

"Nothing," I heard him snarl. "Let's get going."

Then I took a deep breath. "Matt, wait!"

"What you doing?" I felt Steve's hand on my shoulder.

"Matt!"

He stopped and turned to face me once more and it felt like old times for all of ten seconds. "Ames?"

I could feel my heart thumping like a time bomb. "Just be careful, that's all."

He grinned and gave me a wink. "I'm always careful, darling. You know that. But thanks for caring."

I heard Baxter laugh and slam the driver's door shut.

"No, listen." I shook my head in frustration. "You have to listen to me, Matt. It's about Peter."

"Who?" he said.

"Peter Paver. I've heard he's back in Lochinver and he's gone a bit mental. He says he's going to pay back everybody for what they did to his dad."

"So? I don't give a shit." He spat at his feet. "He can burn the fucking place down, for all I care."

I nodded. Same old Matt. "Just so you know, that's all. You're top of his hit list."

57

STEVE escorted me back to the flat and Leanne made us all a coffee. Then she announced she was going to have a duvet day since Steve had offered to drive me home instead of taking her shopping. The chances were she'd be straight on the phone to Mum once we left. Not to spill the beans about the cheque but to warn her to keep an eye on her unpredictable daughter.

"So you and Matt are definitely finished?" he asked.

The rain intensified as we crested the brow of Knockan Crag and he switched on his headlights. We'd overtaken a delivery van and a cyclist on the hill above Strathcanaird. And a solitary breakdown truck headed in the opposite direction carrying some poor beggar's dampened holiday plans back to Ullapool. Otherwise traffic was light.

"Yeah." I braced myself against the back of the seat as he took the first corner into Elphin. "He's changed."

"If you say so. I thought he'd always been a wanker."

"Yeah, well. Prison's made him worse, if that's possible. Steff's afraid she's lost him for good."

"Never mind," Steve said. "You're better off without him."

"I know." Everybody kept reminding me I deserved better.

"He'll be back inside within the month if he keeps hanging round with that Baxter character."

"You think?"

"They're up to something."

"Leanne told me about the van."

"That's right. It'll be Slippy they're working for."

I laughed. "I doubt it. Matt isn't that stupid. Not after what happened last time they got together."

"You'll see. Baxter used to be one of Slippy's couriers, if you know what I mean."

"I can guess."

The rain had cleared giving way to a coiling mist as we approached the loch near Ardvreck Castle.

"Stupid fuckers. Get out of the way." Steve blasted his horn at two men who seemed to be wandering aimlessly in the middle of the narrow road. They were almost invisible with their matching black waterproofs and the hoods pulled up over their hard hats. Each carried a block hammer and chisel, and the taller of the pair had a coil of orange rope looped over his shoulder.

"Hill climbers out in this. They need their bloody heads testing."

"More likely to be geology students staying at the Field Centre," I said. "The Geopark and all that."

"I don't care what they are. They're worse than the sheep on this section of road."

"I know." I couldn't be bothered arguing. My attention had already switched to the vehicle parked at the side of the loch. A nondescript, black pick-up - relatively new, but not Jimmy Jump's judging by the bumper sticker.

SQUADDIES ON BOARD – HONK FOR A BONK

It seemed everyone in this part of Scotland was driving a black Toyota.

58

STEVE left soon after five and I washed our tea things then prepared some ham sandwiches. When Mum got in from work she joined me in the front room, eating from a tray on her knees, just like old times. The only sound the rain again, now drumming against the window.

"This is nice," she said.

"I thought I'd make enough for both of us, seeing as you're working late."

"How was Leanne?"

"Fine. She said thanks for the magazines, by the way."

"I've had a word. They're asking if you can do Thursdays and Fridays one till nine to start with."

"Waitressing?"

"That's what you said." Mum looking flustered as ever. "Don't go messing us about changing your mind because you won't get another chance."

"I won't."

I began to scoop up the evidence of a night spent slouched on the sofa watching E4 re-runs. I'd managed to demolish a tube of Pringles and a half bottle of left-over Shiraz in the process.

"So I can tell them you'll be there on Thursday. Come in with me at twelve and we'll go through everything before the bar opens."

"OK. Don't see why not." The prospect of an entire summer working alongside my mother in Camp

Kommandant mode was hardly appealing. But I needed as much cash as possible for what I had planned, once the school holidays were finished. The five thousand left in my bank account would soon disappear.

She picked up my plate and glass and followed me into the kitchen.

"I bumped into Matt Neilson while I was in Ullapool," I said.

"And?"

"Nothing. I'm just saying. It looks like he's living there full-time now. Got himself a new girlfriend."

"Are you having a coffee with me?" she said.

"Just a glass of warm milk."

"You're better off without him."

"Matt? I know," I mumbled. "I told you. We finished ages ago. We just didn't realise."

"So is there someone else you're not telling me about?"

"What d'you mean?"

"Well, Leanne said you'd been having boy trouble when she phoned. Said you'd told her more than a week ago you were over it but she's still worried. She thinks you're looking tired."

I shook my head in frustration. "God, it was nothing so there's no need to keep fussing."

"So who is it you're staying with when you're not here?"

"I told you, it's just a friend."

"Is it the same boy?"

"It's a girl, if you must know. OK?"

"A girl?"

"Yeah." I counted to ten and waited for the ground to open under my feet as I trawled the mucky thoughts filtering through my subconscious. But it didn't. "I'm having a relationship with a girl."

"A relationship?"

"It is allowed, you know. Even round here. And no, it's nobody you know."

59

TUESDAY morning I had a lie-in. I'd tossed and turned for most of the night. And sometime in the early hours I heard thunder and the power went off - my bedside clock dead.

"You're seeing a girl? Well, that's come out of the blue. But as long as you're both happy."

Mum's reaction exactly what I should have expected.

"And you're always welcome to stay here. The two of you, I mean. If you ever need somewhere to spend. . ." Her words trailed off.

"She's got her own place. But thanks, Mum."

I could turn up with my long blonde hair buzz-cut to the bone, wearing twin lip studs, a pair of overalls and DMs, and Mum wouldn't have batted an eyelid. But the idea of Kay in this bed in this room with Mum under the same roof. I could never imagine that working, despite the show of support.

"You'll have to bring her round for her tea one afternoon so I can get to meet her."

Shit. Kay would have a fit.

And I'd gone and used the word 'relationship' when it was anything but.

I turned my back to the window and tried to block out the light. Summer nights were so short in these parts that Mum had put blackout blinds on our window when Leanne and I were bairns so we could get a full night's sleep.

Eventually I drifted off and had one of those bizarre, half-asleep/half-awake dreams that you sometimes get where everything seems to be happening for real except for one totally weird detail. I woke bathed in sweat and with a feeling of utter dread.

My mobile phone gave one more bleep. Incoming message.

```
 Luv  u  luv  u  luv  u  lil  sis!!!  Y
didn't u tell me? Lea xxx
```

So now it was official.

60

KAZ reluctantly agreed to accompany Matt on his second solo assignment. "I suppose it's better than being stuck at home watching the soaps all on my own. I'd never get to see you otherwise."

Matt had been busy with Baxter the last couple of days. Nothing dodgy. A couple of runs to Inverness and a trip as far as Scourie for an outboard motor. But he wasn't so sure he wanted Kaz for company tonight. He'd seen the brief news segment on STV late last week. A two minute report squashed in between the latest redevelopment plans for Aberdeen city centre and the list of on-off transfers from the SPL. Mysterious explosions on a remote hilltop, miles from nowhere, hardly merited a mention let alone a camera crew and live reporter. Stock footage of a wind farm and a voice-over was the best they could come up with.

"It was fucking dynamite, Kaz. The real deal not that cartoon stuff you see on Roadrunner."

"Cool."

"Not so cool if something had happened."

"Like what? Like getting blown up?"

A ton and a half of dynamite seemed a hell of a lot of bang if all they were trying to do was knock over a couple of wind turbines.

"Is this job for Slippy as well?"

Matt shook his head. "Don't know. It's Tommy who's

organised it." Baxter was the middleman in the operation, but information was strictly on a need-to-know basis. "All they've told me is I'm supposed to meet someone at the Marble Quarry eight o'clock."

"Is it the Land Rover guy again?"

"Baxter didn't say. But Tommy said they'd asked for me personally."

"How cool is that? They must trust you."

"Yeah. Or I'm the only mug crazy enough to do the fucking job."

Once they turned left at Ledmore, rolls of fleecy white began chasing their vehicle from the direction of Glen Oykel. The clouds seemed on a collision course with banks of pink haze above Conival.

"If you're going all the way to the Aultguish again you might as well drop me off in Ullapool," Kaz said. "I need to wash my hair."

"Can do."

But Matt hadn't been given any more details. If he was indeed collecting a second load, the chances were it was destined elsewhere. Maybe the unsightly array of pylons being erected above Garve was the next target.

Matt parked by the large, white boulder marking the quarry entrance. "You're better off getting out here and waiting at the side of the road," he said. "They might not like it if they see somebody else in the van."

"Who's they?"

"I've already told you. I don't know."

"OK, OK, if that's what you want."

Kaz climbed out of the vehicle, turned her back on Matt and took a pack of cigarettes out of her handbag. He wound down his window. "If you see anyone else driving down from the quarry before I'm back, don't let on you're waiting for me."

"So what am I supposed to do? Pretend I'm waiting for

a bus out in the middle of fucking nowhere?"

Five minutes later Matt had reached the end of the twisting, gravel track leading up to the main quarry. The thought of hurtling back down the same road with a full payload of out-of-date explosives gave him the jitters. Half the track had been washed away in places by rainwater runnels, and the potholes were so closely spaced that the suspension continued rattling the entire journey.

A pre-fabricated hut serving as a gatehouse appeared to have been abandoned some time in the distant past. But up ahead on the left stood the weigh-bridge office, a brick building with an asbestos roof. The only vehicle in sight was the black Toyota he'd seen outside the Aultguish three nights earlier. Matt got out of the van and peered inside the office but it looked just as deserted.

The door's hinges had been prised away from the frame and both windows had their glass held in place by strips of gaffer tape. A solitary desk leant against the wall next to a butane heater. Faded rolls of yellow slips bundled together by an elastic band, a couple of tea-stained mugs, a telephone and a clipboard gave the impression that someone still worked here. But it was hardly Corporate HQ. The notice attached to the door announcing blasting times suggested there would be no one on duty after 18.00 any day of the week.

Then as Matt wandered back to his van, unsure whether or not to call out for someone's attention, he heard the roar of an engine close by and the monotonous beep of a piece of machinery reversing up ahead. Slowly he steered the van between the heaps of gravel, keeping to the narrow track skirting pools of grey water and deeper ruts where the hard-standing had been pulverised to water-logged mud by the constant passage of heavy plant. A large, yellow excavator emerged from behind a rusted elevator and slowly turned left to block his advance.

Someone with a clipboard leapt down from the footplate of the tractor. He wore a camouflage top, combat trousers and rigger boots. Very much a weekend soldier living the dream, Matt thought, as he marched forwards and signalled for him to get out of the vehicle.

"Who you looking for?" he shouted above the loud throb of the tractor's engine.

"Tommy sent me."

The man with the clipboard nodded. "How much room in the back?"

"It's empty apart from a few bits. Tools and so on," Matt replied.

"Show me."

Matt opened the rear doors of the van. But before he got the chance to step aside and let Clipboard Man take a look, someone grabbed his upper arms from behind. Then a kick in the small of his back sent him sprawling face-first into the van.

"Hey!"

Matt tried to scrabble to his knees and turn to retaliate but already both rear doors were slammed shut and he heard the tractor's engine begin to rev. Then something made the van judder and he watched the roof buckle. The engine screamed even louder and there followed another bone-shaking crunch as he heard the crump of disintegrating windscreen and twisting metal behind the van's bulkhead.

"Shit. What are you doing?"

The sound of the engine receded a fraction before changing in tone. Then came a sickening lurch as the bed of the van shifted beneath him. It felt as if the vehicle was being pushed sideways along the gravel. The jolting became more pronounced and he could hear the sound of scraping along the vehicle's under-carriage. The scream of metal against rock and, above it all, the constant roar of the tractor's engine.

For a fraction of a second the van stopped moving and tilted, as if about to roll onto its side. Then the sounds changed pitch again and Matt realised his vehicle was being lifted from the ground.

"Shit! Let me out."

He flexed his knees and kicked against the rear doors, desperate to force them apart. But they remained clamped tight, wedged in place by the buckled roof. A triangle of daylight appeared where the larger of the two doors had crumpled under the impact. But Matt realised he'd not escape that way no matter how long he kept kicking.

Finally free fall took over as the front of the vehicle canted forwards. Seconds stretched. Matt lost all sense of direction as the engine sounds faded to silence. Silence and weightlessness. Something hard struck his shoulder and he felt bones crack. Then screaming. Harsh and animal-like. Both hands splayed out to save himself. Knuckles grazed as they caught on something unyielding. A crack to the back of the head that made his teeth snap together. Another roll. The stench of spilt Diesel and a rush of nausea as the van continued to roll over and over.

Then silence and weightlessness again as Matt waited for the inevitable end to it all.

But even that came in stages. First a crashing blow to the front of the van that threw Matt against the bulk-head. Then something heavy struck him and he screamed. A pipe-wrench had flown out of nowhere and glanced off his jaw. Then another eerie silence as the vehicle became briefly airborne again. Another disorientating blast of pain and splintering light then murky darkness as his metal coffin finally came to rest. Not on a rocky shelf at the edge of the quarry but in the milky-grey waters that filled the larger part of the flooded pit.

61

KAZ swiped a finger pad across the screen of her smartphone and scrolled through her latest updates. Wednesday night and nothing doing. Someone out at Rhue selling a set of kiddies' trainers on Ullapool Buy, Swap & Sell. The latest set of dolphin sightings posted by the 'Summer Queen'. Another half dozen selfies of Terri Frazer. A friend request from some random guy with a psycho grin she'd snogged at Cindy O'Connor's party.

Where the fuck was Matt?

In the end she decided to follow the gravel track up to the quarry. There was no way she was going to start walking towards Ledmore and hope someone might take pity on her and offer a lift home.

20:47 and her last cigarette already burnt down to the filter.

Shit!

She straightened her shoulder bag, held it tight against her hip and began walking. A red metal barrier had been erected at the side of the track, presumably to keep out unauthorised vehicles, but it swung open. Creaking on the breeze. If the guy Matt was supposed to be meeting should suddenly appear and warn her off, she'd play dumb. What else could she possibly do out here this time of night?

A battered, pre-fabricated gatehouse sat at the entrance to the quarry on Kaz's right. She paused, wary in case there might be someone in authority seated inside. A security guard or night-watchman. But then she heard the roar of an engine up ahead and an enormous, yellow dumper tractor appeared from behind one of the larger piles of stone chippings.

Two men climbed out of the cab and entered the brick building. No one Kaz recognised. If this was one of Slippy's jobs it could be anybody. Ullapool was full of neds willing to do any dodgy deal for a little extra folding money.

Seriously. Where the fuck was Matt?

Another ten minutes passed then Kaz heard another engine fire up and a black pick-up nosed its way from behind the brick building. She stepped inside the open door of the gatehouse and waited for the vehicle to continue past. The roar of its engine and the rasp of tyres on the uneven track came closer. It slowed as if coming to a stop, but the rattle of its suspension continued as it manoeuvred a way between the worst of the pot-holes. Then the engine picked up speed again and the truck disappeared in a cloud of white dust.

Kaz swore under her breath as she followed the muddy wheel ruts leading into the heart of the quarry. Still no sign of Matt. She swiped the screen of her phone again and clicked onto his number.

```
"Welcome to Vodaphone. The person you
are trying to reach. . ."
```

Bastard.

She had better things to do than this. A large metal barn stood to her left with half of the tin-sheet side panels hanging loose. Inside she could see empty trailers with flattened tyres, sets of snaggle-toothed digger buckets and coils of rusted chain. The entire place resembled a scrap yard rather than a working quarry. No sign of Matt or the van.

Where the Hell could he be?

She followed the deep tread-marks of the dumper truck, clear enough in the maze of tracks that led off in every direction. Then directly ahead she saw fresh scuff marks in the ground. Two deep gouges scarred the surface of the gravel as if something had been shovelled to one side against the low embankment forming the boundary of the yard. A wet patch of spilt oil and a scatter of shattered windscreen glass like diamonds glittering in the gravel made her stomach lurch.

She climbed onto the top of the embankment and almost lost balance. Thirty or forty feet below lay a body of grey, muddy water enclosed within a deep crater. And resting in the shallows of this man-made lake she could see what looked like an upturned boat. A boat with a wheel at each corner and a length of exhaust pipe rather than a keel.

She fumbled in her bag for her smart-phone again.

"Baxter."

"What?"

"Where are you?"

"At the Frigate. Why, what's up?"

"Something's happened. It's Matt. The van's upside down."

"OK, slow down. Where are you? Are you alright?"

"Of course I'm not fucking alright. I'm at the quarry."

"Yeah. And what's this about the van?"

"The van's upside down in a big pool of water. Like a lake at the bottom of the quarry."

"Shit."

The line went quiet for an age.

"Baxter?"

"So where's Matt. Is he with you?"

"I don't know," she stammered. "I think he's still inside the van."

"Christ."

"I'm sure I can hear a noise. Like someone tapping. You have to do something."

"I know. Let me think." Kaz could sense the panic in her brother's voice. "Is there anybody else there with you?"

"God, no. There were two men here but. . ."

"But they're gone," he said. "OK. Go back to the road and I'll pick you up. Give me half an hour."

Kaz whispered a prayer of thanks. "But what about Matt?"

"Fuck Matt. Get your arse out of there now."

62

I'D forgotten how good Thursday nights at the Stag's Head could be when there was live music laid on. As many locals as tourists packed the place after nine to enjoy the craic. The banter. The buzz.

We'd congregated at the bar once my shift ended. Six of us. Marie Jenson was there with one of the trainee chefs from the Lodge. Another Lithuanian. She choked on her orange juice as he tried to slip an ice cube down her cleavage and we all began fishing in the ice bucket for more until Mum intervened and told us to act our age. It was the kind of horseplay we'd revelled in when we were kids.

Then Lauren and Quinn turned up and began to tell us about their next trip to the Far East. Lauren and Caddy could have been mistaken for twins when they were younger. Both girls seemed to find it impossible to hide their feelings. Every single thought that passed through Caddy's mind used to show in her smile, her frown, her bewilderment, her devilry.

Quinn ordered another round of drinks then joined the smokers outside in the beer garden. Most of the abstainers took out their iPhones and began posting snapchat selfies on-line or sharing tips on make-up and clothes. Thankfully Sara came to my rescue.

"So how's things? I've not seen you since God knows when."

I made a feeble excuse for not going to the cemetery at Stoer for Moolie's interment. "I've been staying at Leanne's for a few weeks. Working at the Arches until Mum got me this job."

"I had heard. But you're back for the summer?"

"Looks like it."

"Then what? School?"

"I haven't said anything to Mum yet, but I'm thinking of trying to get into college at Inverness instead of going back. I've only got one term's work to catch up on. Then after my exams perhaps I can look at taking a degree course."

It had been bad enough trying to convince Kay it was for the best. Mum and Leanne were sure to try and talk me out of the idea of leaving home. And now I realised how easy it would be to slot back into the old crowd. I'd never felt part of Sara's group, yet these were as much my friends as Caddy's.

"So what you going in for?" Sara said, interrupting my reverie.

I'd not decided. When I was eleven years old it had been a simple choice between vet and nail technologist. But now I quite fancied Media Studies; specialising in Video. Caddy and I used to laugh ourselves sick at some of the vlogs on YouTube. She used to say I could do a lot worse. But then my long-term career plans had been put on hold.

"I'm definitely not going back to Ullapool."

"Too many bad memories?"

I nodded. "There's other shit I'd rather not get into as well. If I have to, I'll stick it out here. Get a job at the Deli or the Bog Shop."

"Shit. So you're giving up on life?"

I didn't get a chance to reply. Quinn came back in, a sneery grin on his face as he gate-crashed the conversation. "So what's the story about you and Matt Neilson?"

"There is no story."

I saw Sara's eyes light up. "You and him still together?"

"No. We split ages ago."

Quinn nodded. "Only I just heard you gave him a beer shampoo in the Arches."

"Who's told you that?"

He tapped the side of his nose. "Same guy who reckons you and Kay Jepson are spending a lot of quality time together."

"Not exactly. She keeps herself to herself, so I don't know who's spreading stories."

"Just as well," Quinn said. "She's off her head most of the time."

Sara plonked down her glass and fished in her bag for a tiny compact. "I thought Kay had gone back to live with her dad."

Let them think what they want. "I wouldn't know. I don't see much of her but she's calmed down a lot from how she used to be."

"I should hope so," Quinn continued. "Some of the stunts she used to pull."

"You been out to the 'Buie recently?" Sara asked.
"No."

She finished applying her lipstick as the band walked in – two violins, an acoustic guitar and the fourth guy carrying a bodhrán under his arm. The guitarist wrapped his arms around Sara and planted a kiss on the top of her head. "Hi, squirrel. You going to give us a song tonight?"

"Might do."

The place continued to fill and we were forced to huddle in a tight group next to one of the picture windows overlooking the Inver. Out to sea, the sky had

251

already turned salmon pink with streaks of gold chasing the setting sun below the horizon.

"We used to go over whenever there was a ceilidh on at the Hall," Quinn continued.

"To Achiltibuie?"

"Yeah. Rooster always complained how every time we turned up looking for a fight a dance broke out."

Mum came over and asked us if we were wanting another drink before the music started.

"Not me. I think I'll head for home," I said. A quarter to ten and I was knackered. I'd been on my feet since lunchtime and I'd already downed three generous measures of gin and bitter lemon. On the house. "I'll probably be in bed when you come in so don't go slamming the front door."

"Will you listen to this? My own daughter telling me how to behave in my own house."

Sara drained her glass and leaned across to give me a hug and a kiss on the cheek. "It's good to see you again. We should meet up on one of your nights off. Friday or Saturday."

"Yeah. I know."

Quinn and Lauren followed me to the door. "Quinny's got an early start in the morning. You needing a lift home?"

"No ta. The walk will do me good."

But as soon as I stepped outside I saw a familiar vehicle parked at the kerb below the window of Kay's flat. Jimmy Jump's pick-up with its broken rear light cover, though the chances were it wasn't Jimmy paying her a visit. Splashes of grey mud coated its wheel arches. Then I noticed the sticker on the rear bumper that hadn't been there the last time I'd been inside the truck.

SQUADDIES ON BOARD – HONK FOR A BONK

63

PETER Paver answered the door, as I'd suspected he might. The smear of arrogance crossing his face turned his welcoming smile into something altogether more sinister.

"Well, look who it is. You'd better come in."

He sounded drunk but it seemed more of an act than a true indication of how much alcohol he'd consumed. The sweet tang of weed and the throb of a trance track increased in intensity as he steered me along the narrow corridor.

"You're just in time 'cause the party's just about to get started."

I almost gagged at the stench of burning candle wax and hash.

"It's young Amy," he shouted above the din as he ushered me into Kay's living room.

I'd expected to find it packed wall to wall but the room looked virtually empty. A table lamp cast a red glow in one corner and tea-lights ran along the window sill like tiny stepping stones to Hell. The drawn curtains made it almost cave-like. I counted two empty vodka bottles on the coffee table and a third half way to empty. Crushed cans of Coke and Red Bull lay on the floor and a couple of tumblers stood either side of the ash tray. Cigarette butts and discarded ring-pulls spilt over onto the carpet. There was also a pack of tarot cards splayed on the floor and traces of white dust on one corner of the table top.

Then my gaze switched to Kay.

Christ.

She was curled up on the sofa, wearing a pair of tracksuit bottoms and nothing else by the look of it. Her elbows were pressed against her rib cage and she held her hands over her eyes as if desperate to keep out the light.

"Grab a clean glass from the kitchen if you can find one," Peter said. "This is Robbo, by the way."

I'd barely had time to register the third person in the room.

"What have you done to her?" I knelt at my friend's side and began to stroke her hair.

"Fuckin' chill. She's coming down, that's all."

"Turn that frigging noise down," I said. "She looks totally spaced out. Have you given her anything?"

I pulled Kay's hands away from her face and tried to get her to sit upright. But she curled up into a tighter ball and I could feel her trembling.

"I'll get her something to help her calm down," Robbo said while Paver crossed the room and turned off the music.

"What did you give her? Was it coke?" I snarled, turning my attention to Paver's pal. He stared back and let a plume of smoke escape his lips before taking another drag on his cigarette. His hair was close-cropped, darker than Peter's, and his eyes speared the haze like lasers. In a different context I might have paid more attention.

Peter came to stand next to me, arms spread wide apart. "She was already blitzed when we got here, right Robbo?"

"Fuckin' right," he replied.

I knelt closer to her. "Kay? It's Amy. Are you OK, hon?"

Her eyes opened, bloodshot and red-rimmed. Halloween in mid-summer. "I want a voddie."

Peter laughed and I saw him reach for the bottle.

I warned him off with a shake of the head. "Kay, you need to sit up. I think you've had enough to drink."

She tried to push me away as she straightened herself. "I said I want a fuckin' voddie." Then she slid her feet onto the floor and tried to stand.

"Wait. Let me help you up."

But Peter was already on hand. "Come here, doll. I've got you."

I reached out to take over. "Let me have her. I'll put her to bed."

"Nah." He wrapped his arms tighter around Kay and turned her around so her back was pressed against his front. "We came here to party so let's party." Then he started a slow dance, swaying with Kay as he ran his hands over her naked breasts.

Robbo got to his feet as well and I saw him slip a lighter into his jacket pocket. "Maybe we should make tracks, Pete. We've got a busy day tomorrow."

"He's right," I said. "She's in no fit state."

But already I could see Paver's hands sliding up and down Kay's body, stroking her bare skin as he began to gnaw at her left shoulder. "You got any gear left, Robbo?"

"I don't think so," I said.

"We should ask Kay, don't you think?" Paver whispered. "D'you want a little booster, sweetheart? Or d'you want your mummy to tuck you up into beddy-weddy like a good little girl?"

Kay's mouth peeled open in a devil's grin and she eased the tip of her tongue out.

"That's my girl." Robbo reached into his trouser pocket and extracted a tiny roll of silver foil. "There you go." He untwisted it and let the white powder slide onto her tongue. Then he picked up an open can from the table and held it to her mouth. Tilting it gently so she could take a sip and swallow.

"You bastards. What are you giving her now?"

"Just a little GBL, get her in the mood."

"Easy, darlin'," I heard Robbo laugh. Then I felt his hands take hold of mine and lock them behind my back.

"Let me go."

"As soon as you promise to be good."

"You bastards. She's too drunk to know what she's doing."

"Oh, I think she knows exactly what she's doing," Paver said.

Kay's eyes had already begun to glaze over and I watched him as he tugged her tracksuit bottoms down to her knees.

"Let's get you comfortable first, shall we?"

He helped her lie face-down on the couch and finished removing her trousers. Then he pulled off her underwear and held it in front of his face like a trophy.

"Woohoo!"

"Leave her alone," I sobbed as I looked at my friend's naked body laid out for sacrifice. "She never did anything to hurt you."

But Paver seemed more fired up than ever and the air in the room sparked with energy as the tension mounted.

"First or second?"

I struggled to pull free but Robbo was too strong. "After you, matey. Got my hands full for now."

Kay turned her head to one side and I watched as her eyelids fluttered open and her lips shaped two words. "Go now."

Paver was already unbuckling the belt of his trousers with one hand and forcing her thighs apart with the other.

"I'll do it," I called out.

He continued to push his fingers between Kay's buttocks but I could see I'd caught his attention. He turned to look at me and his grin widened. "Do what?"

"She's already out of it, can't you see? If you want your bit of fun, let her go and I'll take her place." I swallowed the bile rising in my throat. "I'll give you both a blow job if that's what you're after. Just as long as you leave her alone."

"A blow job?" He laughed. "We've come here for a proper fuck not a blow job."

I felt something inside me give, as if my heart had broken loose and slid down into the pit of my stomach.

"So are you up for a foursome?" Peter said.

"Look at her," I continued. "She's half-dead. I think you need to leave and I'll put her to bed."

Peter gazed at Kay then straightened up and turned to face me. "But you've already offered to take her place. I'd rather shag a live one than a dead one anyway, so what d'you reckon, Robbo?"

64

ROBBO carried Kay into the bedroom. He was almost gentle in the way he handled her; laying her on her side, pushing a second pillow under her head and pulling the sheet over her body. Then we came back into the living room and Peter offered me a drink.

"Voddie do you? 'Cause that's all we've got."

"Yeah, fine. Make it a big one."

I caught the snigger and the wink as soon as the words were out of my mouth. Paver and his buddy bumped heads like a pair of stags then he stepped closer, eyes taking in every detail.

"So, are you ready to rumble? We can spare a little powder as well, if you like. Make everything that bit sweeter."

I bit back a sob then nodded and kicked off my sensible shoes while Robbo reached into his pocket again. The taste of salt on my tongue came as a surprise and I took a sip of vodka. Straight. It made my breath catch and my eyes water.

Peter reached for the hem of my t-shirt but I turned away. "I can do it."

I pulled it over my head and watched Robbo's eyes follow my every move - mesmerised by my hands as I unclasped my bra, unzipped my trousers, stepped out of them and tugged down my tights.

"Mhmm. Nice," I heard Paver purr as I finally took off

my pants then covered myself with one hand and reached for my drink with the other.

"You sure about this?" Peter asked after I'd drained half the tumbler. "'Cause that means it's consensual. Right?"

I nodded.

Too late for second thoughts.

"Where d'you want me?"

"On the couch and make yourself comfortable. Me and Robbo are going to have a wee snifter first to get us in the mood."

He opened Kay's tobacco tin and measured out a tiny pile of white powder onto the table. Then he picked up one of her tarot cards and used it to form two lines. Robbo took out his wallet and unfurled a twenty-pound note. Then he rolled it into a tube, knelt on the floor and snorted one of the lines. A sharp inhalation then a second one as if clearing his tubes.

"You want a try, doll?"

"Not really."

I sat there and watched while Paver took his turn then they both got undressed and began to massage my feet. The drink helped. And the GBL – if that's what it was. I felt my body go slack as I stretched out on the couch, flat on my back, praying for it all to be over.

"One at a time," I managed to slur. But already I felt as if I'd stepped out of myself leaving the empty shell of my body in the room. Most of the time I kept my eyes closed, but once or twice I turned to look at who was screwing me and who was watching. How could they behave like this? Marvelling at each other's moves like a pair of ten-year-olds seeing who could piss highest in the school toilets.

Paver got to go first. I'd imagined them tossing a coin or playing Rock-Paper-Scissors. And instinctively I felt my muscles clench as soon as his fingers touched me.

"Remember last August?" he whispered. "It was your first time, right?"

I might have nodded.

"I never even noticed the swallow tattoo on your arse."

I said nothing, even though I'd read in one of Mum's magazines that in situations like this silence signifies consent. I didn't need to speak because my body had decided for me – one of its more perverse little tricks. I was wet down there and my nipples were hard. But I still wasn't ready, and I became breathless with panic as he tried to enter me. My reaction seemed to make him even more excited. Eager to prove how much of a stud he was.

I thought of Kay passed out in the next room. One minute we're sharing a pizza and a bottle of wine - doing the washing up like a married couple. And the next. . . I'd never be able to face her in the morning. I couldn't begin to work out how to tell her what I'd done and why I'd done it.

Paver continued, kneading my breasts as he pounded away. I tried to imagine what he was feeling. He couldn't even look me in the eye. Did that mean I didn't turn him on? Or was it simply my breasts and sex that he was focussing on anyway? That erotic combination of vital statistics that makes women attractive to men. Skin texture and colour. Body hair. Scent. Feel. Taste. I tried to blank out everything. He wasn't making love to me any more than those who telephoned Leanne were having a proper date with her. He was screwing a concept. Any female body would have done, as long as it satisfied whatever primitive fixation occupied his tiny brain. This was worse than anything Matt Neilson had ever put me through. Unforgiveable.

Leanne had tried to justify what she was doing by explaining how you often do unbearable things when you're desperate. I'd not bought her excuse back then. But now here I was, desperate and doing something beyond unbearable. I gritted my teeth and squeezed my eyes shut and thought of Paver Senior and his failed attempt to ship me out to Aberdeen. If his plan had worked, I'd be letting men do this to me 24/7, earning him a small fortune in the process.

The irony was that everyone had congratulated me on escaping a fate worse than death and now here I was. That nightmare fate made reality.

65

THE first few times I'd managed to separate what was happening down between my legs from the rest of my body. But I was growing bone weary and Paver must have sensed my detachment.

He pushed a finger between my lips. "Lick it. Let me rub it over your gums."

It tasted bitter. Cold, like menthol rather than minty. Then I felt one side of my mouth go numb.

"Sit up and I'll help you."

Robbo spilled a line of powder onto the back of his hand then he held it in front of my face and passed me a rolled-up banknote.

"Press your finger against one nostril and snort with the other." The sensation almost made me sneeze it back out. "Another deep breath. Get it to the back of your throat, darling."

And I did, and I felt something change. It didn't matter what they did to me anymore. I was becoming attuned to the differences between them. Paver monotonous and detached. Like a frigging machine. Robbo more attentive, more sensual. But a rapist all the same. Part of me had somehow hollowed out and all I wanted was that feeling of being filled. Of being desired again and again and again.

Peter wouldn't let me get properly cleaned up. After

everything they'd done to me, he didn't trust me to keep calm and say nothing to anyone. I'd already put my knickers back on and gathered up the rest of my clothes from the floor while they finished their drinks and roll-ups. Now I picked up my bag and Paver held out his hand.

"Show me." I opened it and tipped everything out onto the couch. Lipstick. Tissues. Sanitary towels. Hand cream. He snatched up my mobile phone. "I don't fucking think so."

"I just need a few bits and pieces." I shook my head. "Just let me get a clean set of knickers. I can't wear these."

Maybe he saw the glint of metal. The nail scissors I'd managed to wrap inside my bra. His hand lashed out making me bite through my bottom lip. Pain instant then done with. He snatched them from my hands and threw them to one side. Then he searched each pocket of my trousers before dropping them onto the floor along with my bra.

"You'll not be needing those," he said. "Keep your eye on her, Robbo, while I go down to the truck. And don't let her take all day about it. We've got a tight schedule."

Robbo stood at the bathroom door while I sat on the toilet and let my stomach unclench. There was no part of me he'd not seen. Not touched. He turned his head away but I couldn't care less what he heard as I emptied my bladder then swabbed myself dry. My head was still buzzing.

What I really needed was a shower, but I knew that wasn't an option. Besides, I was too tender down there. I dabbed inside myself briefly with some scrunched up toilet tissue. Then I swabbed the corner of my mouth. It blossomed red.

"All done?"

I ran the hot tap over a flannel and wiped myself as clean as I could before getting dressed. Then I showed him the blood on the tissue. "My period's starting."

"So what d'you want me to do about it?"

"I'm going to need something from my bag."

"No more funny business." He pulled a set of keys out of his jacket pocket and began jiggling them in his hand. "Grab what you need on the way out."

"What about Kay? Let me see to her, if you like and you two can get away."

He shook his head. "That's not going to happen, doll. Peter's orders. You're coming with us."

66

THE cab of Jimmy's truck stank of cigarettes and greasy fast-food wrappers.

"Budge up next to me." Peter rummaged inside the glove compartment and took out a cable-tie. "Hold out your hands."

"You should have let me stay with Kay. I won't tell anyone what you did. All that stuff you said."

"Sorry, babes. No can do." He smirked. "We're not letting you go 'til we're done."

I chewed my broken lip and stared through the windscreen at the empty street. Ten past five on a Friday morning. Summer be damned, Lochinver was in hibernation mode as usual.

"Done? What d'you mean done?"

"You'll find out soon enough."

I had visions of being taken somewhere else and gang-raped until I could no longer stand.

"Where first?" Robbo asked as he turned the truck around and headed uphill past the Glac and out of the village.

"Skiag," Paver said. "Then we'll do Kylesku."

Traffic was light. A dozen or so sheep congregated inside the visitors' car park just beyond the Skiag Bridge junction. A man with a camera and a black Lab stood on the narrow sandbar linking Ardvreck Castle to the shore and I could make out a campervan at the side of the road a few yards ahead of us. Nothing else was moving.

The surface of the loch was flawless. Not a ripple. Low light cast one side of the ruins in pitch black but the other was bathed in an orange glow. Heavenly. Maybe it was one of them mornings. Or maybe the effect of the cocaine hadn't quite worn off.

"Are we going to wait 'til he fucks off?" Robbo said.

"No. Turn round. We can do it on the way back."

Robbo spun the truck on the gravel and we headed up the meandering road flanking the Eastern slopes of Quinag. Curtains of mist unfurled like layers of lace above the corrie as the sunlight strengthened. On any other morning the scene would have been captivating, unforgettable. But my stomach was still churning with what Paver had told me less than half an hour earlier.

He'd been standing next to Kay's bed when Robbo and I went into her bedroom. "Just checking on Sleeping Beauty here before we go. Wouldn't want her dying on us."

"Can I?" He let me pull back the top sheet and I shook her by the shoulder but she didn't move. I planted a kiss on her forehead. "See you later."

"Sweet." Peter sneered as I pulled the sheet back up to cover her body.

"I thought you and Kay were supposed to be friends," I said.

"This prick-teasing bitch? You'd have been better holding onto your knickers and letting me and the Robster give her one instead. She's had it coming for a long time."

"After what your father's pals did to her? You're all as bad as each other."

"At least I wasn't the one holding her down when they fucked her up the arse."

"They what?"

"She was a real fighter, I'll give her that."

I felt something give inside me and I struggled to speak. "How would you know all that? You were here with them, weren't you?"

"It was my business to know, after the shit Tyler put us through. They were sent here to break the bitch but she had more guts than he ever did."

"What d'you mean?" I said.

"He was like a fucking kid, once we started on his girlfriend, snivelling and gagging for breath. Did you know he pissed himself soon as we got him off the bus?"

What bus?

"You were there when Caddy. . ." A flat statement of realisation.

"The bitch had taken Rick's stash and she wouldn't let on what she'd done with it."

"That's 'cause she never had it in the first place," I screamed.

"What?" The trace of a smile made his eyes look even less human as he absorbed the latest news. "So how the fuck did Kay get her hands on it? 'Cause I know she didn't take it the night of the party at Strathbeg. We both left together."

Christ.

"Speak to Jimmy," I sobbed.

"You what?"

I told him the full story.

"Fuck me."

"Were you here when they raped Kay?" I asked again. I needed to know.

"Nah. I'd only just got back to Newton on PVR that morning. I didn't even reply to her email, but I passed the party invite on to some friends."

"Barto and Damo."

He nodded. "We'd sussed out somebody must have made off with Rick's drugs 'cause the coppers hadn't let on they'd found anything. So when Kay started offering freebies on Facebook we figured out she had Rick's stash, and the chances were she'd know where our money was as well."

"Your money?" I said.

He laughed. "Dad covered the Aberdeen side of the operation. Me and Slippy stuck to the drugs."

"You and Slippy and that Ukrainian pair."

"They usually did whatever I told them to."

"Including raping Kay."

"It wasn't strictly rape," he said. "I can prove it 'cause I got Damo to record everything on his mobile phone."

"You bastard." I reached for the headboard to steady myself. "Kay thought you were her friend. You even came round to see her after the attack."

"Yeah, well. She got that wrong." Peter peeled back the sheet and gave Kay's bare bottom a shove with his foot. "Come on Kay, babe. Shake your booty."

She barely moved.

"D'you have to?"

"Just checking that she's still breathing," he said. "At least she hasn't pissed the bed like she used to. Nothing a few hours' kip won't fix. Now can we go?"

"I need my handbag."

Peter shook his head.

"I need some things. Personal things, if you must know."

"Personal?"

"I'm starting my period." I held up my scrunched-up knickers and the bloody tissue.

End of conversation.

67

"SO why are we going all the way to Kylesku? There's nothing there," I groaned.

"It's a surprise."

"Surprise?"

They both laughed at once.

"Everybody's in for a humongous fucking surprise," Peter said. Then he popped open the glove compartment again and pulled out a black handset. "Did you check the batteries?"

"I tested everything on Sunday," Robbo replied. "According to the spec they're supposed to be good for at least ten hours."

Peter laughed. "Ten minutes should be long enough. Is this channel 1?"

"I've written it down. Channel 1's for the one at Skiag. 2's for Kylesku and 3's. . ."

"OK, shush. Amy here's got big ears. We don't want to spoil it for her just yet, do we?"

I grunted in agreement. Whatever game this pair was playing, if it meant they kept their filthy hands off me that was fine.

Beams of sunlight accentuated the dense shadows cloaking the slopes close to the Stack of Glencoul and closer at hand a pair of young stags on the grass verge raised their heads as we drove past. Lily pads on the roadside loch beyond the Lodges blazed pink in the dawn light. For a moment everything seemed too perfect.

"Was it here?" Robbo asked as we drew close to the turning for the slipway and the hotel.

"No," Paver said. "There's the pull-in further along."

We kept driving a couple more minutes then he pointed to the right. "Swing it round in here so we can get away once it's done."

Robbo slowed down and swept the truck in a semi-circle until we faced the way we'd come.

"OK. Everybody out."

"Me as well?" I said.

Paver snatched the bag from my tethered hands. "Leave that. And remember what I said. No funny business."

It felt as if I was walking on sheet ice as they led me onto the road bridge overlooking the narrows. I'd been on a boat trip here once – all the way from the Kylesku Hotel to the gardens at Kerrachar the summer before they closed down. The Kylesku Bridge spanned the stretch of water where the sea loch connected with Loch Gleann Dubh. It wasn't especially high but it seemed a long way to fall.

"Stop fucking whining. We're not going to chuck you in unless you start kicking off."

We stopped and leant against the railings, gazing West at the tide rippling along the straits.

"D'you want to do it?"

"I think we should let the lady do the honours," Robbo said.

Peter passed me the handset. "See that button. It's press to talk. So all you have to do is press it in."

So this was some elaborate kidnapping and I was their hostage.

"Press to talk?" I said. "What am I supposed to say."

They both laughed.

"Just press it."

The handset was in black, moulded rubber, no larger than a mobile phone but with a stubby aerial almost half as long again. There was a tiny screen with a 2 lit up in white. The button, rough to the touch, was twice as big as the numerical buttons that made up the keypad. I fumbled with it, running my thumb along the edge of the screen before fixing it in place and pressing. The handset gave a bleep. Then I saw the plume of grey-white smoke before hearing the explosion.

68

"**FUCK** me. Did you see the look on her face?"

The billows of white dust cleared and I stared at the handset then scanned the foreshore. A pair of V-shaped struts had supported the far end of the bridge above the sea channel less than thirty seconds earlier. Only two concrete stumps remained, rooted to the rocks. I'd have written it off as a drug-induced hallucination had it not been for the physical clues that confirmed what I'd seen had really happened.

A gust of air laden with sea spray and concrete dust, and flashing white light and the smell of burning came out of nowhere. The entire structure of the bridge trembled and I'd instinctively turned my face away from the blast as soon as the shock wave hit. Then the echo of thunder followed in its wake, sweeping along the narrow inlet beneath us until the sound seemed to drown out all my senses.

Paver and Robbo play-boxed each other before running across to where the metal railings gave way to a low crash barrier. They both climbed over onto the grassy bank and began to contour down the slope to take a closer look at the damage.

"Magic!" Peter yelled as they reached an outcrop of bare rock and clambered onto the top of it. "Both V-legs have gone. And most of the pier that end. Look at the state of the fucking road."

It resembled a section of fly-over with bits missing. As if something had taken a huge bite out of it leaving a ragged edge hanging over an empty space. Fifty or sixty feet of fresh air separated the central span of the bridge from the end anchored to the opposite bank.

They climbed back onto the road and began to walk towards the truck. I felt sick.

Did I just do that?

"Let's shift our arses before the cavalry turns up. If they were still in bed when we got here, they've just had their early morning call."

"Too right. Did you fucking hear it?"

Peter nodded in his pal's direction as he fired up the engine and steered the vehicle back onto the road. "Robbo's a fuckin' genius at demolition. He cracked it sweet as a nut."

I began to blink my eyes furiously. "You're both mad."

"Hear that, bro? I think she's starting to like us."

A battered Range Rover turned onto the road ahead of us from the direction of Kylesku village and flashed his lights but we continued heading back towards Skiag.

"Hope his airbags work."

They both laughed and the sunlight seemed too bright, the sound of their voices too loud. Amplified. Suddenly things began to make sense.

"It was you who blew up them wind turbines, wasn't it?"

I could tell from the beaming smile on Paver's face that I'd been right.

"It's what's called a trial run, Ames. We needed to work out how much det cord to use and how many sticks it would take to bring down something that size when they've been lying around for months."

"Sticks of what?"

"It was dynamite. Christ, what the hell do you think we

were using? Farting powder?"

I heard Robbo snigger as the truck accelerated along the zig-zags below the ramparts of Quinag.

"I still don't see the point. Blowing everything up."

Paver shrugged. "Maybe we got bored playing 'Battlefield 4' all hours of day and night. You can't beat the real thing, right Robster?"

"You heard the man."

"So this is your idea of a game," I continued.

"Hell, no," Paver said. "This is war. What we trained for during the last five years. First rule of engagement, cut off all communication lines. Isolate the enemy."

"What enemy? You're not in Iraq now, or wherever."

"The Sandbox?" Robbo said. "Oh no, we were in the Sand Pit. Bigger stakes. And now we're here. Same sand different desert, that's all."

"You're both mad."

"You've already told us that once. But that's all part of the training. No room for thinking straight or trying to make sense of what you're ordered to do. This is enemy territory and we're going to make sure no fucker gets in or out 'til we've finished." The intense look on Peter's face suggested he was being deadly serious.

"And how long is that going to take?"

"Twenty-four hours max. Once Phase One is complete the real fun begins."

69

WHEN we got back to Skiag Bridge, the campervan was gone but a four-by-four hitched to a caravan sat in the long lay-by just beyond the ruined shell of Calda House. It looked like they'd been there all night and they intended staying put. There weren't many finer spots in the Highlands at which to breakfast.

Robbo pulled up directly in front of them then checked for any oncoming traffic before executing a three-point turn. "What you going to do about this lot?" he asked. "It's not even half six yet."

"I'll sort it." Paver pointed a finger at me before getting out of the cab "You don't move a fucking muscle."

I watched in the wing mirror as he went to the back of the truck and reached in for something. Moments later he reappeared wearing a yellow, high-vis vest and set up a red, Men-at-Work warning sign at the side of the road.

Once he'd done that he tapped on the door of the caravan. It took a while but eventually a middle-aged couple emerged. I couldn't make out what he was saying but within less than three minutes the husband got into the cab of his vehicle, pulled out of the lay-by and they headed off in the direction of Ullapool.

Paver walked round to the driver's door and Robbo wound down the window.

"I need to get closer so I can get a line of sight."

"If you jump over that crash barrier you can walk down

to the shore as far out as it goes," Robbo said, pointing to a low set of crags extending into the loch. "Remember, there's nearly a ton of powder strung across that rock face."

"I'd better get my hard hat. Give me a toot if you see anyone coming. I won't be able to see a thing round that corner."

He wandered off and Robbo began twiddling with the dial of the radio.

"What's any of this got to do with you?" I asked.

"What d'you mean?"

"I mean it's not your fight. Peter's got a grudge with everybody. He always used to go on about how he'd pay back the idiots who teased him when he was growing up. And now the list has grown longer. But none of this is anything to do with you."

In the Hollywood version Robbo and I would have somehow bonded while Paver was out on manoeuvres. He'd have fallen for my feminine charms. We'd have kissed, and he'd have promised to do anything for me. Then we'd overpower Peter when he got back to the truck and between us we'd save the world. But Lochinver's a long way from LA.

"He's on a mission, but I'm cool with that. We've always watched each other's backs. Brothers in arms and all that jazz. One more tour of duty and the Caribbean here we come."

"Caribbean?"

"We sailed round a couple of islands last July. Scoping out where we could hide out if things ever went pear-shaped this side of the water. There's one or two that aren't even on the map."

"Christ. How long have you two been planning this?"

"You'd be surprised."

"But he'll never get away with it."

"You know what things are like round here. By the time anyone figures out they're cut off from the outside world, we'll be half way across the Irish Sea," he said. "The local plod won't be able to do a fucking thing until the reinforcements arrive. And that could take days."

"What about ambulances and things like that. What if there's a medical emergency?"

"What if what?"

"Don't you care that people might get hurt because of this stupid game Peter's playing?"

He pretended to give that some thought.

"You're as much of a bastard as he is."

"Careful what you say. I wouldn't want him hearing you talk like that or you might end up like your boyfriend."

Before I got a chance to ask him what the hell he meant, the truck shook and a massive cloud of black dust obscured the road behind us.

70

PAVER got into the cab, took off his helmet and gave a thumbs up. "Ready to roll."

The bottom half of his face was smeared with dust and blood trickled from a cut above his right eye.

"How'd it go?" Robbo said.

"No one's going to be driving along that bit of road in a hurry, if that's what you mean. I thought the landslide net was going to hold everything in place for about twenty seconds after she blew. But then the whole rock face came down. There's rubble and boulders fifteen feet deep burying the road. I didn't think I was going to be able to get back this side of it without going for a swim."

"Christ."

"I'm soaked up to the balls as it is."

"D'you know you're bleeding as well, bro?"

I bit my tongue as Paver swiped a hand across his face then studied the evidence in the palm of his hand.

"Battle scars. Nothing to get excited about."

Miles of empty road stretched ahead of us. And anyone who might have been able to rescue the situation was stranded on the wrong side of the road block. The chances were that those living in Inchnadamph had heard the explosion and would be first on the scene. Maybe the couple who ran the hotel or someone from the Field Centre. But there'd be nothing they could do to intervene since the road through to Lochinver was impassable.

"What's this about Matt?" I blurted out after we'd continued in silence for several minutes.

Peter cast a scowl in Robbo's direction. "What have you told her?"

"Nothing. Just to watch her tongue unless she wants to end up like her boyfriend."

"So what have you done to Matt?" I said. I was no longer scared of what this pair had planned for me. At least Kay was safe from Paver's clutches and that's all that mattered.

He took a deep breath. "I don't have time for this now."

"Please." Begging. I couldn't believe it.

"Let's just say he's got himself in a bit of a tight situation. I'll tell you all about it once we get to Strathbeg."

They were taking me to Jimmy's. Though I was guessing Jimmy would be nowhere near the chalet park when we turned up.

"Is that what this is all about? Because of me and Matt?"

"Oh, come on Ames. Not everything's about you."

The truck rumbled across the cattle grid and Robbo dropped down a gear as we approached the outskirts of the village. Peter took the handset out of his pocket and began to tap the keypad.

"What d'you reckon, Robbo? Channel 3 or 4?"

Robbo looked genuinely surprised. "4? I only set three charges."

Paver almost sang with pleasure as he explained what he'd been up to while I'd been cleaning myself in Kay's bathroom.

"I got a couple of sticks from the back. Just as a precaution. I managed to wire them up to the spare receiver as well and pre-set the channel."

"Shit. You should have got me to do it."

"No need, bro. I've watched you often enough. I just need something to keep our guest here under control."

I was picturing dynamite under my seat. But that would have been pointless. Paver might have been unhinged, but this wasn't a suicide mission.

"So where've you stuck them?" Robbo said as we passed the police station. All quiet.

"There's a little package underneath Kay's bed. Enough to bring her flat down, give or take a house or two."

"You can't do that!" I yelled.

"Relax." He began to fiddle with his handset again, numbers on its display flickering from 3 to 4 to 3 over and over. "It's already done. So now it's up to you, Amy. Do what I tell you and your friend might get to live a little longer."

71

WE took the Wee Mad, the only remaining road access between the village and Ullapool. Robbo turned the truck into the car park at the start point of the Kirkaig Falls footpath and it all became clear. I realised what they'd been up to with their hammers and chisels and sticks of dynamite during the previous thirty-six hours.

"Neat, don't you think?"

I couldn't answer him.

"Surprising what you can buy over the counter at Maplins. I only need to press one tiny button three times and the whole of Lochinver is in lockdown. Farrell's the only copper on duty and he can't do a fucking thing."

It seemed too easy. Robbo stepped out of the truck and rested with his back against the bonnet while Paver checked my wrists were still fastened together.

"Didn't want to do this while Robbo was here. But you seemed to be getting a little too cosy back there. You never know what can happen when you turn your back on someone you think you can trust."

"Paranoid, are we?"

"Call it being careful," he said. "So are you coming out to watch?"

I shook my head. "Go and play at being soldiers if that's what gives you both hard-ons. I'll stay here."

Paver stepped out and passed the handset to his oppo. The thought of somehow escaping on foot crossed my mind. Less than a hundred metres away a bookshop-cum-café overlooked the approaches to the bridge. Lauren's cousin had worked there one summer serving soup to those tourists who made their annual pilgrimage here. But the place wouldn't be open for at least another hour. Besides, once Paver found out I'd done a runner all he had to do was key in one number to destroy the most precious thing in my life.

I sat and watched the river tumble past. An idyllic morning. And so far I was guessing no one for miles around had a clue they were under siege.

This time I heard the thud before the explosion itself registered. The aftermath was hardly spectacular. Lots of smoke and a spray of water, then the river became discoloured downstream with a mass of floating vegetation. I watched Paver and Robbo wander onto the road to inspect their handiwork. Mission accomplished.

Strathbeg House was empty as I'd guessed.

"Jimmy's having a weekend break. He's catching up with some old friends from Dalwhinnie," Peter explained.

I took that to mean he was lying low somewhere with a bottle or two of single malt to keep him company.

Robbo came out of the kitchen carrying a plate stacked with bacon rolls.

"Where's the tomato sauce?"

"It's not my fucking house. I don't know where he keeps everything."

"Help yourself, Amy."

But I wasn't hungry. No sleep for twenty-four hours, and more gin and vodka than was good for me – as well as various other stimulants. It felt like I was still coming down, and the last thing I wanted was a cosy breakfast date with this pair of creeps.

I sat on the sofa, the same ghastly neon green leather

number with chrome arm rests I'd sat on the last time I visited. It stuck to my bare skin like cling film. "So what's this about Matt?"

"Let's just say he's been taken care of."

Playing games as usual. "What d'you mean taken care of?"

Paver wiped the grease off his fingers. "Remember Slippy?"

"Obviously."

"Well, he owed us big time. When the police were quizzing my dad about the Ukrainians, Slippy's name was never mentioned. Not once. Even though he was supplying them both with drugs as a side-line."

This was too unsavoury for words. "You make it sound like he was running a legitimate business."

Paver took a bite of roll before answering. "It's what's known as private fucking enterprise. I mean, Christ, Ames. How many dodgy deals do you think get made in board rooms all over this country? It's every man for himself."

"So where does Matt fit in?"

"We felt sorry for him getting sent down and all that. He'd kept schtum so Slippy agreed to recruit him. Give him an opportunity to earn a little extra cash."

"But why would you want to help Matt?"

"Just for old times' sake, let's say. We arranged for Matt to run a little errand."

"What kind of errand?"

He smiled as he sucked a stray ribbon of bacon rind from one end of his roll. "He made a delivery. A wee bit of dynamite."

"Matt did?"

"He didn't know who the client was, but he knew exactly what he was carrying. I had to make sure he was reliable."

"What d'you mean?"

"I wanted to make sure he'd turn up alone when instructed. And he did, so fair play."

Robbo nodded in agreement. "Slippy arranged for Matt to come up to Ledmore Quarry Wednesday night."

"Right." I could tell from the casual way he fed me facts that he was enjoying this just as much as Peter and that it was leading up to something bad.

"We had a bit of fun with him. A different kind of party, if you like."

"What kind?"

"Robbo here got him to play Postman's Knock. Matt hid inside the back of his van. Then I played Pass the Parcel before trying to see if it would float."

"Float?"

"For fuck's sake, stop repeating everything I say. All you need to know is that your boyfriend's inside a tin box at the bottom of the quarry."

"He's not my boyfriend." I bit back my words.

"Whatever, he won't be getting out of that in one piece, unless he's Houdini or Jacques fucking Cousteau."

I should have been happy. The one thorn in my side finally removed. But I couldn't get the image of Matt's hands out of my head. The huge blisters and the scarred skin after he'd tried to get me out of that burning minibus. He told me he'd somehow removed himself beyond the pain. He knew his hands were on fire but he'd felt nothing. The same as those people who walk barefoot over burning coals. I took that as a gallant attempt to make me feel less guilty. Less indebted.

"So what next? You going to get rid of me as well?"

Peter looked at Robbo, as if searching for instructions. "Depends. The boat's moored out at Strathbeg Point so you can join us on board for cocktails first. See how Phase Two pans out. Then we'll reach a decision."

A reprieve.

"I still don't get why you want to hurt everybody."

"Because they're all guilty."

"Guilty? And what about you?"

Peter seemed to give my question some consideration, but the sneer on his face revealed his true feelings. "I could tell the nuns back at Portrush a few things about guilt. All the bullshit they fed me about sin and divine punishment."

"Right."

"I've broken every commandment there is. You could say I've gone out of my way to see what would happen. And God's not struck me down dead. Not yet anyway."

Robbo laughed. "Hallelujah. So when do we cast off, Captain?"

Paver pushed the hair out of his eyes and pulled a smart-phone out of his pocket. "Soon as the sun's over the yardarm, matey. Let's just check the tides first."

Things were moving too quickly. "Can I use the loo before we go?"

"What now?"

"I just need to change a tampon," I snapped.

He motioned for me to hand over my bag before I could retreat in the direction of the bathroom. "Empty it on the floor first. Everything."

I scattered its contents onto the carpet and watched as he decided what I could take and what had to be withheld. My mobile phone had already disappeared into his pocket. Now he sifted through the rest of my bag's contents before tossing me a packet of sanitary pads.

"You can take these."

"I need my tampons."

He checked inside the carton. "How many can you shove up there at once, for fuck's sake."

I ignored him and as he threw me the box I tried to

reach for the tiny red cylinder hidden beneath the clutter.

"Don't tell me you need some lippy as well. What's the occasion?"

I could have lied. But if he'd tried to twist the top off and discovered what it really was, any hope of escape would have disappeared for good.

"It's not lipstick. It's spray."

He read the label. "*Pink Heat*? What the fuck is that supposed to be?"

"It's vaginal deodorant," I said. "You can check if you want to. It's up to you."

He threw it in my direction and got to his feet, shoving everything else back inside my bag.

"Go with her. I'll dump this in the bin and get a jerry-can from the garage. Five minutes and then we're out of here. Make sure she doesn't try anything. You'd better give her a full pat down as well. We don't want any Lara Croft heroics once we're on the boat."

Robbo followed me into the bathroom.

"I'd better do like he says." He lifted up my t-shirt and I felt his cold fingers reach into each armpit. Then he slid a hand inside my underwear. Back and front.

"Shoes?"

I kicked them off. "Happy now you've had a grope?"

He eventually retreated into the corridor once he saw me tug down my pants and squat on the toilet. I closed my eyes and relaxed my muscles. It brought back memories of the time Leanne had taken me into our bedroom and showed me how to insert a tampon. I must have been twelve, twelve and a half. Then Matt's throwaway comment came to mind. "There's women come in here with all sorts of gear stuck you know where."

72

THE chalet park displayed the familiar off-season signs of neglect. Lawns either side of the gravel path, once neatly trimmed and mown, were now overgrown and dotted with clusters of reed and dandelion. The four chalets close to the shoreline hadn't been touched in the last four months. Paint peeled off the door lintels, cobwebs like snow-drifts hid in the corners of the windows, and the walls facing the sea had become part-bleached by salt spray.

Peter jogged down the track ahead of us, a jerry-can in one hand and a set of oars in the other. Robbo followed, a short distance behind, carrying a cardboard carton. It contained the few remaining sticks of dynamite they'd not had need of.

"I've stuck something under the bonnet of the truck in case the local bobby turns up and decides to take a closer look," he said. "It's only a bit of wiring and I've left it in plain sight so it might make him think twice."

God.

I wanted no part of this. "You could have left me at the house, tied up in the garage or something. I'm only going to be in the way."

"You're going nowhere until this is over."

The tide was in and Paver's dinghy, a red and white fibreglass job complete with small outboard, lay tethered to a metal pillar a foot or so above the tide line.

"Get in."

I clambered aboard and huddled against the prow while Robbo stowed the carton and oars at my side.

"Don't worry. It's not going to go off."

Beyond where the low, grey headland of Strathbeg Point jutted into the bay, I could make out the graceful lines of the 'Meera Rose'. Paver and Robbo dragged the dinghy along the shingle to the edge of the water and continued to haul it offshore until it floated free. Then Robbo climbed aboard as Paver uncapped the fuel tank and sloshed in some petrol.

"If I fall overboard I won't be able to swim," I said, holding out my tethered arms.

"That's the idea," Robbo said.

Peter, climbed into the dinghy, tilted the motor until the propeller was under the water and handed Robbo the tiller.

"How long is all this supposed to take?" I shouted as the engine spat into life.

"We're not planning on staying around once the fireworks start. We're crossing over to Ireland as soon as it gets dark."

"And what about me?"

Paver grinned and trailed his hand in the water. "We'll drop you off on the way."

"Where?"

"Oh, not far. I was thinking we could cut you loose in the dinghy out in the Minch with a couple of oars to get you home. But we might be needing it."

"So what?"

"It depends," he said. "If you're good, we'll set you ashore on the far side of Soyea. By the time anyone finds you we'll be miles away."

"And if I'm bad?"

"You'll be partying with Rick and Rooster."

73

THEY made me wait in the dinghy while they secured it to the side of the boat and took the fuel can and the remaining explosive on board. Ten or fifteen minutes passed and I heard the engine of the 'Meera Rose' start up and slowly we pulled away from the shelter of the headland into open water. Even this far offshore, the sea was calm. I could smell rain on what little breeze came in from the islands but the plumes of stray cloud capping Lewis remained far enough away on the horizon.

Finally Robbo climbed back down and helped me up the rope ladder.

I'd expected to sense the motion of the waves beneath my feet but the craft sat relatively still on the water.

"Peter says we can go below for a couple of hours."

"You and me?"

He grinned. "You can always get your head down in the dinghy if you prefer."

"No. It's OK." This didn't seem the right moment to be picky.

"He'll moor her up then he's going to stay on top and keep watch."

Paver stood at the starboard side of the boat, a black metal tube balanced on his right shoulder.

"So what's he doing now?" I said.

"It's one of the AT4 rocket launchers," Robbo said. "He's going to try it out one more time. Find out the range."

I thought I'd seen everything, but now the whole situation had become even more ridiculous. "You've got a rocket launcher? Where the hell d'you find stuff like this? Did you steal it from the Army or something?"

"Ever hear about the Troubles?" Robbo said. "Peter's dad still has contacts."

"You mean the IRA and all that shit?"

Peter beckoned me across. "Nine years ago Sinn Féin made a promise that all arms would be decommissioned. We picked half a dozen of these up from a car boot sale outside Derry. So what d'you reckon, Ames? You think I can hit one of the chalets from way out here?"

"Why would you want to do that?"

He tapped the steel tube. "Just a final try-out. I've already seen what it can do close up. Whoosh. I just wish we'd had a chance to try it on something bigger like the 'Artania' instead of some poxy fishing boat."

What fishing boat?

"It says three hundred metres in the manual," he continued. "But I reckon these big boys can launch a rocket at least another hundred if there's no cross-wind."

It was like living inside a cartoon strip, but I knew only too well that Peter Paver didn't waste time on idle chatter. If he was already balancing a rocket launcher on his shoulder he meant to use it.

"I was thinking, it might be more fun if you decide which of the four chalets I should take out."

I humoured him. "The one on its own out on the left."

"Mhmm, good choice."

"Whatever." It had been our so-called love nest. Mine and Matt's.

Robbo came and stood at our side as Peter knelt down then raised his left knee to stabilise himself.

"You'd better cover your ears. And don't go standing

behind me." Paver lowered his head until it rested against the tube and began to line it up at the shoreline. "I'm just trying to remember which chalet we locked Jimmy inside."

"You're winding me up, right?" I said.

"Eenie meenie miney mo. Amy says you have to go."

The short spurt of flame from the tail end of the tube was more of a surprise than the puff of white from its muzzle. Then a section of bare ground appeared through the mushroom of smoke where two chalets had been standing seconds earlier.

"Oops."

"Why are you such a mean bastard?" I said.

"Careful, Amy. There's another four of these stowed up front. Four more rockets to play with. I might decide to make this even more personal."

He rested the empty launcher on the deck and turned to face me. "There's two with the Caley's name printed on their sides. I'll probably send one screaming into the bar later on this evening. It usually fills up on a Friday night. And I'll try and take down the hotel itself with the other one. It might make for some interesting headlines. 'Terrorists Strike Highland Hotel.'"

He stopped mid-speech, as if he'd forgotten his lines.

"What about the other pub?" Robbo said.

"Not so sure now. It seems a shame if there's nowhere left for the poor buggers to drown their sorrows once we're gone. Besides, there's the lifeboat. The jamming hasn't worked as well as I thought it would and we don't want anyone trying to follow us."

Three down one to go.

"What d'you think, Ames? Do we flatten Inver Park with the last one? Or the village centre?"

74

MAYBE Hollywood's version of events would prevail after all. Robbo took me below deck into his cabin while Peter stayed in the wheelhouse. He'd moored the boat in the shallows of the tiny bay facing the White Shore; close to the harbour but still out of sight of prying eyes. Paver claimed it was bad luck to have a woman up on deck when she was menstruating. Except he didn't exactly use those words. He didn't know the first thing about what was happening. I felt as if I'd been walking round with a stone in my shoe for the last half hour. Muscles clenched. Waiting for the right moment.

The cabin was tiny and stifling hot with just enough room for Robbo to undress while standing up. I'd not paid much attention to him at Kay's. All I'd been able to register were the tattoos on each arm and the dark hair covering his chest and shoulders. Enough of a turn-off despite his six-pack and broad shoulders. He smelled of stale sweat and a musky undercurrent of testosterone. Another reason not to get too close.

He signalled for me to lie down on the low bunk attached to one of the cabin walls.

"Don't get any ideas. I need some shut-eye, that's all."

I was in no position to argue. He positioned himself on top of me and one of his hands slid under my t-shirt. It felt good on one level despite my predicament, then I felt him cup one of my breasts and for a moment I thought he was after a re-run.

"You got anything I can take?"

I was feeling pretty chilled, building up to the final scene where the heroine saves the day. Whether or not he screwed me again was hardly going to matter.

"Mhmm?" He seemed more angry than surprised as I struggled free from his clumsy embrace.

"I'm too hyped up to sleep," I said.

He reached for a plastic pouch of tobacco from his jacket and rolled a joint. Then he fumbled in the rest of his clothing on the floor, found his lighter and lit up before passing the joint over.

"It's all I've got left until we get back to Portrush so tiny puffs."

He placed the lighter on the small shelf next to the bunk.

Keep talking.

"What are you going to do once you get back to Ireland? There'll be all sorts of people looking for you."

"Peter's going to suggest his dad comes with us out to the Caribbean. That's where most of his cash is supposed to be."

I took a long drag and felt the hash start to do its work. "Gordon's not going to want to spend the rest of his life on some desert island out on the middle of nowhere?"

"You know Peter. He can be persuasive."

"I suppose." I flexed my stomach as he squeezed himself between my body and the cabin wall, wrapping his arm around my midriff and pulling me closer. "I can be persuasive as well if you let me."

"I bet," he said. "But you're kidding yourself if you're trying to do what I think you're trying to do."

"Seduce you? Turn you against Paver so we can sail away together into the sunset? Do me a favour. I'm not that naïve."

"So what are you saying?"

I slid the fingers of my left hand between his legs. "I don't want to end up like Matt. Paver's going to want me dead when this is all over because I know too much. So if you can watch my back, I'd appreciate it."

"You're wasting your time, sweetheart." He smirked as he finished the spliff. "Peter does whatever Peter wants and nobody can stop him – not me or his old man. Let's get some shut-eye while we can."

"Right." I let my hands slip down onto my stomach and turned my face away from his. "I get it."

The only thing I got was that it was life or death now. I couldn't allow Mum to suffer the tragedy of a second telephone call. "I'm sorry, Mrs Metcalf. We're calling about your daughter, Amy."

75

THE rules of engagement. If Paver was waging war on the place I called home - the place I loved more than anywhere else on the planet - then I had to put up a fight. First step – scope the terrain and identify any hazards or weak points.

Robbo's cabin lay about five metres along the narrow passageway aft of the staircase leading back up to the wheelhouse. There didn't appear to be any other way on deck. I'd noticed the second cabin across from Robbo's. A fire extinguisher was attached to the corridor wall next to it. Both cabins had sliding doors, quiet enough not to be heard up top, but loud enough to wake my bunkmate if I somehow managed to work myself free of his clutches.

This cabin served as little more than basic crew quarters but with a modern, compact finish. Pine cabinets and a built-in wardrobe at one end. Overhead storage cupboards and a tiny oblong port-hole above the bunk. Robbo's clothes lay out of sight on the floor but I could see a rucksack slumped in front of the wardrobe. I also saw the neck of a vodka bottle protruding from one of its pouches. A potential weapon.

The only other signs of domestication were a ceramic mug bearing the crest of some regiment or other on the bedside shelf next to the head of the bunk, a couple of magazines and a rolled-up sleeping bag. In the worst case scenario – where I end up setting fire to the bed - the sleeping bag might prove useful in smothering the flames. But the most important item lay next to the mug.

Robbo had left his lighter in plain view. Close enough to reach if I could somehow extend my arms full length without disturbing his sleep. But it also lay close enough to the edge of the shelf to roll off if I fumbled my grip. Both hands had gone numb long ago. I'd lost count of time, desperate to stay awake despite feeling weary to the bone. I'd grown cold as well – the skin clammy on the tops of my thighs where my t-shirt had ridden up. I could barely move a muscle with Robbo's full weight on top of me.

I arched my back then began to slide my arms from beneath his body, inch by inch.

He stirred. "What?"

"Ssh. My hands have gone to sleep."

I pulled them free in one swift movement than laid them on top of his body. His head now lay between my upper arms and the wall of the cabin, his left hand still cupping one breast. I kissed his hair and began to stroke the ripple of spine running down the centre of his back. He shifted. Tensed up. Then I sensed the cadence of his breathing slip back from Drive into Neutral.

Time dragged its feet once more. I counted to a hundred. Again. Then again. I knew that sooner or later Paver would come looking for his oppo. Desperate to set the campaign back on track. I raised my arms above my head. Nothing. Then cautiously I turned and adjusted my head until the shelf was level with my line of sight. My fingers could barely reach far enough to touch the tiny cylinder let alone pick it up. A deep breath and I stretched further. Every sinew strained until I managed to hook it with a finger and clasp it tight between both hands.

Deep breaths. Calm.

Robbo's lighter was a fancy electronic model with a rubberised body. It had a red slider to adjust the height of the flame and lock it on. It also had a pop-up lid and a nice fat button next to where a jet of blue flame as intense as a blowtorch would appear if I pushed down hard enough. I'd watched him use it. Studied the way he handled it over and over because I realised it might be the only weapon I'd ever be allowed to get my hands on.

But there was no time for a trial run. No opportunity to test how hard I'd need to press that button or to check the sound it might make once the butane ignited. The hiss of burning gas. I had no idea how long the flame would stay alight. How long before I screamed in agony and was forced to let if fall out of reach.

Phsst.

I could see the flame, but guiding it where I needed it first was another matter. The skin inside the wrist of my right hand. That's where the pain began to form. Then it blossomed to the palm. I pulled both hands as far apart as I dared without losing grip of the lighter. I sucked in the pain. Let my fingers uncramp. The flame died but the lighter remained in place wedged between both thumbs.

I rolled it from side to side until I could identify its shape without having to crane my neck to see what I was doing. The button was there under my thumb again. I flicked and almost yelled out as the flare of sudden heat scorched the tips of three fingers. But gradually I was able to tilt it towards my wrists again. Heat returned coupled with the smell of burning plastic. Forcing my shoulder muscles to increase the pressure as I pulled my hands apart, I felt the cable-tie give.

I let my arms drop onto Robbo's bare back; too weak to keep them clear of him any longer.

Shit.

I was bathed in sweat. The lighter had fallen onto the

bed, somewhere in the gap between the cabin wall and Robbo's naked butt.

Could I crawl out from beneath him without waking him? Could I slide open the door and sneak out of the cabin before he discovered I was gone?

I stroked my right arm against his shoulder, hoping the soothing gesture would keep him under a while longer. Then I straightened my legs and spread them apart until I managed to move to the edge of the mattress. He still pinned me down, but most of his weight was now on the left-hand side of my body. I eased down the waistband of my pants with my free hand until they were gaping wide at the crotch. I felt vulnerable. More exposed than ever. But finally I was able to reach the tiny white thread anchoring my tampon in place.

I tried to raise my bottom off the bed. An inch. Legs parted a tiny bit more. Then I unclenched myself and had it between the fingers of my right hand, smooth and as potentially explosive as Robbo's lighter. In one swift movement I felt him roll off me as he transferred his weight to each arm, now positioned either side of my body. Then he grabbed my left wrist, no longer manacled to my right. His eyes flicked open and I felt his spit on my face as he sought an explanation.

"You stupid bitch. What the fuck are you trying to do?"

76

THERE was no time to explain. I raised my right hand and aimed the spray at his face then pressed down hard on the button.

He gagged and gasped, both arms lashing out blindly as the pepper spray took effect. I'd already anticipated his reaction. I had at most twenty seconds before he'd be capable of retaliating. Rather than trying to reach the door, I rolled off the bunk, crawled towards his rucksack and grabbed the first thing I could reach. The bottle was empty but heavy enough to cause damage.

The first lunge caught him on the shoulder. He shrugged it off as if I'd swatted him with a wet tissue.

His hands were already rubbing furiously at his eyes and I could tell he was regaining control of his breathing. Once he recovered his senses, he'd either come after me or call out for help. I struck again. This time the bottle hit him on the jaw. Again. To the temple. He shook his head and almost managed to wrest the bottle from my grip.

For God's sake, why won't you die?

There was no more time for pleasantries. I raised my arm and brought the bottle crashing down onto the side of his head with all my strength. He fell against the wall and I hit him again, wincing as blood spattered onto the sheet and I sensed the damage I'd caused. He slumped onto the bunk, red stains spreading over the pillow. I rolled him to the edge of the mattress and scrabbled for the lighter.

Shit. Where was it?

Then I found it trapped in the tight gap between the mattress and the cabin wall. Flick. Nothing. A second flick and a feeble hiss. A flame of sorts. I muttered a prayer for there to be enough gas to finish what I'd started.

I inched open the sliding door. All seemed quiet on deck. Heads or tails. Do I check if Peter's still in the wheelhouse or do I take a risk? I didn't have a coin handy so I stepped out into the corridor and slid open the door to Peter's cabin. It was unoccupied, as I'd hoped.

There were snapshots blu-tacked to the bulk-head. Guys in full battledress. What would they make of their comrade in arms now? Posters covered the main wall advertising various computer games. 'Call of Duty', 'World in Conflict', 'Blitzkrieg'. And half a dozen 'Guns' magazines lay scattered on top of his bunk. He probably tossed himself off at night fantasizing about holding a real pistol in his hands. A flag hung over his pillow - a swastika superimposed on the Irish tricolour. I set fire to one of the magazines, weaving the flame back and forth beneath the flag until it took hold and began to rise up the wall. Then I gathered up the rest of the magazines and used them to feed the blaze.

Once it became clear that the fire wouldn't burn itself out, I pulled his door to, leaving a gap wide enough to allow in some air. Then I retreated to Robbo's cabin.

I'd seen my share of horror movies. I knew the fatally injured villain always magically recovers and strikes back when we least expect it. I picked up the empty vodka bottle and struck again. Hard. Once. Twice. Once more for good luck. Then I grabbed the sleeping bag to cover the blood-stained bedding, climbed on top of Robbo's body and waited.

77

HIS skin grew perceptibly cooler as the minutes passed. I pulled the pillow from under his head and turned it over to hide most of the blood. Then I straddled him and soaked in the residual heat from his body as smoke began to fill the corridor. Another five minutes of silence. The smell was spreading into our cabin. My eyes were already watering and I started to struggle for breath, conscious I could have set my own death-trap. But then I heard a voice close by.

"Shit!"

The sound of footsteps along the corridor halted and the door moved an inch or two. Then Paver must have realised his own cabin was the source of the fire. I rested my head against Robbo's chest and squeezed the tube tight in my right hand. Counting the seconds.

One. Two. Three. I knew the last thing you should do is enter a burning room. Four. Five. Six. Seven. I made a wish, but presumably Paver had done his share of fire safety training in the Army. I heard him curse again then step inside Robbo's cabin.

"Fuck me. If you'd stop shagging for a couple of minutes you'd have realised the bloody boat's on fire."

I imagined him tugging away the sleeping bag. Eight. Nine. Taking less than ten seconds to join up the dots before I could roll off Robbo, aim the pepper spray at his face and make a run for it.

But give him his due, he didn't waste time checking if his oppo was alive or not. So much for watching each others' backs. Instead I heard the door slide on its runners again. Next came the hiss of the extinguisher as he tackled the blaze. Ten seconds or twenty. I didn't have long. I climbed off the bunk bed and peered through the sliding door. Peter stood with his back to me, one arm shielding his face from the smoke and heat as he tried to enter his cabin. No time for second thoughts. I crept along the corridor then dashed up the staircase onto the deck.

Finding somewhere to hide wasn't an option. Once the fire was out, it wouldn't take him long to realise what else I'd done and come looking.

As I made my way towards the bows, every step seemed to set the boat rocking in the water. The swell of incoming tide was already snatching at the mooring rope attached to the anchor buoy. Surely he'd notice. I grabbed the side rail to steady myself and there to one side lay a familiar cardboard box, half-buried under a tarpaulin. The metal jerry-can stood next to it.

Think!

I could soak the box of explosives in fuel, flick the lighter and let it drop. Suicidal. I'd not have a hope in hell of diving overboard before the fuel ignited and boom.

Think harder!

I tugged off my t-shirt, rolled it up tight and struggled to unclip the cap of the jerry-can. Then I dipped one end of my shirt as far into the open can as possible before pulling it out again. About ten centimetres of garment was soaked in fuel. I'd heard somewhere that petrol fumes are just as lethal as dynamite in an enclosed space. One spark is all it takes. But I was on an open deck and this needed more than a spark.

I took a few steps back until I could feel the low railings against my thighs. Then I held my t-shirt as far from my body as possible, flicked the lighter and whoosh. The immediate shock of intense heat made me drop the burning fabric onto the deck right at my feet. I didn't wait to watch the feeble flame as it struggled to draw breath. Peter had emerged through the hatch alongside the wheelhouse and stood a couple of yards away.

The set of waist-high railings at the bows had become a trap, a dead end. But I resisted the urge to seek an alternative escape route. The familiar stretch of coastline lay so tantalisingly close.

"Oh, you're so fucking dead. You and that junkie bitch." Peter's voice seemed about to break.

And there it was in his right hand. That familiar shape, with its rubberised black moulding and tiny Perspex screen. He raised it as if offering a toast then I watched as his thumb pressed down on the button. But I heard no explosion. Maybe we were too far from the village for the sound to carry. Maybe we lay outside the direct line of sight between his boat and Kay's flat.

I dropped the lighter with its tiny flame locked on and still flickering, sat back against the top rail and let my body fall backwards into the sea.

78

THE sudden shock of cold took my breath away before I surfaced close to the dinghy. There was no sign of Peter but I realised he only had two options left. Come chasing me - since he'd never had any intention of allowing me to escape with my life - or swing the boat around to face the village, open the throttle and complete his mission to blast the hell out of Lochinver.

It didn't take long to figure out which option he had chosen. The tone of the engine changed and I watched as the prow drew closer, despite the boat still being anchored to deeper water. He was taking it personally. I ducked my head under and aimed for the sea bed, hoping the boat would pass over me. I had no idea how low in the water the prop lay and I knew if I timed it wrong I'd end up getting chewed to a pulp.

The water darkened then became light again. I surfaced. The sound of the motor had faded to silence and Paver stepped out from a haze of lingering smoke that enveloped the wheelhouse. He held a cylinder in one hand. Maybe another fire extinguisher. Maybe another rocket launcher. I watched as he lumbered towards the front of the boat and scanned the water. I tried to make myself disappear, but for once the sea was as flat as a mirror. I left ripples in my wake like the traces of a fish gulping for a fly then diving for safety.

I couldn't help myself. I raised my head a fraction

again. No snags this time. I was directly in his line of sight. He crouched. He took aim. He fired and seemed to rise from the deck of the boat at the same moment the rocket left his shoulder. Then the backdrop of summer sunshine transformed into a wall of lurid flame.

There was no sense of piecing together the events that followed into any coherent order. Time pitched forward in a flash of colour and sound and weightlessness. Then I felt water surge all around me and I could taste fuel in my mouth and all I could focus on was trying to control what entered my lungs. Air or water. I knew I was never going to be able to physically draw in breath again unless I somehow pulled myself back to the surface.

After the sting of burning hailstones peppered my left shoulder, the blast of hot air had sent me down deep. There came a time when my entire body slackened, as if all my bones had been liquefied. Dad had once told me the good thing about swimming in the sea is that no one can tell when you've peed your pants. But I'd done more than pee myself as my bowels turned to water.

Once the sky came up to meet me again, I rolled onto my back. Blurred vision. Blue sky. Blue haze. Red haze and stinging eyes. I tried to turn my head to the side away from the direction of the pain but flashbacks from the rocket explosion seemed to go on for ever. Searing heat on my face had singed my eyebrows and hair, but I sensed there was more damage beneath the surface. Splinters of fibreglass and metal shards had showered over me like red hot confetti. Then there followed the taste of something obscenely chemical, like a combination of burning oil and spent fireworks and stomach acid.

I vomited again.

By all accounts, I'd escaped with my life. But instead of relief I felt emptiness inside. Could it be this simple? Or was there a catch that even I, in my paranoid state, had failed to foresee?

White Shore stretched less than a hundred metres away but I could already see the battlefield it had become. Paver's rocket had looped way off-target as the fuel somehow ignited and set off the dynamite. I floated on my back for a while and felt the salt burn my bare shoulder. I was aching all over. I was sobbing and tired and would have gladly let myself drown. But already the water was becoming shallower and I turned onto my stomach and began to crawl towards dry land. Water swirled around me, slick with spilt oil, leaving the rotten stench of burning in its wake.

Then came the familiar scent of the woods - the foreshore reduced to a crater of churned-up shingle and exposed rock and burning seaweed. I retched again and tried to haul myself upright, but the jagged honeycomb of eroded rocks and uprooted mussel shells tore at my bare feet. I fell to my knees, bare flesh scraping against the gnarled outcrop of gneiss guarding the shore. I would not escape so easily. Behind me I could already hear someone else struggling against the currents. Robbo or Paver. I didn't care. All I wanted was to reach that crescent of beach. There. Bare rock giving way to shingle. The ground shifting under my feet. Head under water then into sunlight again.

I continued to crawl on my knees and eventually was able to reach out for a branch part-buried in the churned-up shingle. Its skeletal shape resembled an outstretched arm – radius and ulna - with a withered hand offered in reassurance. On closer inspection maybe two, clasped in prayer. The worst was finally over like they always said it would be. I grasped both hands and held on.

79

RADIO silence. All lines of communication cut off. It took me a while to realise I'd lost my hearing as well as my underwear and was trapped in enemy territory with no means of signalling for back-up. I scanned the rocks within my line of sight for clues. The trees behind me, camouflaged in shades of green and yellow, gave away nothing. I couldn't tell how close Peter really was and whether or not he was armed.

I'd played my part. Over and above the call of duty. I'd entertained the troops, blown up a road bridge, overpowered one of the enemy single-handed and sabotaged Phase Two. I'd done enough to earn a campaign medal, even if I was killed in action.

I rested my elbows on the lip of the crater and tried to haul myself up onto the higher level of trashed beach. But all my strength had drained away. My feet, black and bloodied, didn't seem to belong to the rest of my body. I could just as easily let go now, my mission accomplished.

But I had dreams. Plans. Impossible hopes like birds queuing on a power line ready for some mass migration South. No matter what Paver had done, I refused to revert to being a tiny smear or a stain on this diminished universe.

Shingle slipped under my feet like quicksand. I turned to check the incoming tide, swirling higher up my thighs then draining away as it slowly filled the void then receded. Rising further at each pass.

There had been someone down there; someone with mummified hands and arms reduced to bone and calcified tendons. Hands tethered by a familiar band of black plastic cable-tie. And now he had somehow come to life. He rose to his knees and I saw the blackened ruin of Peter Paver's body try to reach out for me before the sea embraced him and pulled him back under.

Sobbing. Someone somewhere was sobbing. My hearing returned and with it the swelling sense that each sound was closing in on me. Raised voices. The staccato beat of a chopper. The broken-up throb of an outboard.

I gave in and let myself slip down the chute into the rising water. Already I was up to my waist in sand - Paver dragging me down with him. Every last morsel of his being seemed intent on taking me with him. I struggled to fight back but there were other arms. Real arms pulling at me this time not skeletal ones. And I could see an inflatable dinghy with three men in bright yellow water-proofs and red life-jackets. Someone asked me my name. Another wrapped me in a blanket and told me I was going to be alright.

But I knew different. I kept the truth to myself.

I was taken aboard the lifeboat and overhead I could hear the clatter of the rescue helicopter. Two paramedics cleansed and dressed my wounds during the flight to Raigmore but I barely spoke a word. This part was still a dream. I could taste salt water at the back of my throat and smell fire as it overwhelmed the minibus. It all came back to me.

Snow fell outside and smoke billowed into the night. Jimmy wrapped me in his coat and Matt somewhere close by sat nursing his damaged hands and screaming my name.

Even when Mum and Leanne came to visit I couldn't

explain how I'd ended up at the White Shore, filthy naked and looking as if I'd been fighting in the trenches. The stink of shame clung to my body like a second skin, no matter how many times I asked the nurses to swab me clean. Even after I'd told the police about Peter setting off the roadside bombs and his plans to fire rocket launchers into the village, I kept the finer details hidden. They can play funny tricks on you, drugs.

Gordon Paver made a brief statement to the media. The grieving father. Bewildered. He mentioned something about post traumatic stress disorder and how he'd grown distant from his son while locked up in Barlinnie. Gordon made no attempt to quash the rumours that Peter had been involved with three murders long before he left the Army.

He then churned out the usual crap about his darling son being the last person you'd expect to have such sinister intentions. If Gordon suspected I knew the truth, he never let on. He made no attempt to contact me, and even though I know everything, my lips remain sealed. Truth hurts.

The secrets of the last few weeks are locked tight inside my head like time bombs, each with a short fuse ready to be lit by a single misplaced word. Kaz Cartwright's attack on Kevin Waterson. Peter Paver and Caddy. Peter Paver and Rick Tyler. Peter Paver and Matt Neilson.

I mentioned nothing about my part in the disappearance of Robert Cohen - ex-soldier and holder of an Operational Service Medal for his actions in Afghanistan. Another name added to the list of People Lost at Sea. Peter Paver had killed Robbo as surely as if he had bashed that bottle against his pal's head. The consensus of opinion was that Peter had also contributed to his own death, so no one will ever know how good it had felt to kill them both.

I've not breathed a word to anyone about being molested and assaulted in Kay's flat either, or living in fear of my life. I'll never share those horrors, not even with my mum. I'll not let it break me and I can't let what happened inside a mere twenty-four hours define who I become for the rest of my life. Some secrets deserve to be taken to the grave.

80

SO much can happen in five days.

That's all it took for the Highland Council to clear the road at Skiag and declare it safe for traffic. It also took the Army less than five days to carry out their search for more explosives. They'd been helicoptered in overnight. Every room in Strathbeg House and every chalet had been checked. They'd also evacuated the village centre to allow the device in Kay Jepson's bedroom to be dismantled. Peter Paver would have been in his element.

But some things took longer. Repairs to the two bridges involved months of lengthy detours and there was even talk of resurrecting the Kylesku car ferry in time for the Easter holidays.

Matt Neilson had been found – battered and bloody, half-drowned but alive. Four cracked ribs, a fractured elbow and dislocated shoulder the worst of the damage. He sent me a Get Well card and I keep it with those special souvenirs inside my shoe box of memories. The police decided there was nothing to investigate when they realised there was no link between the van at the bottom of Ledmore Marble Quarry and other dramatic events.

There were others who got off less lightly than Matt.

Kay, the shell of the girl I'd known and loved, was taken in by her dad and I heard nothing from her in the months that followed. She has my phone number.

The bomb disposal team found Jimmy's body in one of

the surviving chalets, surrounded by empty whisky bottles. Death by natural causes according to the police.

Two other bodies were recovered – both at the White Shore. The full results of their post mortems would not be made public until the authorities could confirm identity and inform next of kin. But I'd already recognised the charred remains of Peter Paver - washed ashore along with the other garbage following the blowing up of the 'Meera Rose'. His appalling injuries had proved fatal. The second body had lain beneath the shingle much longer. But I realised it was Rick Tyler's as soon as I saw the cable ties.

I survived and I'll return to Lochinver when the time is right. Like Peter Paver, I have unfinished business. But for now I need my own space. A larger space than the narrow strip of beach at White Shore. I need to figure out how to reassemble the fragmented pieces of my disjointed life into a recognisable shape. My relationships with Mum, Kay, even Matt, are on hold indefinitely. For now I'm content with my new life here in Aberdeen. Ironic, I know.

The girly blonde look has gone. I've dyed my hair a fiery red. The military cut suits me well, even if I say so myself, and I wear my battle scars like badges of honour. Some say there's a hardness about me that dares you to avert your gaze. But all I want is a simple life where no one looks twice at a face and sees another that was plastered all over the newspapers weeks earlier.

So much can happen in five days.

Enough to keep the front pages of every British tabloid filled with eye-catching headlines. Enough to clog up hours of airtime on News 24 and keep the cameras and microphones of the world focussed on one tiny village hidden away in the remote top left corner of Scotland.

But a life can change in less than five minutes.

- - -

AUTHOR'S NOTE

Once again I'm at great pains to reassure my readers both characters and plot are purely imaginary.

WHITE SHORE is a work of fiction.

Any locations or addresses portrayed within these pages are based on my own recollections and where altered or enhanced have been fictionalised to suit the story. Likewise, all names and incidents are the product of my twisted imagination and any resemblance to an actual person, living or dead is pure coincidence.

Several unidentified individuals have helped in shaping this book and keeping my writing on track. But I'd especially like to thank the communities of Assynt and specifically Lochinver for humouring my almost perverse determination to portray this unspoilt corner of Scotland as the crime capital of the North-West. Nothing could be further from the truth.

I also owe a huge debt of gratitude to local artist Mary King for allowing me to reproduce one of her photographs on the front cover. Without her optimistic slant on life this world would be an even darker place. Thanks also to Helen Simpson for her constant encouragement – often random but always welcome. And to Nigel Sibbett for all things fish – and for supporting my writing efforts in so many ways as well as scrutinising the final manuscript in search of errors and inconsistencies.

Many of the enhancements are down to them. Any retained flaws are entirely my own fault.

Finally thanks to you for reading.

If you enjoyed WHITE SHORE please consider leaving a short review on Amazon. It would be greatly appreciated.

C B

email: cyanbrodie@yahoo.co.uk

By the same author and available on Kindle and in paperback:

DREAMGIRL (published by Red Telephone Books)

DARK SKY (Book #1 of the Lochinver Trilogy)

When schoolgirl Caddy Neilson is found strangled in a remote Scottish village the police are quick to establish both murderer and motive.
But those closest to Caddy suspect they've got it wrong.
Best friend Amy and part-time student/small-time drugs dealer, Matt, uncover evidence linking the young girl to a major crime.
But the search for the truth not only jeopardises their growing relationship. It also places their lives in peril.

and due out early 2017

BLACK ICE (Book #3 in the Lochinver Trilogy)

Eighteen-year-old Amy Metcalf has made a new start. Life in Aberdeen is good. But when a Polish girl is found dead in one of the city's hotels secrets from Amy's past return to haunt her.
The one-man war waged in WHITE SHORE has intensified as three characters return to Lochinver from overseas. Each of them has an agenda. Each is set on revenge.
Amy and her ex-boyfriend Matt Neilson are caught up in the maelstrom - their lives and their turbulent relationship once more put at risk. But this time they discover that friends can often come disguised as enemies. And giving up on friendship is never an option.

Also for younger readers

TOAD IN THE HOLE AND TOLEY BAGS

-

And writing as Phil Jones:

80 HILLS IN NORTH-WESTERN SNOWDONIA
(published by Gwasg Garreg Gwalch)
available only in paperback.

Available on Kindle and in paperback:

SUMMERTIME BLUES
20 PIECES
(Short Story Collections)

and

80 POEMS

And for younger readers:

THE OUTLANDER

You can contact me at

cyanbrodie@gmail.com

Made in the USA
Lexington, KY
04 June 2018